CHASING
REDEMPTION

CHASING REDEMPTION

Frederick John Loase

Howl at the Moon Press
www.howl-at-the-moon-press.com

Chasing Redemption
Published by Howl at the Moon Press
San Diego California | Poulsbo Washington

Loase, Frederick John, 1944 –
Chasing Redemption / Frederick John Loase – 1st Ed.

This book is a work of fiction. Names, characters, places and incidents either
are products of the author's imagination or are used fictitiously. Any resemblance
to actual events or locals or persons, living or dead, is entirely coincidental.

ISBN-10: 0-9774859-1-9
ISBN-13: 978-0-9774859-1-8

1. Loase, Frederick John, 1944 - 2. Fiction 3. Chasing Redemption – fiction. 1. Title

For Satoko
&
Sean and Madeline

And of course Flo

Also by Fred Loase:

Meditations of a Church Drop Out
Non-fiction | Co-author

Acknowledgments

Albert Camus said that fiction is the lie through which we tell the truth. My longtime friends, Robert Neveln MD and Clement (named after Pope Clement) Wong PhD, whether we were playing racket ball or just talking, always let me know if I was lying. When each of them read my early manuscripts of this novel, they regularly exposed the lies that weren't true. I am forever grateful. Tamera Sellman worked as my editor during the four years I spent completely devoted to writing this novel—after I had retired and had finally decided to quit fooling around with it. Without her dogged enthusiasm, I would never have completed the novel. She taught me how to write fiction. After the completion of my second draft, Tamera could no longer work with me because of ill health. Fortunately I reconnected with Drusilla Campbell who had helped me in years past decide on which of my possible novels to focus. This was while I was still a high school teacher and fooling around with writing. Just a year before she died, she helped me put the final touches on this novel. Her passing was a great loss to the San Diego writing community. More recently, Marni Freedman read my manuscript and thankfully said, "Don't monkey with it anymore!" Thank you Nancy Harmon for straining your eyes, hour after hour, proofreading and setting me straight. I am thankful to my friends Pam Kirpalani and Toni Wood who read early copies of my manuscript and gave me great feedback. My wife Satoko, spent many hours rereading different versions of my manuscript without reminding me of what I knew was true: Her knitting and gardening would have been much more enjoyable. In the novel, Ted gets lost in the painting, which is the cover art of this book. Linda Monfort is the artist and gave me permission to use her art. This painting hangs in my home and I have visited this painting myself most days for the last twenty years. John Abromowski made the perfect digital photograph that graphic designer Monica Holsinger turned into a wonderful cover. Monica also took over the overwhelming task of dealing with the details of formatting the text. She claims to be OCD, and for that I will be forever thankful. And, thanks to David Goodrick (my high school friend with whom I recently reconnected at our 50th high school reunion), who led me through the rip currents and the muddy tidal flats of the modern publishing business.

CHASING
REDEMPTION

1

Phone calls at 2 A.M. invade the cobweb of one's dreams and seldom bring good news.

In his tiny studio apartment, Ted Miller stabbed in the dark at his jangling desk phone, grabbed the receiver, and pressed it to his ear. "Hello?"

"It's your mother, you told me to call if…"

"My mother? Is she…?" Ted groped for the switch on the lamp above his head, but instead he knocked the base of the phone off the ledge above his pillow. "Shit!" The cord stretched, and he strained to keep the receiver next to his ear.

"Excuse me?" The voice on the other end of the line raised a notch in tone and decibel. The voice belonged to his mother's nurse, but he couldn't remember her name.

Ted found the shaft of the lamp. He turned a knob and light cut through the darkness. He shielded his eyes, swallowed to keep his heartbeat tamped down, and breathed in the new, unwelcome smell of bachelorhood. "Sorry… the lamp…." Ted blinked. "My god, my mother, is she…?"

"No!" Her abrupt interruption reached out as if to warn him back from the edge of a cliff. "She's still alive, but the staff doctor said it won't be long. It's in her lungs now; it …it won't be long." Seconds ticked by. "Maybe I shouldn't have called, but you said to call if she was ever able to communicate."

"No, no …it's, okay." Ted twisted his legs over the side of the bed and sat up. "She's talking?"

"She asked for Skipper."

"Skipper?"

"Yes. She asked that Skipper find someone named Sister before it's too late."

"Sister?" The name Sister lashed at the distant edge of his consciousness. Ted closed his eyes and tried to focus.

"So you aren't Skipper?"

"No!" Ted took a calming breath. "I've never heard of this Sister, either." How could he put in words that that name was familiar, but that it was lodged in a part of his reality he had long ago labeled: *crazy*.

When the nurse finally responded, her voice was measured and professional. "I just wanted you to know that your mother is lucid at the moment. You can decide what you want to do about it." Another short silence followed. "But you'd better hurry."

***

Phoenix, Arizona was not ready to wake up, nor was Ted's Datsun 1973 240Z sports car, which sputtered and threatened to stall as he stared, first at the red signal light above, and then at the police car parked just off the road, which was why he had bothered to stop for the signal light.

Four years old, his bright orange two-seater had once represented his one shot at autonomy in his marriage, but now only symbolized his isolation. He wiped sweat from his forehead with his left hand, and tinkered with the stubborn air conditioner's temperature knob with his right. "Shit." He glanced up at an electronic sign on a bank across the intersection that flashed the date, *August 9, 1977*, and then changed to the numbers and words, *90 degrees*. In the desert in August this was, euphemistically, the low temperature of the day. But to Ted, it was just one more reminder that Phoenix has only two seasons. Heaven occurs between November and April. Life is good, temperatures mild, occasional rain. But when May arrives, Hell takes over. Every creature, whether two-legged or four, heads underground or behind closed doors. In August and September, dust storms often darken the sky with orange-brown clouds filled with fine grit that clogs throats and stings eyes. These dirty rampages are followed by monsoon–generated thunderstorms, which drop only enough moisture to muddy the thick coat of dust that had covered every surface and seeped into every crack.

All around him, streetlights glowed in muted amber. Ted shook his head. "Astronomers." Just recently he'd read about the amber streetlights and how (in spite of the fact that Phoenix was going through another growth spurt, spreading asphalt and cement over rattlesnake dens and roadrunner nests) they were holding back the halo of city lights encroaching on the astronomer's view of the heavens. Ted wondered about God's take on the matter. Was He okay with the astronomers mucking around the universe with their telescopes, or was He happier with the old, brighter streets lights that had screened His secrets from their prying eyes?

Ted hit the steering wheel with both hands. "Focus, damn it." He closed his eyes and pictured his mother tied to her hospital bed with tubes and wires. She didn't have a sister. And who was this Skipper? Had his mother begun to hallucinate? For several days she'd been on a morphine drip and uncommunicative. Now she was speaking. But would she make any sense?

A quick blast from a car horn made Ted look to his left. He cranked down his window in response to a wave from the police officer in the sandy-colored patrol car with two round forward-facing red lights on the roof that had moved from the side of the road into the lane on Ted's left. Ted smiled for a moment because the lights had always reminded him of Mickey Mouse, hardly a look that demanded serious reactions from possible scofflaws.

The patrolman leaned toward Ted's sports car. He grimaced, rolled down the cruiser's passenger side window, stared down at Ted and shouted. "What's up?"

Human beings who survive their fourth birthday have already experienced an event in their short lives that has produced an inkling that they are alone and can not always count on someone to save them, and to that event, they react in a particular fashion: withdrawal perhaps, or for others: bombastic displays, or in a myriad of ways which forever become their modus operandi in times of stress. Ted's MO was humor. He cranked down his own window and to the officer's pointed question Ted responded, "Most parts of a giraffe?"

The officer's eyebrows tightened and his gaze momentarily floated away. Then he shook his head and looked back at Ted. "Very funny. But why the hell are you just sitting there?"

Ted looked up through his windshield and pointed. "Just waiting for the light to...." How long had the signal light been green?

***

The early morning wake-up call wasn't the only thing nagging Ted as he left the elevator on his mother's floor of the hospital and walked through a tunnel of lime green. The walls, ceiling, and worn linoleum of the corridor leading to Margaret Miller's semi-private room reminded Ted of his favorite flavor of Jell-O, but he didn't find that disturbing. Nor did he dwell on the rumbling sound emanating from air conditioning registers along the hallway that carried air, cooled only a few degrees below intolerable.

What bothered him now was the overwhelming smell. His nose had taken charge and dimmed his other senses. His mother was warehoused among other lost souls whose lives were now defined by the odor of bodily functions and the chemicals used to disguise them, terminally wounded, hope and dignity slipping collectively into an odorous pit.

"Oh, Mr. Miller."

Ted stopped. A young woman waved at him from behind the counter of the nurse's station. Lois, that's her name, thought Ted. She looked younger than he remembered. Before, she'd tucked her hair under the winged cap that looked like a huge butterfly perched on her head. Today, however, her hair was set free, reaching the middle of her back, a hair style that reminded Ted of a time of peace and love in the mid-1960s. It was probably against hospital regulations for her to wear her hair long, but a pragmatic nurse might prove helpful when he had to make hard decisions about his mother's needs.

The nurse pointed at her watch. "Sorry...I ..."

Ted waved away her apology. "Is she still awake?"

"She was five minutes ago." Lois picked up a chart that Ted could see was labeled *Margaret Miller.* "Go ahead in," she said. "I'll check on you in a few minutes."

Ted lingered at the open door of his mother's room for a few moments, deciding if he was ready for new information that would further upset his life, when he heard the pathetic cries: "Pee, pee. Pee, pee." These were the only English words Ted ever heard from the frail Mexican woman in the bed nearest the door. She used them to get attention no matter what her need. Ted noticed she was holding an empty glass. Duty and empathy drew him to her side. He took the tumbler from her, filled it with water from a pitcher placed just out of her reach, and handed it to her.

"Gracias," she said.

Ted smiled, nodded, and then turned to his mother's side of the room. He pushed the privacy curtain aside and peered into the eyes of a woman he barely recognized. He sat by her side and held her bony fingers, which to his surprise squeezed back with more strength than he imagined she had left. He looked at her hair, pure white since she was fifty, now limp on the pillow, so different from the bouncy permanent waves that were her trademark. Her gaunt face belied the fact that she had once had the cute look of a chipmunk hiding acorns in its cheeks. During most visits in the past, the medication had left her unresponsive and, without the morphine Margaret only cried out in pain, making communication impossible. Now Ted hoped that she might have broken through the hazy medicinal veil.

"Mom, can you hear me? It's me, Ted."

Margaret raised her head a few inches off the pillow and squeezed Ted's hand more tightly. "Ted, it is you." The corners of her mouth turned up ever so slightly. "I'm glad you're here, sweetie." Then her eyes lost their sparkle.

Ted shook his head and sighed. His mother, it seemed, was gone again.

But with her head still raised off the pillow, Margaret breathed deeply and stared into Ted's eyes. "Skipper, tell Jacob that it's time to let Sister come home, before it's too late."

Ted's mouth fell open. He leaned closer. "Am I Skipper?" Ted's mind raced. "Dad knows who Sister is?"

His mother's head dropped to the pillow and she fell back into the clutches of the morphine.

The bird-like sounds of "Pee, pee. Pee, pee" and the smell of death followed him as he race walked down the lime green corridor.

***

When Ted left the hospital, the sun was still tucked behind the mountains east of Phoenix and gave only the slightest hint of where it would rise. His tires squealed and his heart pounded as he chased the ghosts of Skipper and Sister out of the parking lot and onto Indian School Road, a road named for the boarding school a mile away that had for years hijacked Navajo, Hopi, Zuni and Apache children from their reservations and, under the guise of a promised education, instilled an oppressive value system instead.

Ted eased off on the accelerator when the rational part of his brain finally kicked in. He admitted to himself that it was too early to confront his father, and that in all likelihood the confrontation would end in disaster. In spite of the new doubts, he rejected the notion that he could return to his tiny apartment and wait without constant pacing and rumination, so Ted chose to cruise around his old haunts instead. A sign flashing: *Open 24 Hours* caught his attention. He swerved into a parking lot and screeched to a stop in front of *John's Place*, a café where he had spent many hours before his life turned upside-down. The restaurant's eternal schedule was in response to the round-the-clock shifts at the monstrous Motorola plant across the street. For the last year Ted had spent afternoons here—after he had dismissed his last middle school science class and had shooed the stragglers who had stayed behind to feed the lab rats—engaged in heady conversations of semiconductors and silicon with engineer friends Pete and Sam, who spent late afternoons steeling themselves for their evening shift at the electronics giant that loomed in the front windows of the noisy diner. Just last January, a company called *Commodore* had released a personal computer. This had caused a stir at John's Place, and Ted was excited about the possibility of introducing a PC to his students. But that was before the incident in late spring in Ted's classroom that led to his being put on paid leave. Suspended from the job he loved, Ted had avoided John's Place, even when just two months ago in June a small California company introduced the *Apple II PC*, which promised to keep the café's conversation humming.

It was 4:30 A.M. now as Ted entered the eatery. Customers either sat alone at the counter, or sat in small muted groups, and flying in the face of reason since Hades was just outside the restaurant door, were sipping on steaming cups of promised stimulation. Ted sat on a stool at the end of the long counter. His battle with his car's air conditioner in mind, he ordered a Coke with lots of ice and immediately tried to shift away the mental image of his mother lying in her hospital bed.

Because he shared her love of Shakespeare, the image of his mother on which he finally chose to reflect was the royal smirk on her lips when she rendered her impish version of Hamlet's famous Soliloquy. *TB or not TB that is congestion. Consumption be done about it? Of cough, of cough it can.* He chuckled at the memory. Then he felt a sting in his chest when he remembered that recently, his doubts about his ability to take arms against his own sea of troubles had led him momentarily to consider the choice of endless sleep. But of one thing he was sure. It was not the dread of something worse after death that had stirred his resolve to fight on, but rather his dedication to the principle of faithfulness he had learned at the feet of his mother when she read him the Dr. Seuss story *Horton Hatches the Egg.*

At the end of school one day when he was seven, Ted left his second grade classroom resolved to fulfill a promise to deliver a comic book to a friend. He set off with a firm picture in his mind of Horton, the elephant babysitter, perched (if in fact an elephant can perch) on the nest of an irresponsible bird named Mayzie. "*I meant what I said. And I said what I meant. An elephant's faithful, one hundred percent.*" Horton's answer to ridicule from all the other animals, that knew Mayzie would never return, was young Ted's mantra, and he repeated it out loud as he marched toward his friend's house, an impossible seven miles away.

Police had been notified by the time Ted's parents received the phone call from the mother of Ted's friend. "You'll never guess who just showed up at my front door, sweaty and thirsty."

The elephant's determined phrase had also recently echoed in Ted's mind when he thought about his two sons. How could he leave them fatherless? He had remained faithful to his wife, Jan, in spite of the fact that she had sucked the joy out of their marriage not long after their nuptials and had more recently banished him to a studio apartment. Ted gagged on a swallow of Coke. He couldn't blame all their troubles on Jan. He knew he was a disaster when it came to relationships.

"Hey, Teddy boy."

Ted blinked and looked into the eyes of a man he knew well. "Sorry, I was thinking about something. I was…"

"Lost in space?" John's belly laugh let Ted in on the joke and drew annoyed looks from customers nearby.

Ted squeezed his eyes shut for a moment and shook his head. *Shit. Why now? Why would John choose to come in early today?* Ted thought about his teenage years when he and his parents had frequented John's Place, long before Motorola came with its demand that John remain open day and night. In Ted's mind John never changed, perpetually middle aged, a gut that shook when he laughed and, according to his mother, John had exactly thirty-seven hairs combed over the top of his shiny head.

Ted took a breath and stared out the window. "Something like that, John."

"Haven't seen much of you lately." John studied his shoe tops. "Hear what happened to Pete and Sam?"

Ted feigned surprise. "No." He avoided John's stare.

John continued his examination of Ted's face. "I haven't seen them since they got busted for possession of cocaine—snorting that shit in my restroom for Christ's sake."

Ted's look of shock continued its lie. "Arrested?" Ted swallowed and risked a glance up into John's eyes. Yes, he had heard about the arrest. But thankfully, his friends hadn't implicated him. He knew that they were out on bail, but they hadn't answered their phones or returned Ted's calls in response to the messages he'd left on their answering machines.

John's expression sought the truth. "You never messed with that stuff, right, Teddy?"

Ted shook his head. "No. Of course not." In truth he hadn't touched a line since his personal shit storm in the spring. But before that, what Pete and Sam used to stay sharp throughout their evening shift Ted inhaled to ease a lifetime of guilt and depression. In the end, it was just another wild animal taking up shop in his crowded psyche, but he did still have a taste for this beast. The only reason he had stopped was because his engineer friends were his only source. Ted had waited all his life to let this tiger loose. One good snort of the chalky substance and his self-confidence soared. All his fears and self-doubt flitted away. This was his tiger, and it roared when the powder exploded in his nose. Thankfully, no one else but his engineer friends knew about his forays into the divine. But, his suspension was not related to the drugs. In fact, it had everything to do with his lack of focus when his tiger was in its cage.

Ted evaded John's stare for a moment when he thought about his last envelope of cocaine hidden in his car's glove compartment, waiting for when he needed it the most.

John released Ted from further scrutiny. He sighed, looked up at a large clock and returned his attention to Ted. "You're here pretty early."

Ted puckered his lips and breathed in hard through his nose. "Can't a guy just get a soda?"

John took a step back. "Teddy. I know you got problems, but..."

Ted looked down at his Coke, picked it up slowly, and took a swig. He glanced at the large clock on the wall behind John. "I should probably get going."

John leaned on the counter. "She never liked me. Jan, I mean."

Ted stood and searched his jeans pockets for change to pay his bill. Jan had always used the word common in the pejorative sense whenever she referred to John and his café. Now he could imagine her using the same word to describe he himself to her friends. Separation. What a stupid word! A sinking ship better described what was happening to his marriage, and worse, his two young sons were hanging on to the ship's railing without a lifeboat in sight. Ted's laugh was explosive. "I'm on the Titanic John, and we're taking on water fast."

Ted felt pressure on his right arm. John had come around the end of the counter and was standing beside him. "Teddy boy, get hold of yourself." John pushed Ted back onto the stool. "Don't worry about the bill. You got enough on your mind. I heard about the job thing too."

Ted's chest tightened. He drained the Coke glass and coughed when some of the liquid went down the wrong way. He forced a laugh. "Even my windpipe is indecisive." He thought of Paul, his principal, when they'd spoken in Paul's office the day after the school board made their decision to suspend him. Paul was furious that Ted had made a joke about the situation.

"Who are you?" Paul had asked. "You laugh when you should cry." Ted remembered the feeling of Paul's finger poking his chest. "Who's in there? What's in there? That's what I want to know!"

Even sitting here in John's Place, Ted remembered how numb he had felt when he looked at Paul, spread his arms, and gave his best imitation of Porky Pig's phrase that ended every Loony Tunes cartoon: *Th-th-th-that's all folks.*

Ted stood and brushed past John. At the door he stopped for

a moment and saw that Paul's question was in John's expression. He shook his head and, with a voice rising in volume, repeated his version of Porky Pig's exit line. "That's all there is folks!" A hush fell over the restaurant and heads turned in his direction.

Ted pushed his way out of the café, and slammed into a wall of heat. He hesitated in front of his sports car. The reflection of the restaurant's neon sign shimmered in the sheen of the polished hood. He looked back through the glass door of John's Place in time to see the owner still staring in Ted's direction, mouth agape. The look reminded him of Jan when she had glared at him and accused him of never being able to be serious about anything during their recent session with a marriage counselor. Ted opened his car door, collapsed into the driver's seat, nursed the sports car's engine to life and squealed out of the parking lot. He glanced in the rearview mirror and watched the restaurant recede from view. "Screw them if they can't take a joke."

A block later the quizzical look he had received from John still haunted him, so Ted pressed a button on his dash and filled his car with a duet from Mozart's opera, *Marriage of Figaro*. As usual the voices of the sopranos spilling from his cassette player broke his heart, even though when translated into English their words were merely a plan to punish an unfaithful man. It was to music Ted could flee when his human frailties were exposed. Whether it was the sonorous tones of classical music, the complicated riffs of modern jazz, or even the sappy oldies of the fifties, it was in the music he could hide.

But as he arrived in the neighborhood of his youth, not even the music could relieve the pressure in his chest that increased as the distance to his father's house dwindled. The memory of his mother's fragile fingers squeezing his hand as she made her shocking request kept his foot from jumping from the brake and accelerating his car away, past his father's home and the impossible task within. So with his mother's poignant petition as a guide, he pushed harder on the brake, swerved to the right, and slid to a stop in his parents' unpaved driveway.

He knew his father would be up with the sun, but he waited. The miniature dust storm he had created subsided and revealed a sunken front yard. His mother and father lived in an older section of Phoenix where water was diverted weekly into their yard from one of the irrigation canals that meandered through the city, where it flooded and greened their lawn. And later, further downstream on the fringe of the city, the artificially diverted water assisted farmers in their efforts to tease crops like cotton, melons, and alfalfa from the parched and barren desert soil. The front yard was a foot lower than street level and the land upon which the home rested. The driveway was at street level, and a narrow berm separated his parents' yard from their neighbor's yard.

Ted's father had always kept the yard neatly mowed. Now in the yard where Ted had waded and caught the occasional fish that had washed in from the canal on irrigation day, dark green grass enriched by nutrients from the canal grew higher than the edge of the driveway and waved at Ted. Watching the grass undulate in the warm desert breeze, he wondered. In which of his father's worlds would Jacob be entrenched today? The more he thought about his father, the less confident he felt about finding out about Sister. He searched his memory for an alternative plan and thought of the family pictures that lined the long hallway of his boyhood home and the boxes of memorabilia in a closet. Maybe he had missed someone's face. Who might be hiding in the family archives?

Ted opened his car door and exited slowly, conflicted, squinting as he watched the sun clear the horizon and take charge of the day. Above him a vulture glided in a rising air thermal as though waiting to help him pick the bones of his history. He walked quickly to the front porch of his childhood home and dodged out of the vulture's view. He tugged on the screen door and it fell open, hanging precariously on one hinge. Ted sighed. He turned his key in the main door and mentally added his father to the list of people he had failed.

The rush of cool air that engulfed him the moment he cracked open the heavy oak front door brought with it the sharp odor of a marsh. Homes like his parents', built in the 1950s, had bulky square evaporative coolers instead of the modern air conditioners that were regularly installed on homes in the new sub-divisions, homes that were steadily filling in farmland and desert on the outskirts of Phoenix. Water circulated through padded vents on three sides of the boxy unit attached to the side of Ted's old home, then a large fan inside the swamp cooler drew air in through the vents and forced relatively cooler air into the house. It didn't substantially lower the temperature of the house, forcing the occupants to stand directly in the blast of air to get relief from the oppressive desert heat. In the Miller's yard, irrigation water would soak into parched soil in a few hours, but its river smell would last for days. The cooler sucked in that boggy odor from the yard, and it combined with the fetid smell of algae that had grown in water pooled in the bottom of the unit. Nothing in the house was safe from the relentless surge of dank air. Windows refused to budge in their swollen wood frames and the piano, always out of tune, was a victim of the persistent humidity.

Ted hesitated in the home's small vestibule. How would he broach the subject of this mysterious person, Sister, with his father, whose only reaction to uncomfortable reality was to retreat? He stuck his head into the living area. "Dad?"

Jacob looked up from his favorite chair. He was already dressed in a suit and tie, in spite of being retired. Ted noticed how his father's body caved inward, as if a vacuum cleaner had sucked him into the center of the overstuffed recliner. Jacob's deep-set eyes brightened when he recognized Ted. "Son!"

Ted was hopeful, but his mind buzzed, struggling with his desire to approach Jacob carefully and with his desperation to know more about Sister. His reckless need to know won out. "It's about Mom."

Ted stood motionless in Jacob's gaze. He felt like a young buck that had locked antlers with an older deer that was losing its authority. His father's eyes didn't wander, but Ted could see a change. It was as if a light had begun to dim.

"She'll be right back, she just stepped out to..." Jacob hesitated. "... To the market."

Ted flopped into a chair. "Sh... it." The word sounded like the final hiss of a steam engine coming to a stop. He knew the moment was lost. Asking about Sister now was pointless. Nevertheless, Jacob had stirred a familiar response within Ted, a response that he would, as usual, soon regret. He felt as though he was nine years old again, helpless, unable to catch his breath or to stop the seething anger that bubbled up from his chest and caught in his throat. "Face it. Mom is in the hospital! She's...." Ted paused to watch his father squirm deeper into the chair. "Look, Dad...." Ted fought to keep a patronizing tone out of his voice, but he couldn't control the raising volume. "For Christ's sake. Mom isn't coming home. Not today, not next week, not ever!"

Ted swallowed hard to stop the lump forming in his throat when the lights in Jacob's eyes clicked off. He thought of the many times in the last few weeks that he had busied himself so that he too could enjoy a moment of denial. How could he blame his father for blocking the terrible truth of their impending loss?

Jacob struggled out of his chair. "Dirty, he said."

Ted knew that, although the remarks about his mother that had pierced his father's shield of denial would have been enough to send Jacob fleeing to the bathroom, it was his profane use of Christ's name that was his major transgression. A few moments later Ted heard the sound of the shower running, which was soon overcome by yips and howls as Jacob purged himself of the evil brought into his home by his son.

Ted leaned back in his chair and closed his eyes. That his father barked in the shower wasn't the only problem. True, Jacob's barking over the years had caused much consternation, especially during Ted's formative years when Ted was sure that every kid in the city knew about the canine noises emanating from the Miller's bathroom window. But Ted became accustomed to the side-glances and amused expressions, even the outright teasing. It was what caused the barking, a family trait of loony behavior that worried Ted most. The gene which had caused his father to misplace his sanity might have hitched a ride on the back of the one-in-a-million sperm that united with the unfertilized egg in his mother's fallopian tube on that day, 33 years and nine months ago, when he was conceived. According to his mother, it was not long after Ted's birth that his father, who was at the time also thirty-three years of age, found religion and lost his grip on reality in the span of six months. She was hazy about which event came first, but she had no doubt that they coincided. For his entire life, Ted had watched his father sink deeper into the morass of mental illness. As Jacob Miller's mental state deteriorated, the frequency and duration of his showers increased, for it was in that enclosure that he found temporary relief from life's grime and dirt. Satan and his demons were responsible for this constant barrage of filth. Jacob's only recourse was to bark and howl, scrub and yelp, until he had driven every contaminated demon down the drain, back to the sooty, fiery pit from which they had come. Back to the hell Jacob Miller knew full well existed, for he had created it. He had been there.

Ted groaned. "Crap, he'll be in there till the hot water runs out." He shook his head and snorted a quick laugh. Ted thought about his mother. Once when he was younger and distressed by Jacob's barking she had hugged him. *"He sounds like a poodle today, doesn't he?"*

Ted sat for a few moments wrapped in the glow of that distant hug. Then he stood and wandered from the living room into the long, dark hallway of his parents' ranch-style home and fiddled with the wall switch that controlled the hallway ceiling light. "Come on, Dad, light bulbs are cheap." Ambient light from an open bedroom farther down the hallway helped, but he had to stand close to see individual faces on the family pictures lining the hallway. He paused briefly at each picture, searching for a face he might have missed over the years. But most of the photos revolved around him: baby pictures and events of his first 13 years of life in Florida, then shots of his high school years here in Arizona and a few of his short stint in the Navy, and more recent pictures of his wife and children. He stopped and stared at his high school graduation picture, which was out of order in the parade wall of his life. Was that boy staring back at Ted really him? Ted still had the unmanageable cowlick that fell on his forehead. But these days several strands of gray hair twisted through the wave, their presence their only comfort. And of course there was the matter of the bare spot on the crown of Ted's head and the obvious thinning above his temples. He stepped closer to the photo. The boy's eyes were a puzzle; they should have been full of wonder and anticipation, but it troubled Ted to see a look of sadness, introspection, and shame. He wanted to reach out and comfort the boy. But the boy and his innocence had faded.

Ted lingered for a few moments, and then looked to his left. "When did they move that?" Squeezed in between the next two pictures was a wall plaque that had been relocated from a prominent place in the living room. *As for my family, and me, we will serve the Lord.* Jacob wouldn't have moved it. Less radical about her faith than Jacob, Margaret had always kept her feelings to herself. Had she begun to challenge him?

Tell Jacob that it's time to let Sister come home, before it's too late. His mother's recent words haunted him. She only called his father "Jacob" when she was angry. Had a conflict about this Sister opened between his parents before Margaret's hospitalization?

Sunlight streaming in from the open bedroom door distracted

Ted from his ruminations. The beam of light fell on the last picture on the hallway wall. It was a photograph of his maternal grand-parents standing between his parents. Both sets of Ted's grand-parents had died before his birth, and this picture was one of the few memories he had of them. Although there were a few pictures of all of his grandparents in family albums, this was the only picture that had ever been displayed on the wall.

He stepped back for a moment. The light was bright enough to see the expressions on their faces and the fedoras, popular with men in the 1940's, perched on the heads of both Jacob and his grandfather. But something he saw on the left side of the photo made him move closer. It was odd. Although it was a group photo, Jacob was standing more than a person's width from his father in-law and was near the center of the picture frame because there was a gap between the right edge of the photo and the frame. The other three were huddled more closely together, with his mother on the end next to the left edge of the picture frame. Margaret's dress, light colored with polka dots, flowed out of the black and white picture, but overlapping her dress at hem level, it looked like the edge of another dress, darker in color.

"Jesus." Ted took the picture from the wall, entered the bedroom behind him and placed the frame upside down on the bed. His hands shook as he released the pins holding the photograph against the glass of the frame. When Ted pulled the picture free, he noticed that a little more of the photograph was revealed. An elbow pressed against his mother's arm. Someone had been neatly cut out of the picture.

Ted had to find some answers. But the only two people on earth who could shed some light on the mystery either could not, or would not, help. He moved to his parents' closet, opened the door and reached up for a box that contained family memorabilia. But as his face brushed one of his mother's neatly hung dresses he stood, wrapped for a moment in the familiar smell of her perfume, knowing well that soon it would fade forever.

Ted sighed and pulled the box from the shelf, turned and plopped it on the bed. Inside the box he found a worn red scrapbook, one that Ted hadn't looked through since childhood. His mother had written on the cover in neat script: *Teddy's Baby Book*. He gingerly opened the book to a page of firsts: first formula, first carrots (promptly spit out), first passed gas. None of these observations helped until he came upon a page that had been partially torn out. The tear had interrupted a word in the middle, leaving only a capital "**S**" and a lower case "**i**". The next page, exposed by the tear, was blank, but Ted noticed that pressure from his mother's pen had created a permanent impression on the blank page. Quickly he found a pencil and lightly shaded over the indentations.

He read the now exposed sentence:

Sister loves to give Skipper his bath.

2

This time it wasn't the omnipresent odor of his mother's hospital wing that distracted Ted the following day as he left after yet another frustrating visit with his mother, who was again unresponsive, still locked in her medicinal prison. Although the odor had followed him, embedded in his mucus membranes, it had faded as he reached his car in the parking lot.

It was that damn song he couldn't shake.

Itsy bitsy spider climbed up the waterspout, down came the rain and washed the spider out.

He stood statue still, staring at the window of his mother's hospital room in spite of the summer oven threatening to cook him on the spot, his left arm braced on the open door of his car and the other arm on the edge of the roof. The children's song haunted him now as it had on many other occasions. In his memory the song was sung by the same voice. It was melodious and sweet, a young girl's voice. Like an apparition from the past, it often nibbled at his heels, trying to get a grip, pulling him back from the present. It was not his mother's voice. The song always came to Ted in that space between when one is aware of reality and the mystical zone of a full on daydream. In that fleeting moment, pleasant or unpleasant memories jump from the shadows and quickly recede before you can slap them with meaning, a time tinged with danger and hope.

Finally he gave in to the sting of heat on his right arm and climbed into the sweltering cabin of his car. He redirected the hot blast from the air conditioning vent, which had come on with the start of the engine and promised not to cool down until he was almost to his destination. His fingers tap-danced on the searing steering wheel as he drove away.

The song followed Ted out of the parking lot and for several blocks, only receding when the tightness in his chest and increased heart rate announced his return to his default physical state when under stress, which centered in his stomach. Ted was in his early thirties, but he had the guilt and shame of a sixty-year-old soul. Inside him resided a volcano with a bulging lava dome ready to burst. He fought the desire to turn his car around and flee in the opposite direction with no destination in mind, free of the terrible responsibility his mother had set like an anchor in his soul. Yet Ted knew that he must talk to his father again, so he steeled his will to accept the risk of setting loose the howling demons of his father's shower if it would lead him to Sister.

***

Ted's heart raced when he found the front door of his parents' house unlocked, something unheard of since 1958 when Ted was 13, and he and his father had made an exploratory trip west to Arizona in search of a new life. Jacob was always running away from something. Ted tried often to connect with him, but Jacob's eyes always shifted away as if dreading closeness, ever on guard. On that trip they stopped at a New Mexico motel where Ted left his suitcase leaning against the door inside their room. His carelessness paid off later that night when someone unlocked their door and shoved it open. The sound of the falling suitcase wakened Ted and Jacob and scared off the intruder. Since that night Jacob had religiously checked the locks of his exterior doors at least twice before going to bed and always kept the doors locked during the day.

Ted quickly searched the house, investigating each of his father's favorite places to keep cool, each nook containing furniture strategically placed under air vents: the overstuffed chair in the living room, the desk in Ted's old bedroom (reclaimed by Jacob as a den) and the kitchen table, which was oddly off-center in the room. Air was going to waste in all of Jacob's retreats.

Ted released a calming sigh when he opened a side door and found his father standing under the only air duct in the garage, tying fishing flies. Jacob hadn't employed the lures to catch a fish since the end of 1958 when Ted and his family had completed the move from Florida to Arizona. Most ocean fishermen in those days used less complicated lures. Jacob was one of the first to use flies similar to the ones used for trout, but much bigger and stronger to catch the larger ocean fish of the Gulf of Mexico. But Ted expected odd behavior from his father. To watch him here in the desert tying fishing flies large enough to catch a marlin just blended into the everyday craziness.

Ted noticed that Jacob's tongue stuck out as he secured the multicolored feathers to the shaft of a large hook. Ted knew that he hadn't inherited that high level of focus. He respected Jacob's ability to imagine what the fly would look like when completed. If only Jacob could have shown as much interest and enthusiasm in the activities of his only child. For a moment, Ted wondered how it would have felt when he was a boy to have had Jacob hold him as tightly as he held these fishing lures now as he inspected each one for flaws. But in those days Jacob cared too much about saving Ted's soul and not enough about nurturing his spirit. Because of that, including his brief foray into the world of drugs, Ted had for years worn thin a path in the soil next to the road of rebellion but had yet to step up on the pavement and feel the exhilaration of mutiny that would free his pagan heart.

Ted sauntered to the bench on Jacob's right. "Mind if I try tying a couple?"

"Sure, go ahead." Jacob glanced in Ted direction. "The fish will be grateful."

It was true: Ted knew he couldn't tie a functional fly if his life depended on it. But fishing had always been the one thing he and Jacob could discuss without his father's religious fanaticism invading the conversation. Now, if Ted could rein in his impatience, talking about fishing might smooth a path to a conversation about the facts he really wanted to reel in.

After mangling a lure and managing to stick himself with the hook, Ted cleared his throat. Despite standing near enough to Jacob to feel the air blasting from the single air vent, Ted felt warm beads of perspiration on his forehead and a fluttering in his chest. "Say, Dad." Ted squinted as he tried to tie the final knot in the fly. "When I was a little kid..."

Jacob pointed at the clump of thread in Ted's hand, which should have been a clean knot. "You couldn't tie off these things then, either."

Ted took a long breath. "Did you ever call me Skipper?"

His father continued wrapping thread around the fly he was working on without any sign he'd heard Ted's question. Finally he bit his lip and looked heavenward for a moment. "By golly, come to think of it, we did call you Skipper when you were real little. Why?"

Ted studied the mass of thread and hook in his hand as if he could wish it into the best tied fly ever. "Mom called me Skipper when I visited her yesterday."

Jacob dropped his handiwork, struck dumb for a moment. "Your mother will be home soon." He retrieved the fly and returned to his task.

Ted stared at his shoes. "Mom said to tell you that it was time to let Sister come home. Do you know where Sister is?" When Ted looked up all he could see was the back of his father's head. "Don't leave. I need you to listen this time. Please don't go to the shower. Not now... Dad?"

Ted was too late. Jacob Miller was on a mission. Ted had again brought evil into the house. The dirt, and the sin that caused it, needed a thorough scrubbing. His yelps, echoing from deep in the house, reinforced the reality: Ted had struck out again. So where could he turn for help? Divine guidance was certainly out. Ted had learned early in his life that he and God would be adversaries, competitors for his father's attention.

Once in the mid-1950s, when Ted's family still lived in Florida, his father took him to visit a traveling evangelist who preached from the rear of a converted Airstream mobile home. The back end of the trailer would lower and become a stage with a pulpit. The preacher and his family traveled the country hauling the big silver whale, swallowing up souls as they went.

Joey, the preacher's son, was pretty for a boy, even angelic. Joey had memorized many verses of the Bible and would hold his chin up with a big smile when he told Ted exactly where in the Bible each verse could be located. Ted's father compared the boys and suggested that Ted should try to be more like Joey. As usual, Jacob had set the bar high for Ted. Always just out of reach.

As soon as Ted and Jacob entered the mobile home, Joey and a boy Ted had never met came out of one of the bedrooms. Joey asked Ted if he would like to join him and his friend Jimmy to mess around in his room while their fathers weighed heavenly questions. Joey looked at Jimmy. He raised his eyebrows and grinned. "We got something neat to show you."

Ted was cautious. On previous visits Joey had been polite, but distant, when he and Ted spent time alone.

"Go ahead," said Jacob. "Maybe Joey will help you memorize Bible verses."

Ted followed the boys to the back room of the mobile home, which would transform into a stage with the flip of a lever. Ted loved anything mechanical and was immediately drawn to the maze of cables and pulleys that lowered the rear wall. Ted turned to ask Joey to show him how the door worked but was surprised to be confronted by Jimmy instead. Jimmy was at least three inches taller than both boys. His lip had a permanent sneer that matched his greasy black hair, combed in a tight ducktail at the nape of his neck, a persona he had obviously adopted from Elvis Presley, then a new rock and roll singer who had recently struck a chord with America's youth.

Jimmy thrust an opened magazine toward Ted. "Which do you like best?" He laughed and flipped down a third pleated page. "Her big tits or her ass?"

Ted felt his face get hot. "Should we be looking at these pictures?" He glanced at Joey and then toward the bedroom door. "What about our dads?"

"What a wimp." Joey smiled as if he had just recited a Bible verse. "Don't you like girls?"

"Yeah, maybe he's a queer," Jimmy said. "I'll bet he wears pink and green on Thursdays."

Ted tried to move past the boys.

"Hey." Joey reached with two hands and shoved Ted backward. "You'd better not tell your dad."

Ted pushed back and the testosterone gauge in the room hit the top of the scale. Jimmy grabbed Ted, threw him to the floor and sat on Ted's chest. Ted struggled to replace the air forced from his lungs. He grabbed Jimmy's left arm and, with all his strength, twisted to his right and pulled. He used his last bit of air. "Shit!" He felt Jimmy roll off.

At that moment, Jacob Miller entered the room. He hauled

Ted to his feet and, in the same motion, pushed him back on his knees in front of a bed.

Joey took a step back and glared at Ted. "He's been swearing since he got here."

Jimmy scrambled to his feet and pointed at the girly magazine spread out on the bed in front of Ted. "Look what he brought."

Jacob grabbed the magazine and rolled it up, then shook it in Ted's direction. "Pray for God's forgiveness."

A few minutes later on the drive home Ted felt a heavenly divide when he looked at his father. "You've got to believe me. They had the magazine. They were beating me up. They were afraid I would tell."

Jacob stared straight ahead. "I heard that evil word from your mouth!"

Ted noticed that his father's knuckles had turned white and his hands made an abrasive sound as they twisted back and forth on the steering wheel.

"Father." Jacob began to pray. "Forgive Teddy for bringing shame on you and his family."

In his mind's eye, Ted visualized God as he had on other occasions, an old man with a gray beard, arms folded with a smug smile on his face.

The yips and howls that had drowned out Ted's protests on that long drive home nearly twenty years ago were the same sounds now coming from his father's bathroom. The contest was rigged in God's favor. In his quest, Ted was alone.

He hesitated at the front door. Although he could feel a rush of air on the back of his neck, valiantly fighting to keep the house cool, the doorknob was warm from the inferno just outside the door.

Leaving his father's house, Ted walked into the oven of August. On the horizon, ominous brown clouds promised to engulf him if he didn't hurry. As usual he had to alternate his grip, from hand to hand, on the steering wheel as he drove away. The AC groaned, competing with the stifling heat.

"God-damn-it!" Ted swore at the heat. "God-damn-it!" He swore again out of frustration with his father. "God-damn-it-to-Hell!" He swore yet again. He was off to see his mother again, whom he missed as much as if she had already died.

***

The afternoon sun turned a dirty orange and grew fainter as Ted steered into the hospital parking lot and maneuvered into an open parking space. He opened the car door, and a gust of wind ripped it from his grasp. Ted had barely exited the car before another circuitous blast of sandpapered air blew his door shut. Dust stung his eyes as he ran toward the hospital's large glass doors. Once he was inside, the doors automatically shut out the worst of the storm behind him. Ted paused for a moment in the waiting room to compose himself.

"Daddy!" To his right, one of the two boys sitting in the waiting room waved a Superman comic book in his direction.

"Josh, Eric. What are you guys doing here?"

"Mom's up with Grammy." Josh, Ted's oldest son, punctuated the word up with an upraised finger. Ted looked into Josh's perceptive eyes. He recognized a ten-year-old copy of himself, thin and professorial.

"And we're being good." Eric, Ted's seven-year-old, ran to him and in one fluid motion, jumped into Ted's arms. The firm athletic body Ted held bore no resemblance to Ted's whatsoever. Ted breathed in the musty scent of an active boy.

"Why can't we go see Grammy?" Eric stuck out his bottom lip.

Ted pointed to a sign attached to the receptionist's desk. "Because you aren't twelve yet, Tiger."

"It's not fair." The lip didn't budge. "Daddy, when are you coming back to live with us again?"

Ted let Eric slip down to the floor. "It's complicated."

Eric crossed his arms. "What's complicated mean?"

Josh studied the green tiles beneath his feet. "It means he won't be home any time soon."

Ted reached out and pulled Josh to him, and the boy buried his head in Ted's chest.

***

Ted hesitated outside the closed door of his mother's room. They were both in there, the only women he had ever loved. One wanted him to completely realign his existence so that he fit into her worldview. The other clung to a secret that churned in his belly.

The door suddenly swung inward, eliciting a gasp from Ted.

"Ted. How long have you been standing out here?" Jan's hair floated and bounced—free of the bobby pins that had for years held it locked in a bun and stretched the fun out of her face. A glint of surprise in her eyes took him back before their marriage, when he had bathed in the glow of her approval. Too soon, though, her precisely painted lips pursed into an accusation and her eyes clouded with reproof.

Ted steeled himself against his pattern of acquiescence. "I just got here." His gaze shifted quickly away from her eyes and into the room. "How is she?"

Jan turned and led the way into the room. "Sleeping." She continued past Margaret's bed and stopped at a window where widely spaced raindrops struck the pane and flowed downward, creating brown streaks where dust had accumulated. Jan stared out the window. "The nurse had to increase her morphine."

Ted smiled at and walked past the Mexican woman propped up in her bed, pulled up a chair and sat next to his mother. He held her fragile hand. "Did you have a chance to talk to her?"

"Not really." Jan turned away from the window. "She was hallucinating. She asked for someone named Skipper several times. Oh... she said something about her sister." Jan moved to the foot of Margaret's bed. "She doesn't have a sister, does she?"

"No... at least not one she ever mentioned to me." Ted stood and faced Jan. "But I found out that I'm Skipper... at least I was. Skipper was my nickname when I was a baby."

Jan crossed her arms. "Oh." She frowned and stared at Ted. "But what about the sister?"

"I found my baby book at my parent's house. It seems someone called Sister took care of me when I was an infant."

Jan put her hand to her mouth. "Oh, my God."

"What?"

"Your mother said that Sister has a letter for Skipper that will explain everything."

3

Ted stood for a moment in the parking lot of his apartment building. He breathed in the last wisps of humidity left by the monsoon that had retreated as quickly as it had appeared. He was mesmerized by shimmering waves of heat that danced on the asphalt amid the last rays of the sun. Then he plodded to the door of his tiny apartment—the memory of his activities since leaving his father's house a blur. He fumbled with his keychain, chose a shiny new key and slipped it home. Once inside his claustrophobic cell, Ted closed the door, leaned against it and let the darkness of the cloistered space hide him from the ghosts of his day. They refused to remain hidden, however. Their evil one-eyed agent, the answering machine he had recently attached to his telephone, flashed its insistent tidings: *Three, three, three.* Three messages waited impatiently for him, three bits of news that would demand some kind of action or response. Ted tried to ignore the annoying red light, but an apparition of his mother, reaching to him from her hospital bed, sent him lurching through the dark toward a lighted button labeled PLAY.

"Ted, you can run, but you can't hide." The reedy voice of Phillip Morris, Ted's personal psychiatrist, provoked a sigh from Ted. "Remember, every session you miss without notice is twenty bucks out of your pocket."

Ted hit the DELETE key. "Crazy fuck."

The psychiatrist was Ted's concession to the school board after the episode in his classroom last spring, the reason he was on suspension from his teaching job. Morris's job was to rummage around Ted's psyche and banish every last neurosis. That the psychiatrist's voice sounded almost identical to the bellhop in the old Phillip Morris cigarette commercials from the 1950s made his task difficult. Ted often lost the gist of Phillip's conversation as he imagined the doctor in a small round cap with a chinstrap, shouting: "Call for Phillip Moor –ay – is."

"Ted, are you there? Please pick up. I know you can hear me." The second message was from Jan. She had a thing about answering machines. Jan was convinced that people used them to screen calls and that they would answer if she were persuasive enough. "Paul just called. He wants to talk to you. Sounds like he has good news about your job. Don't blow this, Ted. Eric is wetting the bed again. He needs you. Are you just sitting there listening to me babble on? I won't ..." (beep)

Ted dropped onto the single bed, which was, at that moment, imitating a sofa. "Saved by the beep," he said.

Ted smiled at the mental image of his wife standing with the phone in one hand and the other hand on her hip. Life was simple to Jan: things were either black or white, with no danger of the two touching and giving off the slightest hue of gray. With such a clear view of how life should be, Jan had great difficulty fitting Ted into her ordered existence. In Jan's view of life, being distractible or spontaneous was a sign of weakness. Her major complaint was his lack of focus. Ted had a hard time defending himself. It was his daydreaming that had facilitated the class-room incident, which was the last straw for her. The separation followed soon after.

Ted wanted to love her. He cherished their fleeting moments of happiness that floated back to him like goose feathers returning to the ground after a joyous pillow fight. Though it hadn't happened in years, he missed the touch of her hand moving lightly through the hair on the back of his head when they kissed.

Had it really been 11 years since their hurry-up wedding? They had only known each other five months when they married. Josh had covertly attended their wedding. Jan tried to hide his presence by wearing a loose-fitting wedding dress. Since then she had toiled to reconcile the moment she had let down her guard on their first date.

"Mr. Miller? It's Lois, your mother's nurse."

Ted stood and hovered over the one-eyed monster.

"I thought you should know. Your mother's sitting up and she's talking again. If you hurry…"

Ted closed the door of his apartment on the nurse's message.

***

Ted stepped off the elevator at his mother's floor, but he could go no farther. He willed his legs to move forward, but they refused. It was safe to be in that room when his mother, numbed by the medication and pain, spoke in riddles. But now she was lucid.

Ted steadied himself on the frame of the elevator. His free hand explored the familiar territory of his solar plexus where he felt a twist in his gut. For as long as he could remember whenever he felt stressed his intestines had, like a frustrated Boy Scout, tried again and again to tie the perfect square knot.

It was easy to forget the anger that welled up within him about his mother's condition when she was sedated and delirious. But now that she was alert, would he confront her with his worst fears? Many times he had counseled her to divorce his father.

Jacob subscribed to the fundamentalist belief that wives must be subservient to their husbands, to which Ted had heard Margaret respond, *phooey*. But his mother was, if anything, longsuffering, and now Ted was convinced that she had ignored the pain in her gut until it was too late, choosing liberation through death. His mother's possible revelations about Sister and the mystery letter only added to his paralysis.

Ted felt a tug on his shirtsleeve. "Mr. Miller, are you okay?" Ted pulled away, and the young nurse recoiled.

"Sorry…" Ted held up his hands as if in surrender. "Yes, I'm fine." Ted nodded in the direction of his mother's room. "Is she…?"

"Talking a blue streak. Her doctor doesn't know what to make of it. She should be in terrible pain."

Ted wasn't surprised.

In 1955, when he was in sixth grade, Ted's father had moved his family from Saint Petersburg, Florida to Graham, a small North Carolina town, for almost two years. After that they returned to Florida for a summer before the move to Arizona.

Central Florida is Southern by latitude only. Most of the residents moved there from the northern states, and Ted could have just as well grown up in New York, where he was born. North Carolina on the other hand was steeped in the glory of the Old South.

It was in North Carolina that his mother first encountered the beast that had now, in Arizona, returned after all these years to finish its dirty work. The surgeon at that time in nearby Greensboro was surprised that Margaret had colon cancer at her relatively young age, but was sure that he had removed it all.

Ted ran into cultural trouble at school a week after his mother came home from her surgery. In social studies class, he suggested that the South had actually lost the Civil War. He found no support from the teacher, the other students, or the social studies textbook that seemed to imply that the war had simply ground to a halt. A small group of boys from the social studies class waited for Ted a few blocks from the school. He could still see the look of horror on his mother's face when he came home and admitted to her how he had acquired his bloody nose and puffy, purple eye.

The gray, damp winter had a strangle hold on Graham the next day, but Ted knew that it wasn't the bite of the wind inciting his mother to clench her teeth as she marched him toward the school. The night before, he'd overheard her telling his father that she wouldn't take the pain relievers prescribed for her because they made her feel loopy.

At Ted's school, when the principal heard why Margaret had brought Ted to the principal's office he laughed and leaned back in his chair. "I was in the Army, Mrs. Miller. Why, I got teased every day about my slow speech and odd expressions. But those old Yankee soldier boys didn't really mean any harm. I'm sure the kids here didn't mean any harm either." The principal leaned forward and clasped his hand together on his desk. "It was just a little roughhousing. You know how it is with boys this age."

Ted noticed that his mother's hand, which gripped the back of the chair she had refused to sit in, had turned white. She closed her eyes, her other hand pressing her stomach precisely where Teddy had seen her incision the night before. Then she straightened her back and glared at the principal. "Roughhousing?" Margaret turned and pulled Ted from his seat. She pointed at his swollen eye. "You have the nerve to say those bullies were just roughhousing?"

"Mr. Miller" Lois crossed her arms. "Are you sure you're okay?"

"What? Oh yeah. My mother does have a high tolerance for pain." Ted sighed. "So her medication ran out?"

Lois nodded. "But she didn't complain, she just started talking ..."

Lois was interrupted by a commotion down the hallway. She looked back at Ted as she hurried away. "It's your mom's room."

Ted arrived just in time to see another nurse adjusting his mother's IV. Margaret's eyes fluttered, then closed, as Ted joined Lois at his mother's bedside.

"The pain was too much." Lois looked at the other nurse. "Good thing Jill was nearby."

"She was shrieking with pain," Jill said. "It's amazing she could stand it so long."

"I should have come sooner." Ted searched the young nurse's eyes as if they reflected the answers to the mysteries hidden behind his mother's medicinal veil. "Did she say anything about Sister or a letter?"

Lois thought for a moment. "When we spoke earlier she only asked me about her cancer and what was happening to her... Jill?"

"I heard the same, but..." Jill nodded at Margaret's neighbor. "Too bad Mrs. Reyes doesn't speak English."

Ted shifted his attention to the familiar smiling face in the bed near the door.

Jill continued. "She must have heard everything, even what Mrs. Miller said before we found her talking and called you."

Hopeless looks flashed between Ted and the two young nurses. Then they left Ted alone with his mother and Mrs. Reyes. Ted turned to Margaret, cradled her limp hand, and watched her chest rise and fall.

"Mom, what am I going to do?" he asked. "I want to find Sister for you, but I don't know where to look."

"Mister Ted?"

Ted turned toward the door. "Yes?" He strained to see who had called him.

Mrs. Reyes smiled and waved at Ted from her bed. "It's me, Mr. Ted, I called you."

"You speak English?"

"Si, I mean yes."

"But I thought..."

"I know, it's a long story, but it's better for me and my family if they think I speak only Spanish."

"Then why tell me?"

"You are a kind man, I know I can trust you." Mrs. Reyes pointed toward the door. "But we don't have much time. When your mother was not under the influence of the morphine, she talked to me about her cancer, and you, and her grandchildren."

"Then you didn't hear anything about..."

Mrs. Reyes held up her hand. "Mr. Ted, please, I did hear something while she was dreaming, something that will help you."

Ted walked closer to Mrs. Reyes's bed.

She reached out and took Ted's hand. "Your mother wants you to go to your old neighborhood in Florida. She said to find Mr. Calvinato. She said he knows what happened."

***

Early the next morning Ted was physically present at a marriage counseling session with Jan, but mentally he was miles away. As usual he was lost in a painting that hung on the wall behind their therapist.

Each time Ted explored the painting, he was drawn behind the slim trunks of aspens that dominated its center, deep into the inky black background that absorbed all color and light. Although the branches of the trees eventually broke into blue sky at the top of the painting, Ted seldom followed their arc. Only rarely did he notice that the leaves on the branches sported fiery rust colored coats that were bathed in the bright sunlight above them. It was to the darkness Ted retreated, hiding behind the forest of skinny tree trunks, escaping the harsh reality of a void in his life. The voice that sang about the spider always came from an empty place, so similar to the impenetrable spaces between the tree trunks in the painting. Peace and contentment eluded him, hiding just out of reach in the shadows.

This morning, however, Ted tried desperately to hide a different emotion in the blackness of the painting, a feeling that had welled up when Mrs. Reyes mentioned his former neighbor in Florida and still weighed heavily on his mind. Now he had a name for feeling. He had acquired a sense of shame early in his life but had stuffed it into darkest corner of his soul.

When Ted was ten years old, he hung around with three brothers who spent the hot, muggy days of Florida's summers free of significant discipline, abandoned daily by their single mother to the incompetent care of their grandparents who lived around the block from Ted's house. Twins, Donnie and Ronnie, who were Ted's age, were, at best, immature, and at their worst, corruptible. Their younger brother, Howard, however, was different story. Cats in the neighborhood had learned to avoid him, and mothers hauled their children into their homes whenever Howard was nearby.

One day the four of them were in a large chicken coop behind the grandparents' house. High pitched squawks pierced the air and feathers swirled around Ted and the twins as they watched Howard try to reinsert an egg into a hapless chicken's rectum.

"Howard! Stop torturing them Goddamned chickens!"

Through the chicken wire cage Ted saw the unshaved, toothless face of the brothers' grandfather poking out a window in the back of the house.

"The rest of you get the hell out of that hen house!"

Ted and the twins moved toward the door.

"Wait," Howard said.

The three boys turned and watched Howard heave the violated hen into the flock of perplexed chickens huddled in one corner of the coop, and then the boys ducked as Howard pegged the egg in their direction. Ted felt the egg graze his hair and heard a splat on the door behind him.

"Twins." Howard waved the two boys to where he stood. Ted shivered when Howard glanced at him and smiled as he whispered to his brothers.

Moments later Howard led his two older brothers to where Ted was standing. "Hey Teddy," he said. "Want to be in our special club?"

Howard nudged Ronnie.

"Yeah Teddy, join the club."

Donnie nodded encouragement.

Ted then asked a question he would always regret. "Okay, but what do I have to do to join?"

The initiation Howard described didn't quite ring true with Ted, but the three boys pestered him until he finally agreed. They were all to strip off their clothes and then, naked, they would chase the chickens around the coop.

Ted watched the three for a moment as they unbuttoned their shirts. Ted turned around to avoid their stares and undressed. He finished removing all his clothes, except his shoes, and was surprised when he turned around that none of the boys had even removed their shirts. Ted gasped when Howard rushed him and grabbed the clothes he held bunched below his stomach.

Ted watched in horror as the three brothers ran out of the chicken coop and headed to their grandparent's house. The last thing he heard before they disappeared into the house was Howard's voice. "Sucker!"

Ted left the hen house in a dead run holding his hands as if they were the fig leaf he had seen on a painting of when God threw Adam out of the Garden of Eden. The fastest route home was along Lealman Avenue, which was paved and a main road in the area. Cars passed him, but he kept his eyes on the sidewalk as he ran with an awkward duck-like gait. Just before he reached his street, the driver of a passing bus blew his horn and startled Ted. He looked up just in time to see several sets of eyes glued to their respective windows.

At that moment Ted fully realized his predicament. His ears began to burn as if they were two tiny torches. Tears appeared and ran like rivulets of hot lava down his scorched face. He turned at the corner around Old Man Rothamul's house, and as if tossing aside the fig leaf, he churned his arms as he sprinted toward home, down his dusty street.

Ted sighed, looked away from the painting, and surveyed the drab office of the marriage counselor. He and Jan had attended four of the twenty sessions his medical plan—thankfully still intact while the school board evaluated his position—allowed, and Jan had attended another session alone. Ted couldn't shake the image of an insurance executive picking numbers from a hat. How else could he have decided that twenty sessions was just the right amount of time to put the spring back into the step of a couple dragging toward connubial disaster? The counselor, Ms. Stella Bloomberg-Stein, who was as fresh and new as her shiny PhD desk plaque, informed them that it was her moral obligation to see to it that her couples found harmony and bliss at least a session or two before the deadline.

Sometimes studying the painting provided a different kind of escape for Ted, an excuse to ignore the ingratiating psychobabble of the hyphenated counselor and the litany of complaints about Ted that Jan felt needed a fresh airing each session. At this latest visit to the counselor, Jan had arrived with a list that was shorter than usual.

"Ted." Jan's lips hardly moved. "Ms. Bloomberg-Stein asked you a question."

"Stella, please just call me Stella."

Ted's face felt hot. "Sorry... Stella. Would you mind repeating the question?"

Stella nodded and smiled. "How does it feel?"

To Ted, Stella was a dead ringer for Bob Dylan. Every time she used that phrase, Ted could hardly stifle the urge to respond, *out on my own,* or, *like a compete unknown,* or, *like a rolling stone.*

"How do I feel about...?"

Stella leaned closer, her chin cradled in her hands and her elbows pressed against her knees. "About what your wife just said."

"Like a rolling stone?" The words tumbled out before Ted could stop them.

Jan opened her mouth as if to speak and took a short breath of air. Instead of words, she released a brief squeak.

"Now we're getting somewhere." Stella swung in a triumphant arc to an upright position in her chair. "Jan..." The counselor acknowledged Jan with a sweep of her hand as if she were Cleopatra, motioning to throngs of her subjects. "Jan just said that you are never satisfied, that you're always searching for something more. And you, Ted..." Stella leaned in for the kill. "When I asked you how that makes you feel, you said, 'like a rolling stone.'"

Ted smiled. "And that's good?"

"Good?" Stella smiled and squeezed her eyes shut. "Ted, for four sessions I've waited for you to dig down and express a real feeling.

For a few moments, Ted and Jan lingered in Stella's approving glow. When Stella grabbed her appointment book, Ted cleared his throat.

"Look, Stella," Ted leaned toward her as he spoke. "I hope this won't mess up your plans for us, but I'm seriously thinking about leaving town for a while."

"What?" Jan joined Ted and Stella in what resembled a football huddle.

"It's about this Sister thing." Ted hesitated. "I need to go to Florida for a while."

"Ted, that's crazy." Jan sat back upright and folded her arms. "If you go, I'm finished."

Stella, looking like Moses just before he separated the Red Sea, lifted her hand in the air. "Wait," she said. Then she closed her eyes.

Stella sat deep in thought. Ted guessed she might be reviewing lectures on crisis intervention wondering how she was going to get the two of them through the next fifteen sessions.

Stella opened her eyes. "There's no harm in taking a break, even if it's for a week or two." Stella paused, then smiled at Ted. "Would it be possible for you and I to have our one-on-one appointment before you make your final decision about leaving?"

Ted thought for a moment. "Sure, I don't see why not."

"Okay then. You two just relax and do some deep breathing while I step out and arrange things with my supervisor."

As soon as the door closed behind Stella, Jan turned to Ted. "I've tried to be patient, but this trip sounds like another excuse to avoid counseling. If you leave now Ted, I swear, we're finished."

Ted tried the only card he had left in his hand. "It's for Mom. I've got to find out about Sister before Mom dies. You know that Mexican lady who shares Mom's room?"

Jan crossed her arms. "What about her?"

"She can speak English."

"So?"

Ted told Jan what Mrs. Reyes had said. Jan's face softened for a moment, and then she shook her head. "I can't make any promises. I just can't take much more. What about your job? Paul sounded hopeful." She sighed. "Think about the boys, Ted. It's not just about you and me, you know."

"I know, I know. I'll talk to Paul and to both of the boys... soon."

Jan looked squarely at Ted. "Tell me one thing. I've just got to know."

"What?"

"When you were off in dreamland ... and don't think for a minute I bought the rolling stone B.S... where were you?"

Ted sighed and motioned toward the painting. "In the woods?"

4

Jan had just shaken her head in response to Ted's answer about being in the woods. She would not relent until he agreed to visit his principal at North City Junior High School immediately. So now, an hour after leaving the counseling session, Ted stood for a moment in front of the school. He was here partially to placate Jan, but he also knew that he couldn't put off the possible show—down with Paul much longer.

Ted felt a sting of nostalgia as he walked down the covered walkway in front of the flat-roofed, sun-baked, single-story rows of classrooms that stretched like octopus arms from the central office complex. He didn't miss the buildings. The architecture of Phoenix has little historical significance. Most old buildings had long ago been torn down and the soil paved over in the constant wrestling with and reclaiming of land from the desert. No, it was the bumping, shoving mass of hormone-driven protoplasm that had surged into his science classroom everyday that he missed.

Ted hesitated before opening the office door. Paul was a friend as well as his principal. But how would he react to Ted's need to leave town? The new school year was just days away, and it sounded as if the board had finally agreed to reinstate him.

Ted's gut tightened, and he felt dizzy. What about his boys? They weren't handling the separation well. What if he left town? Would Jan really pull the plug on the marriage if he left? Would leaving really solve anything?

Ted gripped the handle of the office door. The door flew open without warning. Ted threw up his arms to protect himself, but the door smacked his nose.

"Oh my God, Ted, I'm so sorry. Are you all right?" It was Jeannie, the school secretary. Since it was August and the fall term had not yet begun, she wore tight peddle-pushers and a casual blouse under a sweater Ted thought she must have thrown on because of her boss' notorious need for cranking up the air conditioner.

Ted held his nose. "Don't worry, I'm sure I can straighten it."

"Oh, shoot. It only hit your nose?"

Ted laughed, leaned down and gave the startled woman a hug. She had to stand on her toes to keep from being lifted off her feet. "That's what I like about you, Jeannie, that sensitive nature of yours."

"Then I guess you won't believe me when I say we've missed you since the..." Jeannie pulled herself from Ted's grasp and studied her fingernails. "...Incident."

Ted's smile disappeared and he looked in the direction of the principal's office. "Is Paul here?"

Jeannie raised her eyebrows and frowned. "Oh, he's here all right. Better grab a whip and chair before you go in, though." Jeannie pushed past Ted who was still in the doorway and wedged the door open wider. She hesitated for a moment. "Ted...

Paul got a letter from the Superintendent this morning. I think it's about you. I hope the news is good."

Ted continued to stare past Jeannie's desk at Paul's office. When he stepped into the office he looked back in Jeannie's direction, hoping to ask her more about her comment, but she had disappeared, and he heard the door click shut. He sighed and closed his eyes. He thought about his mother and Sister, his job, and Florida. Things were about to get even more complicated.

Looking out the office window he caught a glimpse of the boys' restroom where, while on duty one day during lunchtime, he'd found two eighth graders having a pissing contest, seeing who could pee higher on a wall. He winced when he remembered how little he had to say to them, since they effectively punished themselves. In their haste to tuck away after hearing Ted's voice, they both had walked away with growing circles of urine forming on the front of their pants. Then his gaze turned to the lunchroom where he got in trouble with the cafeteria manager, Mrs. Price, who could not see her own feet when she was standing, and whom the kids called Attila the Bun. Ted chuckled to himself at the memory of her arms crossed over her belly and her protruding bottom lip when she called him on the carpet for telling the kids that studies had shown that nitrates in hot dogs—hot dogs that according to her were government issue and had to be served—could cause cancer.

"Jeannie!" Paul Reynolds' bass voice preceded him out of the partially opened door marked Principal. The face that followed was no match for the voice, more the face of a tenor reaching for the elusive high "c" note. At six inches over five feet and no more than 130 pounds, he was definitely not back-row-of-the-choir material. That he had chosen to wear a suit and tie made his fixation on cooler temperatures more reasonable. Since Paul was looking down at a letter in his hand as he walked, Ted could see that the shiny crown of Paul's head had lost more territory to his retreating hairline.

"Jeannie, I ..." Paul looked up from the letter. "Ted, for God's sake, have you been out here long?"

Startled, Ted reacted with gibberish, which led to a bout of nervous laughter from both of them.

"So," Paul said. "Still trying to leave us, huh?"

"I guess so. Maybe I really will get sucked into my shadow."

Paul frowned and shook his head. "That's not funny."

Not funny indeed. Before the classroom incident Ted had described to everyone, including his students, his daydreaming as being sucked into his shadow. Shadow, as other teachers reported to Ted, was what his students were calling him behind his back. On the day of the incident he lived up to his reputation.

The assignment was simple. The kids were partnered up, looking at slides of bacteria. Ted, distracted by hummingbirds fighting for territory in the bushes just outside the classroom windows, was yet again adrift. The haunting melody of a spider, fighting its own battle with torrential rain, repeated itself in a soft voice in his head.

His reverie couldn't have lasted more than a few seconds when he heard a scream and an explosion that sounded like a large firecracker. An investigation later revealed that two boys in the back of the lab had been making a plastic soda bottle bomb when one of them mistakenly combined vinegar and baking soda too early. Normally the baking soda is kept in a plastic bag in the bottle, having no contact with the vinegar. The boys later admitted that their plan had been to shake the bottle, thus releasing the baking soda, and blow it up out on the school grounds after class. The scream had come from a girl who saw the bottle begin to foam. One of the boys panicked and threw the bottle into a trashcan in the back corner of the classroom where it exploded.

The incident might have remained a disciplinary situation for Ted to handle. However, one of the students who sat near the front of the classroom told her parents that Ted had been missing in action.

Paul turned around abruptly, returned to his office and sat behind his desk. Ted followed him, easing into one of the uncomfortable chairs designed to make kids who visited the principal sit upright.

"Are you getting anywhere with your shrink?"

"I'll never get anywhere with that crackpot. He's crazier than I'll ever be."

"God-damn-it Ted, your career's on the line. Take this seriously."

Ted felt like a 14-year-old in the torture chair.

Paul closed his eyes for a second and took a long breath. "I'm sorry. I just got off the phone with the superintendent. He wants to add a hundred more kids next semester but he doesn't think we can rent portables in time for the first day of school." He raised his hands as if pleading with the gods of school finance. "Says I'll just have to wing it."

"Hey, don't be sorry. I'm the one who barged in on you. I could come back later."

Paul shook his head. "No, it's okay. I can't do anything about the room problem right now anyway." He picked up the letter he had been holding when he first ran into Ted. Paul looked out his door at Jeannie's empty desk and dropped the letter back on his desk. "I yelled at Jeannie this morning, so God only knows how long she will be on her potty break."

Ted smiled and nodded.

Paul leaned back in his chair and sighed. "Adding extra kids wasn't the only thing the superintendent and I talked about this morning."

"Oh?"

"He seems to think that you and your shrink are doing well. That's why your answer pissed me off."

"Morris said I was okay?"

"He told the superintendent he was okay with cutting you loose, said that he couldn't find any reason to keep you out of the classroom."

"So...?"

"So..." Paul stood, tapped the letter on his desk, braced himself, and leaned toward Ted. "The board has given me the go-ahead to put you back to work. "

Ted stood up and circled behind the torture chair as if he was taking cover in a gunfight.

"What's wrong?" asked Paul. "This is good news, no?"

"Good news, yes." Ted studied the scuffs on his shoes. "But... but I don't think I can come back just yet."

"Can't come back? What the hell are you talking about?"

"Look, I appreciate everything you've done. I..."

"You bet your ass I've done a lot for you. I've been out on a limb so far it's starting to bend. I've..."

"Paul." Ted held up both hands in surrender. Just let me explain."

Paul slumped into his chair.

"You're my friend, I know how hard you've worked to help me." Ted slowly circled back to his seat. He took a deep breath. "Something's happened."

Ted spent the next few minutes telling Paul about his mother and why it was so important to find Sister. He talked of the pressure from Jan and his concern for his sons. During a long silence, he stood and leaned on Paul's desk.

"For years, I've felt something has been missing from my life. Not like love." Ted took a deep breath and returned to his seat. "It's more like I'm missing a piece of me. It's as if there is a chunk of my soul missing." Ted studied an area at his feet where the carpet was worn. He looked back at Paul. "Maybe finding Sister is a key to that. Do you understand at all?"

Paul nodded. "What I understand Ted, is how much you feel it. So, what next?"

"I need to go to Florida. Where I was raised. My gut tells me that if I'm ever going to be whole, I've got to start there."

Paul frowned. "I can't make any promises about your job." He picked up a pen and doodled on a piece of paper. "If it was up to me I'd hire a substitute to start the year in your place, but..."

Ted leaned forward. "What are you saying Paul?"

Paul dropped his pen on the desk, stood and walked to the window. Ted could see that although Paul was looking out the window, he wasn't focusing on anything in particular. "The superintendent wants your answer now." Paul turned to face Ted. "I can stall him for a day or two, but..." He shrugged.

Ted took a deep breath. "Then there's even more at stake here." He thought about Jan and his boys for a moment. "I could lose everything."

***

As usual, Stella, ready for their one-on-one appointment, was perched on the edge of her chair as Ted dropped onto the sofa across from her the next day. Ted, on the other hand, fought to keep his eyes open. He sat alone in the middle of the sofa in the space usually left vacant when Jan sat on the other end. For the first time, he hadn't lost himself in the painting above Stella's head. He had even arrived early. One thing hadn't changed, however. Ted wasn't paying attention to Stella.

"Bibles?" Ted repeated her last word in a lame attempt to prove to her he had been listening.

"Gideon Bibles."

Ted closed his eyes for a moment and sighed. "Oh... So Jan...?"

Stella shifted. She changed from right leg crossed over

her left leg to left leg over her right. Her loafer bobbed, warning Ted to pay attention. "Jan gave me permission to talk to you about anything she and I discussed in our private session, including any insights I might have about Jan." Stella cleared her throat. "I was most interested to hear what you had to say about stealing Gideon Bibles from motels."

"Stealing... I never stole..." Ted spread his arms to show that he wasn't concealing any holy books. "They encourage you to take them, take this Bible with you if you want to, or words like that are printed on the first page of the Bibles. Anyway, what does that have to do with Jan and me?"

Stella uncrossed her legs, folded her hands in her lap and leaned even farther toward him."Jan said you had some life-long problems with your father and his relationship with God thrown into the mix. I thought maybe you should talk about that. The Bible thing sounded interesting. I thought it was a good way to get into some of those issues."

Ted leaned back. "Okay, I guess I get it." He sighed. "Look, I've been fighting with God for my Dad's attention for as long as I can remember. It was kind of a joke the first time I took a Bible the Gideons had left at a motel. But after a while, I think I did it for spite. I thought, okay God, you keep screwing with my relationship with my dad and..." Ted's eyes welled up. He took a long breath. "And I'll keep taking your fucking Bibles."

Ted stared into space. Stella stood and walked to her coffee machine.

Ted thought about the day he moved in to his studio apartment and hid his Bibles on the top shelves of the closet. Jan insisted he take them with him, and he didn't have the energy to argue with her. The weariness he felt that morning had always been with him—not only a physical tiredness, but an existential exhaustion as well, a condition that Philip Morris suggested came from Ted's poor self-image. Ted's negative feelings about himself were easy to understand. Jacob's constant reminder to Ted as he grew up was that without God's help, Ted would remain, in God's estimation, lower than a whale turd.

As soon as the Bibles were put away in his closet, Ted had blocked them from view with boxes of the flotsam he had brought into the marriage that Jan had rejected and stored away years ago. He wasn't ready to discuss the pain associated with his collection of Bibles with his boys.

While Ted composed himself, he noticed that Stella had returned to her chair with a cup of coffee. She looked as though she could hardly conceal her joy.

Ted spread his hands in front of him. "What?"

"I call it the champagne moment." Stella grinned. "A breakthrough! You can't start healing until you allow yourself to be vulnerable. Once you've done that, it's like you popped your cork."

While Ted pondered that thought, Stella rose, gave Ted the Styrofoam cup of coffee she had poured and walked back to the coffee maker. She began filling a cup for herself. "Jan told me more about this Sister person." Stella let that comment float for a moment and sat down. "From what I've heard about you from her, this trip to Florida may be the thing necessary for the healing I mentioned before."

What...?" Ted spilled coffee on his hand. "Crap!" He wiped his fingers on a napkin Stella handed him. "What did Jan say?"

Stella returned to her perch. "Enough for me to get a fix on you."

Ted opened his mouth but didn't speak.

Stella leaned in. "And... with your written permission, I spoke to Dr. Morris who filled in some blanks.

Ted leaned back in the sofa. "So, you've got me and my life figured out, huh?

Stella smiled. "Not completely. You're a pretty complicated guy."

"Everyone is complicated."

Stella nodded. "Good point. But there's a sadness in your eyes that is going to make my job harder." Stella's phrase danced between them for a few seconds. "I don't think you understand it completely yourself. But..."

Ted stared at Stella. "But?"

"But..." Stella crossed her arms. "I think you're hiding something from me."

Ted immediately thought of John. *"You haven't messed with that stuff, have you Teddy?"* Ted stared at the floor. He wasn't sure if he had steered John away from his demon, but he was sure he didn't want to discuss it with Stella. This was one monster he wasn't ready to release. He looked at the cup in his hand for a moment then set it aside. "If you know me so well you know that my life will go to hell if I leave, right?" He didn't want give Stella a chance to return to her observation. "So I'm pretty sure I can't go to Florida."

Stella held up her hand. "You have to go."

Ted's mouth hung open.

"Saving your soul is never easy." Stella bit her lip. "Remember what Bob Dylan said in his song about losing?"

"You knew?"

"People have been making jokes about me looking like Dylan since I was a kid. I may be new at the psychologist game, but I'm not stupid. I picked up on your rolling stone reference right away."

"Sorry... I..."

"Forget it." Stella's smile was impish for a moment, and then it changed to an inclusive grin. "Actually, I thought it was really funny." Slowly her grin faded into thoughtfulness. "But getting back to losing. The song goes, 'when you got nothing, you got nothing to lose.'"

"Yeah I know." Ted sat back and crossed his arms. "Finding something is only worth it if you have something to risk, right?"

"More than that, Ted." Stella paused. "If you don't fill that big hole in your soul, the relationships you do have aren't ever going to mean anything or go anywhere."

Ted nodded. "So you did talk to Morris. Did he tell you everything? His recommendation about my job?"

Stella bit her lip and took a deep breath. "Yes...but things are more complicated than you think."

"What do you mean?"

"Jan dropped out of counseling."

Ted tried to wrap his mind around the words, the finality and harshness they represented buzzed in his thoughts like an annoying bee. He tried to swallow, but his mouth was dry from hanging open, so he gagged. When he finally opened his eyes, Stella was standing next to him holding his Styrofoam cup, now refilled with water, in her hand. Ted took the water from her. It was cool and sweet. "So," he said finally. "Alone again."

Stella sat back down. "That's not what I was hoping you would take from this."

Ted crushed the empty cup. "What else?"

"I spoke to my supervisor. It's a little unusual. But she thinks... if you agree, of course... that I could take you on as a single client."

"So you think I still need therapy?"

Stella closed her eyes, took a deep breath and shook her head. "Ted. Don't you think you need therapy?"

Ted's silence said it all.

"And now that we have the Dylan thing out of the way." Stella raised her eyebrows. "I think we could work together, don't you?"

"But what about Florida? What if I go?"

"You could call. Pay phones are still a dime to start a conversation, and there's a phone booth on every corner." She shrugged. "I could encourage you if you get down."

Ted nodded. "Okay, but are you really willing to get involved in this? I'm not even sure if I'm going yet." Ted looked at the painting. "I wonder," he said. "Can we ever know the truth?"

Stella smiled and shook her head. "Oh, you're going. And I wouldn't miss this for the world." She leaned closer. "I assume you have the same problems with Jesus as you do with his old man. Right?"

Ted raised his eyebrows.

"Well, if I can remember, Jesus is quoted as saying something like, 'You will know the truth and the truth will set you free.' Remember that?"

Ted nodded.

Stella leaned back and crossed her arms. "Well, I say the truth will set you free, but first it's going to piss you off." She leaned forward again, retrieved her coffee cup, and held it up. "Cheers."

5

"Eric, don't mess with the answering machine." Ted immediately regretted his sharp tone. He couldn't stop thinking about his meeting with Paul the day before or the meeting with Stella earlier that morning, before he picked up the kids for an overnight. Paul's lack of ambiguity about Ted's future at his school if he didn't choose soon to return to work clashed with the persistence of Stella and her rally cry for a quest of personal salvation and the search for truth. Although noble and convincing, Stella's challenge paled in the presence of his boys. A sting of guilt shot through Ted's chest when he thought of them abandoned. Ted reread a math problem he and Josh were working on. They were sitting on two stools at the bar that separated his tiny kitchen from the main room of his studio apartment. Behind them, Eric was sitting on the sofa bed, 12 feet away. When he yelled at Eric, they had locked eyes. Sweet defiance as usual greeted Ted.

Once when Eric was just two years old he had joined other kids rolling down a grassy slope. Ted yelled just loud enough to sound serious. "That's far enough!" Eric stopped in mid-roll and looked uphill at Ted. Then he took one more complete roll and looked up at Ted again. "Is that far enough?

Josh nudged Ted. "Dad, stop day dreaming. I need help." Ted massaged Josh's back. "Come on kiddo, you're good at math, concentrate."

Josh shrugged Ted's hand away. "If I'm so good at math, why do I have to take summer school?"

"Because your mom and I don't want you two sitting around all summer." Ted glanced over his shoulder. "Damn-it Eric, I told you not to…"

"But Mommy said your machine must be broken. She says you never answer her messages." Eric pushed the PLAY button again.

Jan's recorded voice filled the tiny apartment. "Ted, are you there?"

Eric's voice raised an octave. "Hey, it's Mommy!"

"Paul called. He said you haven't returned any of his messages. He has to have your decision by tomorrow."

Ted jumped up, and his stool hit the carpeted floor behind him with a thud.

Jan's voice continued. "You can't go to Florida…"

In his haste to hit the PAUSE button, Ted knocked the answering machine off its perch next to the sofa. He looked at Eric, who had fallen backward off the sofa to avoid Ted and now sat on the floor. "Are you okay?"

"Yeah, but why did you turn it off so fast?"

"Sorry Tiger, but some of that stuff is private."

"Private? You're leaving and weren't going to tell us?" Josh, who had twisted on his stool to watch the action, stared at Ted for a moment and then turned back to his homework, reminding Ted that Josh was ten going on forty.

Again Ted recognized how deeply Josh and Eric would be affected by his hasty plans to solve the puzzle his life had recently become. He righted his stool and sat back down at the counter. Josh twisted around in his bar stool again and stared at Eric who was as silent as the answering machine. Ted leaned his elbows on the counter, held his head in his hands and looked straight ahead. "I'm sorry, guys. I really was going to talk to you about all this. It just that it's all so…"

"Complicated?"

Ted turned toward Eric. "Exactly."

Josh didn't budge. He closed his eyes and a tear streaked down his cheek. Ted reached over and put a hand on Josh's shoulder, but his son pulled away from his touch.

"Look." Ted stared at the hand Josh had rejected and turned back to the counter. "Grammy asked me to find someone for her."

Eric got up and ran to Ted. "Who?"

Ted felt the pressure of Eric leaning against him. He turned and put his arm around his son. "We think Grammy might have a sister. A person we never met before."

Josh turned, wide-eyed. "Grammy has a sister?"

"We're not sure. You remember we told you Grammy sleeps so much?"

Josh nodded.

"Well, she hasn't been able to tell us anything else."

"Does her sister live in Florida?" asked Josh.

Ted squeezed Eric. "That's what I need to find out."

Ted sat on the edge of the roll away bed he had just unfolded. The boys had finally drifted off to sleep, but he saw very little chance of joining them any time soon. Eric slept on the single bed against the wall on the left, which also served as a sofa. That bed butted up against the solid side of a hollow corner unit into which the other single sofa bed, which was along the other wall and at a ninety-degree angle, could slide in one-half of its length when not in use. Although it was supposed to save space, Ted never pushed the bed in. It had become his laundry system when the boys weren't visiting. On that bed, two piles of clothes sat perpetually, one dirty and the other clean. The system was easy. When the dirty pile grew significantly larger than the clean pile, it was time to wash clothes.

Josh moaned and rolled over as if to protest, one last time, his turn on what the boys had named the Laundry Bed. The last thing Josh had said to Ted was that he hated the bed. Ted knew the comment had nothing to do with the bed. He looked around the apartment and shook his head. "What have I done?" Ted closed his eyes and the answer to his question, posed to the universe, floated into view in his mind's eye as an image of Jacob chasing him around the house.

Ted was only ten when he took a sharp right turn into the living room of their house in Florida, with his father in close pursuit. He heard the report of Jacob's belt striking the doorjamb, a blow he had barely avoided. He circled around a large coffee table, keeping it between him and his father, just out of the flailing belt's reach. "What did I do?"

Spittle flew from Jacob's mouth. "You know exactly what you did."

Ted caught a glimpse of his mother charging into the room. She grabbed at the belt. "Ouch! Jacob! No more!"

Jacob stopped, caught his breath, staggered backward and sat in a chair when he saw Margaret nursing her swollen hand. "I'm sorry... is your hand...?"

"What did Teddy do?" Ted's mother hid her injured hand behind her skirt. Ted moved behind his mother. He cowered under Jacob's glare.

Jacob stood up. His hands shook as he pointed in Ted's direction. "His Sunday school teacher called. Teddy's been questioning God's word again, and I'm going to beat the devil out of him."

Ted felt his mother push him farther behind her. "That's foolish! Teddy's just curious. Why can't he ask questions?"

The roll away bed squeaked as Ted stood and reassured himself that the devil wasn't behind his decisions that threatened to throw his life down a shit hole. He tucked Josh in and then he picked up the laundry Josh had thrown on the floor. Ted paused for a moment next to Eric, his face bathed in the red glow of the answering machine. He reached over his younger son, unplugged the machine from the phone, followed the electrical cord down the wall to the wall socket, and killed the monster with the fiery red eye.

In the bathroom, Ted brought the machine and its blinking eye back to life. He turned down the sound and pushed the Play button. He listened to the message left by Jan. Again, he heard about Paul's final demand. The news about his mother wasn't any better. The rate of her decline had accelerated. The doctor couldn't predict how long Margaret would remain on this side of the chasm between the known and the unknown. Then there was the developing problem with Eric. As if the bedwetting wasn't enough, now there was news of a note from his summer school teacher outlining some acting out behaviors, which were a complete surprise to his teacher. Next came Jan's latest accusation that surely Ted must be, at that very minute, hovering over the answering machine, letting her go on and on. Then came Jan's ultimatum.

Ted looked at his reflection in the mirror over the sink. He could see the white flags waving. Everyone in his life depended on him. His own salvation would have to wait.

***

"Ted?" Stella sighed and looked at her watch. She had arranged an early morning appointment for Ted before her regular clients arrived.

Ted repositioned himself on the couch across from Stella and rubbed his eyes. "Sorry, I didn't get much sleep last night." Ted pointed at the painting on the wall behind Stella. "Guess I'm still lost in the woods."

"Woods?" Stella turned and looked at the painting. "Those woods are pretty dark. Tell me more."

"Not much to it, really." Ted squeezed his hands together. "I've spent my life in the dark, bumping up against things, never getting anywhere. I guess the blue sky above in the painting is the goal, you know, to make sense of things."

"And what do you think you have to do to reach the blue sky?"

Ted thought for a moment. "I know I've got to solve the puzzle about Sister." He frowned. "But that's not going to happen."

"Oh?"

"That's why I'm here." Ted looked up at the painting. "I'm not going to Florida."

Stella leaned toward Ted. "What happened?"

Ted laughed. He laughed as he often did in awkward social situations: explosive, nervous and inappropriate. Like in Navy boot camp, when the drill instructor grabbed the front edge of his t-shirt collar while he was still wearing it, to see if it had been washed. The instructor's nose was so close to Ted's face that he could recognize the smell of the petty officer's Aqua Velva aftershave lotion. Not every ill-timed response brought consequences as serious as a hundred pushups. But the looks Ted received from those on the wrong side of his incongruous outbursts made him regret his neurotic trait.

Ted sucked in a breath. "What happened? My life is falling apart, that's what happened." Ted lowered his voice. "Jan says that if I go, she files the papers. Eric is wetting the bed and pissing his summer school teacher off, and Josh refused to speak to me when I dropped him off this morning." Ted took another long breath. "What happened? My mother is getting worse, and I don't know how much longer my father can keep it together." Ted stood up and moved behind the sofa. "My principal says he can't hold my job for me, and you ask what happened?" Ted stopped his monologue and crossed his arms.

Stella folded her own arms, crossed her legs and put her loafer in motion. "How will things improve if you stay?"

Ted looked at Stella as if she had asked him to do somersaults around the room. "I'm staying so things don't get worse." He returned to the couch.

"That's not what I mean. Look…" Stella unwound her legs and arms, leaned forward and braced her elbows on her thighs. Then she put her hands together in a prayerful position and pressed the tips of her fingers against her bottom lip. "How can you really help any of the people depending on you if you don't heal that big hole inside you?"

Ted sighed and leaned back.

"And what about God?" Stella asked.

"What does God have to do with this?"

Stella smiled. "You tell me. After all, you're the one who took His Bibles from motels, and you're the one who's fighting with Him over your father's attention."

Ted closed his eyes. "So, you're saying I can't settle any of my issues by staying here?"

Stella shook her head and smiled. "Ted, these issues have been haunting you here in Phoenix for years, right?"

Ted nodded.

Stella leaned toward him again. "And, how's that been

working for you?"

Ted shifted his position. He hated that phrase. It made him feel trapped. "But what about my marriage?"

"Oh, you mean that relationship you've been running away from for years?"

Ted sat up. "Me, run away? ... I love Jan." Ted folded his arms. "I'm not..."

"Look me in the eye... Look at me, and tell me that all this disappearing into your shadow isn't your way of either consciously or unconsciously sabotaging your relationship with Jan."

Ted stood quickly and walked to a window. He watched as the world went on with its business. People in cars and people walking, scurrying around, probably doing a much better job at running their lives than he. His heart pounded in his throat, and his gut knotted up. "Why would I...?" Ted froze.

"Why would you what?"

Ted continued to stare out the window. "Why would I try to sabotage my marriage?"

Stella answered his question with another question. "Who else in your life besides Jan can't accept you as you are?"

Ted thought for a few moments. "Jesus." He focused on a mountain in the distance. "I married my father."

Ted's mind whirled. He could hear Stella's response, but she sounded as though her voice was coming from the mountains he could see in the distance. "It's common. People often marry some-one who is like a parent with whom they have unresolved issues."

Ted closed his eyes. His face felt hot.

"Ted?"

Ted turned around.

Stella cocked her head to one side. "How do you feel?"

"Like a rolling stone rolled over me."

Stella looked at her watch. "We have about fifteen minutes until my next client shows. Why don't you take a break while I make a quick phone call?"

Ted took a long breath and nodded.

Stella stopped at the door and turned back. "Oh, and while I'm gone, here's something to think about." Stella toyed with her hair. "Are you worth saving?"

The door closed and Ted returned to the sofa, sat, and retreated into the painting. He looked at the trees. He would have to climb one of them if he was ever to reach the blue sky. They were slender and all the branches were near the top. There was nothing to grab and nowhere to rest on the way up.

Ted wasn't surprised to feel the knots forming in his stomach. Anxiety had always walked hand-in-hand with indecision. Stella had made it clear. Staying meant status quo, stuck. If he went to Florida, there was a chance that things could change. But leaving was also a leap into the unknown. What would he find if he chose to rummage around in his family's past? He might find out too much. Maybe he had come from a long line of lunatics, or worse, maybe he would destroy his life.

Ted looked at the office door. Like a cobra rising out of a snake charmer's basket, Stella's question swayed in front of him, tongue darting, threatening. *Well?* The door opened. "Yes," he said.

Stella returned to her seat. "Yes, what?"

"Your question. Yes, I think... I am worth saving."

"Does that mean you've changed your mind about Florida?"

"I don't know, I..."

"What are you afraid of?"

"Afraid? You know, my marriage..."

Stella held her hand up in the Moses position. "No, we've been over those things. What else are you afraid of?"

"What else?"

"There is always something else, Ted. Deeper. Think."

Ted look at the ceiling, hoping the answer would be written there. "My kids, my job..."

"Bullshit."

Ted stared at Stella.

Stella leaned even closer. "Ted, of all the things I could ask you to do, you know, the things that would save you, what is the one thing that scares the shit out of you? Fill in the blank: Ask me to do anything, but don't ask me to…"

Ted closed his eyes. The day of the girly magazine incident flashed into view. He wasn't really any different than those boys. The real shock that day was that he wanted to look at that picture. He was a fraud. Secretly he wanted to be just like Jimmy. Why couldn't he slick his hair back like Elvis? Why couldn't he play cards or go to the movies?

After that day at Joey's mobile home he'd lived two lives, one for his father and one for himself, sometimes confusing the two. He'd run with two crowds. One group was associated with the church. When he was with them, all conversation was Jesus talk. With the other group, he took secret puffs on Lucky Strikes, lingered over lingerie adds in the Sears catalogue, and had conversations peppered with words like bullshit and God-damn-it, the latter always used with just a hint of reverence.

With confusion came shame. Once, when he was in high school, Ted was watching a football game on television with some friends from church. When the quarterback on his favorite team fumbled the ball, Ted said, "Oh, shit!" The looks he got from his friends brought a burning feeling to his face and the knowledge that he was on a slippery slope to damnation.

Ted opened his eyes and looked in Stella's direction, avoiding her eyes. He wasn't ready to use the word fraud, nor was he ready to dig around in his psyche with the purpose of routing out the pain of his double life. Ted chose an easier, but related path. "Expose myself."

"Expose yourself?"

"You know, look inside. I'm scared to death of what I'll find."

Stella leaned toward Ted. "Yes, I do know. And I think you know that exposing yourself is the only way to save yourself."

Ted nodded. "I think I'm ready now."

"Ready to…?"

"Let the world see the real me. Go to Florida."

Stella smiled, but it wasn't a triumphant smile. She turned and looked at the painting behind her. "Remember what you said about what you had to do to get to the blue sky?"

"Yeah, find Sister."

Stella turned back. "I've been meaning to talk to you about that."

"Oh?"

"Finding this Sister isn't the answer, you know."

"But…"

"Finding Sister will just be the beginning."

6

Ted woke to the sound of a paddle wheeler churning water as it steamed up river. He rubbed his eyes and realized that what he heard was actually the sound of his motel's air conditioner fan splashing the water it had sucked from the stifling Florida morning air. Summer air in Florida isn't breathed, it's slurped in small mouthfuls. He moaned as he scratched his arms and neck and slapped the side of his head in response to an insistent whining in his ear. He breathed in a sharp odor, a smell that brought memories of the boys' shower room at the Saint Petersburg YMCA and the indoor pool where hoots and screams from Ted and his friends had echoed in the wooden rafters. He blinked at sunlight streaming through an opening in the curtains he had given up trying to close the night before. Blood on his hand verified he had killed the source of the high-pitched sound near his ear.

A quick glance around the sparsely furnished motel room reminded him that his luggage had, indeed, been lost during the course of last night's red-eye flight from Phoenix. A call to the front desk confirmed that Continental Airlines was in no hurry to reunite him with his property. The prospect of spending another day in his still damp clothes added to the gloom invading Ted's psyche. Ted opened the side table drawer. A Gideon Bible held his attention for a moment, but he grabbed the local phone book. Only the fact that an Anthony Calvinato was still living in Ted's old Saint Petersburg neighborhood, a place relegated to the memory of a 14-year-old, gave him reason to drag his butt out of bed for a shower that would benefit him for no more than ten minutes.

In the shower he thought about the message he'd just left on the Calvinato's answering machine. After 19 years, he just happened to be in town and wanted to drop by for a visit?

True to its name, Ted's rented Ford Pinto bucked as he popped the clutch and left the motel parking lot. His shirt was already soaked and sweat stung his eyes as he turned the air conditioner switch to high and swore when all he could feel was a rush of hot air. "We try harder." Ted mocked the slogan of the rental car company.

On the other hand, he was grateful that the rental car attendant had insisted that Ted take a map of the area. Things were smaller than he remembered, and new structures confused his sense of direction and distance. He passed a café that he knew was once a coin-laundry his mother had frequented. His stomach growled at the thought of flapjacks and eggs, but his mission kept his foot firmly on the gas pedal. He slowed to avoid two boys on skateboards, blond hair flying in the hot wind, so out of place in his 1950s memories of this place.

But some things were familiar. Fields of knee-high palmettos still waited patiently for a shin to slice with their sharp edged fronds. Tall oak trees, as they had long ago, invited boys with bodies browned by the omnipresent sun to build forts in their solid branches. Unpaved secondary roads beckoned cars to send fine dust billowing, where the grit would seep into the adjacent homes and settle on furniture, as it had when Ted was a boy. Here in the outskirts of St. Petersburg, it was still a wonderful place for adventurous children to grow up. After a short detour to the West, Ted verified that within a ten-minute drive the warm waters of the Gulf of Mexico still waited to drench squealing bodies in deep blue pools of salt water formed by pure white sandbars.

But a disquieting feeling hovered over Ted as he backtracked and drove through old childhood haunts, like the memory of conversations between his mother and father cut short when he entered a room. There were unexplained weekend visits somewhere up north by his parents and hours of arguing and tears when they returned. But more disturbing was the voice he had often heard before, louder and more insistent now, struggling to release itself from the Never-Never-Land of early childhood memory, that sweet voice singing about a tiny spider's adventure.

Ted finally turned down his old street and, in a cloud of dust that he had created, he reined in his Pinto in front of the Calvinato home, which had a familiar shape but had grown appreciably. The house had always been a work in progress. Mr. Calvinato, a first generation immigrant from Italy, lived the American dream in installments. The process had obviously continued after the Millers' departure for Arizona. New rooms hung off the original structure, impossibly designed by a mad architect. Ted remembered his mother saying that Mr. Calvinato built with his heart and without the city's approval.

This constant state of remodeling had, over the years, contributed in part to Ted's sexual awakening. Elisa, the younger of the two Calvinato girls, was six months younger than Ted but much more worldly. Once, when they were jumping from the empty window frame of a room addition into a pile of sand, Ted looked up at Elisa, who had delayed her leap. Although Elisa's mother was an Irish Catholic and had undoubtedly given Elisa the "keep your legs crossed" lecture, Elisa chose that day to give Ted an unfettered look up her loose-fitting shorts. Ted's face had burned, but he couldn't shift his gaze from the vision of that moist V of flesh, the revelation that until that day been denied him by the ghosts of the mothers of all the girls his age, ghosts who urged their daughters to hide the mystery between their legs. On yet another day Elisa charged Ted ten cents to peek into a room through an opening into which Mr. Calvinato planned to hang a door, where her sister Clio, who was four years older, pranced around the room taking her new bra for a test ride.

Ted fumbled with the memories and the unfamiliar handle of the rental car's door. When he finally opened the door, a rush of sweltering heat assaulted him. All thoughts related to shorts and bras were quickly dispelled. Ted sprinted over the lawn of St. Augustine grass, a weed in any other state except Florida. Sand spurs hitched rides on the cuffs of his pants, reminding him of painful barefoot forays in his old front yard next door.

The oak front door of the Calvinato residence had beautiful inlay patterns, but in the spirit of the unfinished nature of the house, it remained unstained and unvarnished. When the door opened, Ted leaned into the blast of refrigerated air that enveloped him. He found himself eye to eye with a young woman. He backed up, not far enough to lose contact with the cool air, but far enough to stay out of her personal space. Her fragile facial structure didn't match his memory of either Elisa or Clio, and she seemed lost for words.

Ted cleared his throat. "Hello, my name is Ted Miller."

Her eyes widened. "Si, Signore Ted...I..." She held up her right thumb and index finger, a quarter of an inch of air squeezed between them. "Sorry, little English."

Ted spoke slowly but purposely tried not to patronize. "I'm here to see Anthony Calvinato?"

"Si, Si, Tony." She waved Ted into the house. "Favore."

The young woman led Ted through a maze of warren-like

hallways, looking in various rooms as if they were playing hide and seek. In the air was the scent of fresh paint.

When they reached what Ted calculated had to be the last unexplored room in the house, she let out a happy shriek and pointed at a disheveled man in a wheelchair who looked to be in his late seventies. "Tony!"

Mr. Calvinato looked at Ted, and his smile broadened. "Tony!" Mr. Calvinato's enthusiasm matched the young lady's zeal.

"No, I'm Ted. You're Tony," Ted replied.

Mr. Calvinato smiled as if everything was normal. "No, I'm Ted. You're Tony," he said.

Ted was stunned. He tried again. "Mr. Calvinato, my name is Ted, your former next-door neighbor? Jacob Miller's son?"

"Jacob Miller's son?" Mr. Calvinato's smile didn't change a bit as he parroted Ted's sentence.

Ted stepped closer. "Yes, my name is Ted. I was hoping I could ask you some questions about my family."

Mr. Calvinato nodded his head and raised a finger. "I was hoping I could ask you some questions about my family."

Ted closed his eyes and sighed. Mr. Calvinato was even loonier than his own father. He turned to leave but felt a tug on his sleeve. The young woman laughed and pointed at Mr. Calvinato.

"He's a funny guy, no?"

Ted smiled. "He's a funny guy, yes."

He tried again to leave, but he felt another tug on his sleeve. This time, however, it was Mr. Calvinato, who had wheeled up behind Ted.

"Barks in the shower." Mr. Calvinato said. "Howls at the moon."

Ted turned, squatted and looked into Mr. Calvinato's eyes. "Yes, that's right. My father, Jacob, barks in the shower." Ted braced himself on the arms of the wheelchair. "This is great, I didn't think you could talk to me."

Mr. Calvinato beamed at Ted. "This is great," he said. "I didn't think you could talk to me."

Ted lost his balance and fell backward. He would have landed hard on his backside but, instead, he was grabbed from behind and gently lowered the short distance to the floor. He heard a female voice. "Hey there, pervert. You giving my daddy a hard time?"

Again, Ted found himself looking up the shorts of the same redhead he had admired over 19 years ago.

"Pervert?" Ted laughed. "You knew what I was doing back then?"

"Of course, I knew. Otherwise, back then I would have worn panties." Elisa held out her hand. "If you're finished looking now, I could help you up."

While Ted struggled to gain his balance and composure, Elisa spoke to the young woman in Italian. Elisa still had the fiery sparkle in her eyes Ted remembered that seemed to reflect her shiny red hair, now swirled into a bun. The conflagration of freckles on her face contradicted the language she was speaking. It would have been more appropriate that she speak in an Irish brogue, a heritage brought to her by her mother, who, as Ted now recalled, was born in Dublin.

Ted watched Mr. Calvinato, who was smiling broadly while his daughter spoke. But Ted saw that the old man's focus was elsewhere, outside the house, beyond the earth's atmosphere. Time and dementia had taken away much from the wiry man Ted remembered scurrying around this house, but the smile and distant look in his eyes were actually the same as he'd had in the past. The only difference was that in the old days, Tony was constantly distracted by what he wanted to do next on his eternal remodeling project.

Elisa finished speaking, and the girl grabbed the handles of the wheelchair and whisked Mr. Calvinato out of the room. Elisa explained that the young woman was a distant relative named Maria who watched over and cooked for Mr. Calvinato when his daughters weren't around. Tony's dementia had been a recent surprise, as had the phone call she had received earlier that morning from Maria trying to pass on a phone message from a Signore Ted. Elisa led Ted to a room dominated by two large overstuffed sofas and a chair, then disappeared into yet another side room. Ted collapsed onto one of the sofas and breathed in the cool air washing over him. When Elisa returned, she brought Ted an offering of iced tea and pointed to the window in front of him. "Recognize that?"

Ted smiled. "I liked the view from outside better."

They laughed, and for a few minutes Ted was able to tuck away his disappointment that Mr. Calvinato was in no shape to help him, as if he were quickly cleaning a room before a guest arrived, stuffing things into closets and drawers. But Elisa wasn't fooled. She cut their talk of the old days short and quizzed him about his sudden arrival and what she had overheard when Ted was talking to her father. He told her about his situation, about the strange events recently, and of his mission to find this mysterious person called Sister. Elisa was intrigued, but being younger than Ted, she had no more insight into that time period than did Ted.

After that, like a bee moving from flower to flower, their conversation touched various topics. She told him that she had married at 17 and had three children, one already a teenager. Ted was in the middle of a story about his boys when Elisa's eyes widened, and she touched his hand. "Ted, I just remembered something. Something my mother said not long after you and your family left for Arizona."

"Your mother, of course. She would know..."

"Ted, my mother died ten years ago."

"I'm sorry, I didn't..."

"It's okay." Elisa moved to the edge of her chair. "She talked about a young girl who used to live next door in your old house when you and I were babies. The girl babysat my sister Clio."

Ted sat up on the edge of the sofa. "Clio? Does she live nearby? Could we talk to her?"

Elisa looked at her watch. "It's too late to see her today."

"She's at work?"

Elisa thought for a moment. "Yeah, something like that. Maybe we could catch her tomorrow… early?"

***

The next morning memories and sunlight flooded the room. Elisa had insisted Ted stay at her father's house overnight. She said that her dad would be amused by it and that Maria loved to cook for guests. Then she had left for her own home and responsibilities.

After a quick shower Ted checked the condition of his undershorts that he had washed out and hung in front of the air conditioning vent. Glad to find they had dried, he slipped on the boxers and pulled on a pair of Bermuda shorts and a Hawaiian shirt that hadn't been washed for two days and now had the faint odor of the nearby swamps. The swamps were a mysterious place where he and his friends had thrown rocks at alligators submerged up to their eye sockets. The water was crystal clear because of the upwelling of a spring below. Once the alligators moved away, Ted and his buddies swam in the chilly water until the toothy reptiles returned to reclaim their territory.

The curtain-less window of the room he had chosen the night before overlooked his old house and its backyard full of tropical fruit trees. A guava tree, laden with ripe fruit cracking open and ready to fall to the ground, made him think of his best friend Dewey and their guava fights. They called the guavas "Florida snowballs" because they exploded like snowballs when they hit. His mother always handled the situation the same when he and Dewey stood at the back screen door, dripping slimy red guava pulp and seeds.

"You two are not coming in this house." Margaret's frown always faded, the corners of her mouth beginning to creep up. "Get over to that hose." She consistently beat them to the hose and, by the time the first jets of cold water hit them, she was laughing as if she were a lunatic.

Another type of memory pushed and shoved its way into Ted's thoughts, the type of memory that comes in flashes, harder to catch than a mosquito whining in one's ear. It was a memory from before Ted's fourth birthday and, for the first time—most likely because of the proximity to his old house—he had a glimpse of a face that matched the voice he heard in his head singing about the spider. A sweet face, a young face, but gone in an instant. Before Ted could take another swipe at the fleeting memory, giggling at the entry to his room interrupted him.

"Buongiorno, signore Ted," said Maria.

Tony smiled up from his wheelchair. "Buongiorno, Signore Ted."

Ted turned and nodded in turn to each intruder. "Good morning, and good morning."

Ted smiled. Mr. Calvinato looked as if he wanted to jump out of the wheelchair and give Ted a big hug. But there was also a look in his eyes that Ted found disturbing, as if Mr. Calvinato had already vacated the earth. Was he was no longer constrained by the inhibitions and responsibilities of society because he had already left? Ted worried. Was this a preview of his future?

Having accomplished their mission the happy duo backed out of Ted's room, leaving him to his musing. By the time Ted caught up with them, they had reached the kitchen.

"Mr. C." Ted called Mr. Calvinato by the nickname given to him by the neighborhood kids years ago. He was a father figure, always willing to teach Ted how to pound a nail or how to properly use a paint roller. "Do you remember me this morning?"

Mr. Calvinato sat up in his chair. Instead of looking at Ted, he seemed to be looking through him at something on the wall behind him. "Mr. C," Mr. Calvinato said, "Do you remember me this morning?"

Elisa breezed into the kitchen as Ted finished Maria's Italian version of huevos rancheros.

"Come on, dude." Elisa moved behind Ted and squeezed his shoulders. "Clio sounded sober when I spoke to her on the phone a few minutes ago."

The afternoon before, she had mentioned that Ted shouldn't get his hopes up about how much information Clio might give him. Now he was beginning to get the picture.

Elisa moved around the table and leaned over her father. "No doubt about what you had for breakfast." She laughed as she wiped egg yolk and bright red salsa from around her father's mouth.

"No doubt about what you had for breakfast," Tony answered. There was nothing in Mr. Calvinato's smile that indicated Elisa had any special significance to him.

Ted saw tears well up in Elisa's eyes as she kissed her father on the top of his head. "I love you too, Daddy."

***

Ted took the phrase, 'she's kind of let herself go,' and twisted it in his mind. He punched it as if he were making a pillow more comfortable; he stood it on end, but nothing he did could make that phrase match the woman standing before them. The phrase mocked Elisa's attempt at softening Ted's reaction to her sister's appearance. To say Clio had 'kind of let herself go' was like saying that a car hit by a speeding train had been damaged. Damaged, Hell—pieces of the car had been strewn for a hundred yards along the side of the track.

Some quick mental math verified that Clio was not yet forty, but she looked much older. Her face hadn't followed the rest of her body into the heavy weight category, but her leathery cheeks and neck had given in to the sun and too many cigarettes. She carried her increased weight like a juggler who has added one too many bowling pins to his act.

"Well, are you two coming in, or are you both going to stay on the porch staring at the fat girl?" Clio pointed the way into her apartment with her left hand, which gripped a can of Schlitz beer covered with droplets of condensation. In her right she held a cigarette with a two-inch ash, and she used it to prod Ted and Elisa in the direction of the beer that had made Milwaukee famous, though Ted could tell that it wasn't being offered to either of them.

Once they were in the apartment Clio brushed by them. "Sit where you can."

Ted helped Elisa remove magazines and empty TV dinner boxes from a sofa that was covered by a slip cover that had likely never seen the inside of a washing machine. When they sat down, Ted had to move closer to Elisa to avoid a spring that had worked its way out from the bowels of the sofa, close enough to the surface to feel, but still hidden from view. Ted counted six over-flowing ashtrays that accounted for an acrid smell that hung in the room competing with the overwhelming smell of poverty.

Clio had yet to sit down and the conversation, like a newborn calf, had trouble staying on its feet. "Did you think any more about the young girl who Mom talked about?" Elisa asked.

"Girl?" Clio was perplexed. She was obviously deciding how she was going to sit in her dilapidated La-Z-Boy without putting down either her cigarette or the beer.

"You know. We talked about it last night on the phone. The young girl! Come on, think, Clio. I'm talking about the girl who lived next door when Teddy was a baby. Mom said she was your babysitter."

"How the fuck do you expect me to remember that?" Clio plopped down in her chair, stuck her cigarette into an ashtray, and busied herself brushing away ashes that had fallen on her large breasts. "Shit, I hardly remember what happened last week."

Ted noticed how much larger Clio's breasts had grown since he had paid to watch them bounce around in her new halter. He was ready to judge their visit another dead end when Clio nudged him back in the general direction of hope.

"I do remember something about Teddy's house, though."

"My house?" Ted leaned in, intent on hearing Clio over the voice of Bob Barker blaring from a television that occasionally caught Clio's attention as she spoke.

Clio lit a fresh cigarette. The tip of the cigarette glowed bright red as she inhaled and held the smoke in her lungs for a moment. When she exhaled she recycled some the smoke back through her nose. Then she examined her beer can for a few seconds and took a long swig. Finally she screwed up her mouth, searched the ceiling for a moment, and then looked at Ted. "I remember someone singing a stupid song about a spider climbing up a waterspout."

Ted jumped up and bumped the coffee table in front of him. Ashes from an ashtray on the table clouded the air. "Can you remember who was singing?"

"Nope, just the song." Clio placed her beer can on a table next to her chair and took another long drag of her cigarette. This time she exhaled the smoke from her nose and mouth as she continued. "I do remember what a little pervert you were." She pointed at the mess on the coffee table. "You were sloppy then, too."

Elisa laughed. "And he's still a perv."

Ted sighed, flopped back down on the sofa and nodded his head. "Guilty." He turned down Clio's delayed offer of a beer.

Elisa, rose to her feet and mouthed the words, 'I'm sorry.'

He shrugged and stood up himself. Then, he reached across the coffee table to help Clio, who was struggling out of her chair.

Clio ignored Ted's outstretched hand and on the second attempt got to her feet. "What about the old lady who lives on the other side of Teddy's old house?"

"Lives next door to my old house?" Ted sat back down. "Mrs. Rothamul is still alive? How about her husband?"

"He died years ago." Clio steadied herself on the arm of her chair, picked up her beer and took a swig. "But I see her walking around her yard sometimes when I visit Daddy."

Elisa reached down, grabbed Ted's hand, pulled him off the sofa, and glared at her sister. "So that must have been quite a while ago, huh?"

"Don't be such a bitch." Clio brushed past Elisa and nudged close to Ted. "Teddy, talk to her. She's as old as God, but she's still sharp. And remember when we worked for her husband that summer?"

Ted thought for a moment, then his eyes lit up. "She remembers everything about everyone." He wrapped his arms as far as they would reach around Clio's body and squeezed and whispered in her ear. "Thanks, Clio."

7

An hour after leaving Clio's apartment and driving back to the old neighborhood, Ted and Elisa shared a reflective moment in Ted's rental car that was parked in front of the Rothamul house. The aged house had always been as out of place in the lower-middle-class area as a masthead on a rowboat. The three story Victorian lorded over the surrounding low-slung homes like a castle where, from its high porches and turrets, Old Man Rothamul had ruled the neighborhood. Ted smiled as he remembered when he and his friends made a game of hiding in bushes nearby as the old man scoured the vicinity with his ever-present binoculars. The rules were simple: The children were to stay well away from, and out of earshot of, the Rothamul's property. Ted and his friends took turns dashing out from the bushes, waving and shouting. When the binoculars turned in their direction, they ran back to their hiding places before Mr. Rothamul could make a positive identification. This was important since the old man was a source of income to Ted and his friends. Old Man Rothamul ran a sweatshop in his garage. He used Indian-head pennies to pay neighborhood kids five cents for each rubber doormat they made.

"I was just thinking about Old Man Rothamul." Ted rubbed his eyes. The sting of perspiration dripping from his forehead had interrupted his thoughts. The engine and air conditioner continued running, but for the moment the heat and humidity were winning.

Elisa shook her blouse to keep it from sticking to her skin. "God, he was such a curmudgeon."

Ted shook his head. "No, a curmudgeon has at least a touch of humanity."

In the old days, the neighborhood kids were convinced that Rothamul had something other than a heart pumping the icy fluid that flowed through his veins. They were also sure that the screams that occasionally emanated from his house were not from a cat being kicked by the old man as their parents suggested. The screams, they were convinced, were from the Indians on the Indian-head pennies, the ones he used to pay them and kept in a large jar on his mantle, coins that he pinched day and night.

Ted stared at the old house again. "Remember working in the old man's garage?

Elisa, lost in her own thoughts, only nodded.

The doormats were fashioned from narrow strips of old rubber tires pressed onto thin wire rods. Five small rubber grommets separated the rubber strips on alternate rods that created the wavy pattern of each mat. The grommets caused all the problems. If a grommet had been inadvertently left out early on, there would be a slight change in the overall pattern of the mat. Of course, the old man would notice right away. His face would turn red, he would wheeze and sputter. Then he would utter the word they dreaded: "Unacceptable."

He would refuse to pay the measly five pennies to the mat's maker until the mat had been taken apart and redone. The mats took at least twenty minutes to complete, an eternity for an eight-year-old. A redo made the task unbearable.

Thankfully, even the old man answered to a higher power: Harriet Rothamul, his wife, Queen of the neighborhood. Mrs. Rothamul knew every person within a mile of her house and, though she seldom spoke to anyone, she knew everyone's business intimately. Even the most outspoken residents deferred to her judgment. She held court, privately making decisions about how the locals could improve their lives, doling out edicts in handwritten notes to be delivered by the children. She remembered everyone's birthday with either a piece of candy for the kids, or for the adults, bunches of fat bananas that grew wild on her property.

After a few mat re-dos, the kids learned to take their grievances to the Queen. She would arbitrate on their behalf with her slave driver husband. After a glare from the Queen the old man would swear and throw the mat in the bin of completed mats. Then he would frown and toss five shiny pennies on the workbench. The routine never varied. From Ted's perspective, Rothamul never gave up hope that one day the decision might go his way.

Ted wiped the sweat from his forehead. "Thank goodness for the Queen."

Elisa leaned closer to an air vent. "What?"

"Sorry," replied Ted. I was thinking about Mrs. Rothamul."

Elisa tied up her rusty hair in a rubber band and let the breeze, cooler now that the air conditioner had turned the corner in its battle with Florida's sultry heat, wash over her face and neck and down her low cut blouse. "I was just wondering why we put up with that old prick and his doormats."

Ted nodded and redirected one of his air vents. "We needed the money." Then Ted leaned back in his seat. He reconsidered his answer to Elisa.

That the neighborhood children worked for Old Man Rothamul back in the day was actually an oddity explained by the lower-middle-class life they lived. Here in the neighborhood where Ted had lived, the word allowance was unknown. Ted and his friends had to rely on delivering newspapers, babysitting and odd jobs for spending money. Rothamul and his rubber mat outfit had unwittingly provided the kids with a hard lesson in economics. To have money, they needed to work for a bastard like Old Man Rothamul, who represented uncaring bosses for whom they were inevitably destined to work. The Queen, on the other hand, fore-shadowed the unions Ted's friends would eventually depend on to watch out for their interests. While Ted had escaped that fate by moving to Arizona at age 14 and later going to college, he didn't feel special. In fact at this moment in front of the Queen's home he felt humble—and anxious.

Ted leaned forward and surveyed the upper floors of the Rothamul estate. He knew the old man was dead, but for a moment he thought he saw binoculars pointed out of one of the tower win-dows. He switched the engine off. "Well, ready to face the Queen?" He opened his door and was slapped by heat that threatened to take his breath away. He strode quickly to get out of binocular range.

Elisa joined him as he reached an old wrought iron gate that complained when Ted pushed it open. A combination of appre-hension and hope accompanied him up several cobbled steps, on to a wide porch and up to a large oak door, its fading finish a victim of years of exposure to the unrelenting sun. Hope, however, was stretched as thin as the cotton tee shirt that had restrained Clio's mountainous breasts as earlier she'd waved good-bye, scattering cigarette ashes in the air. Ted grabbed and raised the bulbous door-knocker, sculpted in the shape of a bulldog's face. Then he froze.

Elisa let out a long sigh. Ted felt her hot breath on the back of his neck as she braced her left hand on his left shoulder and reached over his other shoulder with her right hand. "For Christ's sake Ted, knock." She pushed the back of Ted's hand, and the knocker hit the metal strike plate with such force that the sound echoed on the other side of the door. Startled, Ted knocked three more times.

Moments later the old door cracked open slightly, then swung open. In the doorway stood a woman about their age.

Ted's eyes widened. "Paula?"

Paula was the Rothamul's granddaughter. The feature that made her instantly recognizable was her teeth. Kids in the neighborhood used to say that Paula's teeth always entered the room before she did. Her grandparents could have easily afforded braces for her, but she refused to wear them.

"Teddy Miller?"

Ted stared at his shoes. "Guilty." A hot shadow of shame moved across his face. Like Elisa, Paula had also been a big part of his sexual awakening. She had been much more overt, however. He could almost feel her protruding teeth cracking against his own teeth as he thought about their first kiss behind the Rothamul's garage.

It was a few days after that kiss that he was first introduced to social hierarchy. Ted and some of his friends were standing in front of the Rothamul house, trying to avoid the old man's binoculars. Paula and her mother walked past their group. Her mother stopped and looked directly at Ted. "I don't want you playing with these kinds of children."

Of course, Paula did just the opposite and got very much involved with Ted. Once she suggested that Ted look through her bathroom window while she took a bath. Although the bathtub was on the first floor, Ted remembered his precarious toehold in a slight break in the siding of the ancient house and how his fingers ached as he gripped the window ledge. Paula hid herself in a tub full of bubbles and raised her hips up through the bubbles just far enough for him to glimpse her pubic bone. She kept her budding breasts hidden under a large washrag and was slowly revealing one of them when her grandmother burst in the room. To his chagrin, Ted had ignored the sound of a window slamming shut a floor above him just moments before. He quickly surmised that the old man had caught sight of him clinging to the window-sill and had reported him to the Queen.

The shame of being caught in such a compromising position lashed and pummeled his body to the point that, later that evening, the belt Ted's father took to his bottom offered a strange kind of relief. Paula had acted shocked when Ted was discovered that day over twenty years ago, and they had not spoken again until this day.

Paula crossed her arms. "What are you doing here?" Her gaze shifted to Elisa. "And what is she doing here?"

Ted could see in Elisa's glare evidence of a history of her own with Paula. He took control before Elisa had a chance to respond.

"We..." Ted glanced at Elisa, who was still staring at Paula. "I mean... I was hoping I could speak to your grandmother. You see..."

"She isn't well."

Ted took a deep breath. "It's very important. My mother is dying, and your grandmother might have some information about my past that could help me."

Paula uncrossed her arms and closed the door halfway. "I'm very sorry about your mother, but Harriet can't be bothered. She's too ill to speak with you."

"Paula, who is that at the door?" Ted recognized the ghostly voice echoing from the bowels of the house.

"It's nothing, Grandmother. Go back to your room." Paula shut the door until only her face protruded.

Ted stood on his toes and looked over Paula's head. "Mrs. Rothamul, it's Ted Miller. I..."

Paula's face disappeared, and the door clicked shut.

Ted turned around and leaned on the door, "...hoped to have a word with you."

His back braced on the Rothamul's front door, Ted noticed a black cloud moving their way. Summer thunderstorms in Florida are like bumper cars at a carnival ride. They can sneak up behind and hit without warning. Often they are small weather cells no more than a quarter of a mile wide. One side of a street can be deluged by torrents of rain, while the other side of the street remains relatively dry. When observed from a distance they can look innocent enough until, from within these puffy pods, blazing fingers of lightning splay across the sky. Seconds later, the flash of lightning is followed by mind-numbing cracks of thunder, extending their threat with a rumble to warn those in retreat to remain alert.

Ted and Elisa had little time to consider their failure to communicate with the Queen. In seconds, one of those meteorological bad boys blasted them with a flash and a bang, followed quickly by a cloudburst.

Ted grabbed Elisa's arm and guided her down the front stairs and toward the car.

Elisa pulled free of his grasp. "Screw the car. Running is faster."

Ted could hear her shrieks as she sprinted toward her father's house until he closed his car door on the downpour. He drove his car two hundred feet, parked in front of the Calvinato's house and waited. Although his car shook with each blast of thunder, it was no match for the storm his encounter with Paula had unleashed in his mind. Finally he braved the downpour and ran to the house, where he stopped for a moment on the Calvinato's covered front porch. Though still disturbed by Paula's rebuff, he closed his eyes and let the earthy smell of air—momentarily scrubbed free of its thick coat of humidity by the cleansing deluge—seep into his lungs. Refreshed, Ted entered the house, determined not to let this setback change his quest.

In his room he stripped off his soaked clothing, which he had already worn for the second day, and put on a bathrobe Elisa had given him the night before. Ted looked up to see Elisa entering his room.

She had obviously changed her own clothes, mismatched and only partially buttoned, in a flurry, and was swirling a towel around her matted hair creating a turban. "What a bitch. She hasn't changed a bit."

Ted nodded. He decided not to say anything that would elicit further elaboration of Elisa's personal issues with Paula.

"Scusi?" Ted noticed that Maria was biting her lower lip as she leaned into the room, extending her hand, which held a note. Her long black hair, knotted in a ponytail, accentuated her high cheekbones. Elisa took the note and spoke to Maria in Italian. Maria nodded and disappeared. Elisa handed the note to Ted.

Ted understood the word: *telefonata*, but *albergo* and *bagagli* made no sense to him at all. Elisa laughed and told him that it was a phone message. Ted's luggage had been dropped off at his motel by an airline delivery service. He should pick it up as soon as possible.

Elisa disappeared for a few minutes then returned with pair of Bermuda shorts and a shirt. "These are my dad's. They should do until you get your own clothes."

***

Ted returned to the Calvinato residence later that evening with more than his luggage. The tempest in his mind had returned, but now it was a hurricane. As if to match his discomfort, the storm outside still raged, larger now and more intense. At the motel, Ted had received a message from Jan. *Call me. Your mother's nurse, Paul, and even Stella, are trying to reach you.* Ted now regretted not calling anyone with his new contact number. Because of his reluctance to face reality, he realized that he was virtually cut off from anyone in Phoenix. He tried to convince himself that although Stella had promised to help, in reality she was busy with her own life and career. He was also sure that neither Paul nor his mother's nurse could possibly have good news. So for the moment he let the message from Jan hang in limbo.

Elisa had already left by the time he came back from the motel. She'd told Ted earlier that, although she felt lucky to have full support from her husband as far as helping Ted, she didn't want to push her luck. She promised to talk more about what they should do next the following day. That worked for Ted. Maria and Mr. C were preoccupied elsewhere in the house and, for the time being, Ted didn't plan to look for them. He needed some time alone.

Ted sat in front of a large plate glass window to watch the lightning dance over trees on his family's former property. When he was a child, his father had often sat with him at a window counting the seconds between a flash of lightning and its companion clap of thunder. According to Jacob, the number of seconds counted was equal to the distance in miles from where lightning had struck the earth. Ted had treasured these fleeting moments of peace with his father between the abusive remarks and beatings and the episodes of barking which peppered most of his childhood.

Ted pulled his chair even closer to the window. An especially bright flash, which Ted quickly verified was only a mile away, lit up the side of his old house. The sight of the bathroom window that had leaked his father's barks and howls into the neighborhood drew him in and stirred memories that had long ago settled to the back of his brain.

Ted was only five years old. It was late and he was in bed when he heard knocking and shivered when it increased in volume. "Who's there?" Ted could barely hear his father's voice.

The loud answer to Jacob's question was as clear to Ted as if the stranger was already in the house. "The sheriff."

How surprised he was to hear that a sheriff was at his front door. Until then, the only sheriffs in Ted's experience rode the radio airwaves with the Lone Ranger and Tonto.

"Open the door."

Ted heard his father bump into the wall as he stumbled past Ted's bedroom. "Hold on. I'm coming."

Ted cracked his bedroom door open. Muffled voices from the living room confirmed that the sheriff was in the house. Curiously, the sheriff spoke to Jacob in the same way adults spoke to Ted when they didn't think he understood something.

That memory faded as another came into focus. Ted and his father were at an amusement park that included a corral with ponies to ride. Teenagers walked the ponies, mounted by young riders, around a circular path surrounded on both sides by a hitching post fence. Ted stiffened when a boy helped him onto the saddle.

"Come on, kid. Don't be a baby."

Something felt wrong. His feet didn't feel secure in the stirrups. Ted watched his pony butt the older boy. The teenager swatted the pony's ears, and the tiny horse bucked and backed away. Ted gripped the saddle horn as if he wanted to strangle it. "Stop! Let me off!"

He lurched to get off the pony. It took another step backward and bumped Ted's leg against the side rail. He let go of the saddle horn and grabbed the colt's mane. The pony jerked the reins from the teenager's hand and bolted down the path. Ted's feet were out of the stirrups and the saddle horn was jammed into his solar plexus. As the pony galloped, it twisted its head from side to side to loosen Ted's death grip on its mane. Every few yards it bumped Ted's leg against the rail. Even now, Ted could remember the feeling of a scream caught in his throat.

Ahead, Ted could see the other ponies at the starting point. The teenager waved his hat and the pony stopped suddenly, throwing Ted even further forward. But he held on. When Ted was eased down, the boy had to pry Ted's hands off the pony's mane.

In the car a few minutes later, Jacob chided Ted for his embarrassing behavior. "You are such a disappointment. Why did you spook that pony?"

Then Ted's memory returned to the sheriff's visit. That night Ted's history of disappointing his father had crept down the hallway with him. He didn't want to be discovered cowering in the hall, but he had be near the action. There was a sheriff in the living room and he brought with him the sweet, sharp smell of burning pipe tobacco that Ted remembered from Old Man Rothamul's pipe when he leaned over Ted's shoulder to check on the quality of a doormat Ted was assembling.

Ted heard his mother's voice join the others. "Jacob, be reasonable. It's for your own good."

"Arresting me isn't necessary. I know the drill. I worked there for many years, for crying out loud." For crying out loud was as close as Jacob Miller ever came to swearing. "I want to know who ordered this."

"Please stay calm, Mr. Miller." The sheriff used the voice reserved for five-year-olds again. "We're not arresting you, we're accompanying you. It's the law. If you worked there, you know that."

There was a long silence. Then Jacob spoke again. "At least take that pipe back outside. We don't allow smoking in the house."

The front door opened. Ted heard the sharp report of something tapping on the porch.

"How could you go along with this?" Jacob voice sounded like a cobra's hiss.

His mother sounded as if she were begging. "You need help, Jacob."

Ted moved closer to the living room. It was dark and he didn't see the broom. The sharp slap of its handle on the hardwood floor startled Jacob, and he turned toward the sound.

Jacob's voice exploded. "Teddy?"

Ted ran to his mother, who instinctively pushed him behind her. "He's just curious. He has to know why you're leaving."

Jacob took a step toward them. "Who said I was leaving?"

Ted felt his mother stand straighter. She looked back at Ted, took a deep breath and turned back to face Jacob. "The barking, it's getting worse, and I'm frightened. It's... It's time to get some help."

A loud crack of thunder brought Ted back to the present. The rain had shifted direction and danced on the window, blurring his view of his old house. He tried to remember where Jacob had worked when they lived in Florida. In Phoenix, his father had worked as a business manager for a hospital until he retired. But as far as he could remember, Jacob was usually around the house when they lived in Florida.

Ted looked at an alarm clock perched across the room on an antique mission style dresser. Even with the time difference it was still early enough to make return calls to Phoenix. First, though, he wanted to take another stab at breaking through the repetitive communication gap with Mr. C.

Once in the hallway, Ted heard a commotion on the other side of the house. He followed the laughter until it led him to the kitchen. Maria waved a piece of broccoli, enticing Mr. C to eat it. The old man would have none of it.

Maria puffed out her lip. "Tony, mangiare, per favore."

Mr. Calvinato puckered his own lips and repeated her request. "Tony, mangiare, per favore."

Ted reached across the table, took a piece of broccoli and popped it into his own mouth. Mr. C laughed and ate a piece of broccoli himself!

Maria smiled at Ted and held up her thumb. "Bravo, grazie."

"No problem." Ted took a seat across from Mr. Calvinato and waited until he thought he had the old man's attention. "Mr. C, do you remember where Jacob worked?"

Mr. C thought for a moment. Then his eyebrows raised and his mouth opened wide, giving the impression that he had received a great insight. Without hesitation, he reached out, grabbed another piece of broccoli and tossed it into his gaping mouth. He chewed the broccoli. Then in a clear voice he repeated Ted's question. "Mr. C," he asked. "Do you remember where Jacob worked?"

Maria, happy that Mr. Calvinato was eating, laughed and joined him in eating the broccoli, piece by piece. Ted shook his head, stood, and walked back through the warren-like hallways to his room. He sat on the edge of his bed and picked up the phone on the bedside table that Elisa had told him to feel free to use. His first call was to Jan.

Her tone of voice and manner reminded him of their life together for the last few years. Jan kept a distance of a least four feet between them. Whenever he would move toward her, she would move away far enough to maintain the four-foot gap. As she spoke now on the phone, she was ready to retreat again. Her conversation was a laundry list of the reasons why he should give up this idiotic venture in Florida and get back to Phoenix where he belonged. The boys missed and needed him. There was no way she and Ted could work on their relationship with him in Florida. Paul had called her to say that he was interviewing candidates for Ted's job and that, unless he was going to be heading home soon, there was no reason to call him back. When Jan hesitated for several seconds, Ted imagined her taking time to reload. He was under attack and looked around for a rock to duck behind.

What came next was new.

"Your father is in the hospital."

"What happened? Is he ill?"

"Mentally. He's at 24th and Van Buren." Jan used the Phoenix intersection commonly used by locals when they referred to the Arizona State Mental Hospital.

Ted stood and paced as far as his phone cord would allow, then back again. "Have you seen him? What the hell happened?"

"Who do you think you are, swearing at me? I'm the one who's holding the bag while you're gallivanting around God knows where."

"Okay, I'm sorry. Do you know exactly what happened?"

"Call Stella."

Ted knew exactly where this conversation was headed. He took a deep breath. "Did Stella give you any details?"

"A neighbor checked on Jacob. He must have stopped taking his medication. The neighbor called the police."

Ted plopped back down on the bed. Silence on the other end of the phone line indicated that, like boxers at the end of a round, Jan and he had retreated to opposite corners.

Jan must have handed off the phone, because moments later Josh came on the line. "Dad, when are you coming home?"

Ted sat up at the sound of his son's voice. "As soon as I can, Sport. How's your math coming along?

"Eric, stop pulling on the phone. Go use the extension."

Before he could ask Josh about his math again Ted heard a click and then Eric's voice. "Dad, Josh won't let me watch the Giants game." The Phoenix Giants, a minor league team affiliated with the San Francisco Giants, was Eric's passion. Josh, on the other hand, couldn't care less about baseball.

"He always gets his way. Tonight, I'm watching Welcome Back, Kotter," Josh said.

"Please Dad, let me watch the game."

Josh's voice intervened. "Forget it Eric. Mom said I could watch Kotter."

Ted raised his voice and immediately felt guilty about it. "Boys, please, I don't have much time. I've got to call Grammy's nurse. Eric, if your mother says Josh can watch his show then..."

Eric began crying. "Josh is a butt, he always gets his way."

Ted heard a click. "Josh, are you still there?"

"I'm here."

"He's only seven."

"But Mom said I could." Josh's voice trailed off. "Dad... Mom said maybe we could visit you if you're going to be in Florida for a while."

Ted felt his chest tighten.

The last thing he said to Josh was that he would think about it, though after he hung up the phone the thought of the boys coming to Florida set him pacing around his room. The momentum of his pacing increased, as if he could outdistance the anxiety catching up from behind. His ruminating covered all of the territory of his impossible situation. Finally, thoughts of his mother sent him back to the phone. A nurse on his mother's wing answered.

"I'm sorry, Lois has the night off. Can I help?"

"How is Mrs. Miller?"

"I'm sorry, who is...?"

"Her son, Ted Miller."

"Oh yes...Mr. Miller. I..."

"Oh my God, she isn't...?"

"No, no... she's about the same. In fact she's..."

"Talking again?"

"Mr. Miller, I'm trying to tell you... apparently your mother said something to her roommate, Mrs. Reyes last night."

Ted played dumb. "Mrs. Reyes? She doesn't speak English..."

"That's just it. She does. And just before she..." The nurse stopped for a moment. Then she continued. "Mrs. Reyes told us she had a message for you."

Ted let a few seconds go by. He didn't want to alienate the nurse. "Then perhaps I should be speaking to Mrs. Reyes."

"You can't... she was transferred this morning."

8

The King is Dead! Ted stared at the headline. He sat on the front steps of Camp's Store reading the morning paper. He was three blocks from his old house and what seemed like an eternity from his former home. Through the screen door—still hooked to a foot-long spring that slammed it shut every time someone entered—he could see the large clock that had kept him on time until his family's move to Arizona. His burdens then, like being on time for school in the morning or for starting his paper route promptly in the afternoon, were eased by the big clock's reassurance that, if he hurried, he wouldn't be late. He was sitting exactly where he, as a fifth grader, had folded the *Saint Petersburg Evening Independent,* a job that supplemented his meager income from Old Man Rothamul.

The paper he held at the moment, claiming that Elvis Presley had died sitting on his toilet, was the *Independent's* rival newspaper, the morning *Saint Petersburg Times.* The Times article was betting on a massive heart attack as the cause of death. Still, it held out the possibility of contributing factors, such as Presley's dependence on prescription drugs. Elvis prowled the night with the bats and, like a bat, retreated to a heavily curtained cave at the first rays of daylight. The drugs made his nocturnal life feasible. The death of Elvis, though shocking, didn't create in Ted any particular feelings of regret or loss. In 1956, he and his friends joked about Elvis tripping on his blue suede shoes. All the girls Ted's age worshiped Elvis. He was simply a rival.

Ted wiped his forehead. The sudden thunderstorms from the day before were gone, leaving behind moisture that saturated the air. The first rays of sunlight peeking through the drooping fronds of a palm tree across the street verified that it was much too early in the morning for Ted to be this sweaty. He folded his paper and began to retrace his steps back to the Calvinato's and air conditioning. Though Ted was glad his old haunt still existed, he moved away as quickly as he could through the weight of the humidity and fought the mental fog of recent pressures brought upon him by the phone calls of the previous evening. Considering the untimely death of Elvis, and just four days earlier, the first launch of the space shuttle *Enterprise* from the back of a Boeing 747, he realized that earth shattering events were occurring, and he began to feel a bit selfish. Still, that Josh and Eric needed him was no small thing, nor was the fact that his job and marriage were on the line. His conversation with Stella, the last phone call of the previous evening, was the only thing delaying his next anxiety attack. Stella had assured him, that since she already had Ted's written approval, she would use her influence to track down Jacob and find out how he was doing. She also promised to look into Mrs. Reyes' transfer, and if possible, arrange for Ted to speak to her.

As he trudged along, Ted shielded his eyes from the bright rays of the sun that had just cleared the top of a palm tree rooted between the road and sidewalk. A block away, the Rothamul mansion loomed over the neighborhood. Coming closer, he instinctively surveyed the upper balconies. Had Paula assumed her grandfather's role as guardian of the fortress?

All clear.

His confidence bolstered, Ted circled down the narrow alley that separated his family's former property from the Rothamul homestead. Forty feet down the alley, the Rothamul's fence changed from a solid block wall to vertical wooden planks separated by four-inch gaps. Behind this section of fence lay the Rothamul's garden, where the Queen had held court, settling disputes between Old Man Rothamul and the children who toiled in his sweatshop.

Ted froze. Through one of the spaces in the fence, he saw a woman bent over, tending to low-lying greenery. Her face was hidden. All he could see was the top of a hat. It looked like the hats he had seen on Chinese peasants in social studies films at school when he was in the fourth grade, round brim and pointed top. He moved closer. The hat popped up and Ted was confronted by a glare through the fence that made him feel like a ten-year-old with no logical excuse for his behavior. The woman rose and moved to the alley gate. Moments later, the gate opened. Ted recognized the white shocks of hair refusing to stay bunched under the garden hat. It was the Queen.

To his relief, the Queen recognized Ted, and he asked if she would be willing to talk to him there in the garden, out of view from the main house. She pointed out a gazebo where they could sit, protected from the sun that had moved even higher in the sky.

Ted sat carefully and then shifted his weight on the hot and narrow seat of a metal garden chair. He used his shirtsleeve to wipe sweat from his forehead and looked into the Queen's eyes. Something there had changed. Though she still held the steady gaze of a sovereign.

Ted shifted his weight again. "Do you remember a young girl ever living with my family?"

Mrs. Rothamul searched the heavens. Ted followed her gaze as if he could intercept the answer she seemed to be searching for and to help her remember. All he could see in the cloudless sky were ripples of heat radiating from the parapets of the house.

She abruptly shifted her attention back to Ted. "You were just a baby... an infant when your family moved in next door. Your father had a job... at a hospital... was it in Tampa or was it north of here? I don't remember now." Mrs. Rothamul squeezed her eyes shut and frowned. "But he lost the job soon after your family moved here."

Ted leaned forward. "And the girl... do you remember a girl?"

She opened her eyes and returned Ted's stare. "My goodness, there was a girl... not long after you moved here... she couldn't have been more than fifteen years old." The Queen's triumphant smile disappeared as quickly as it had appeared. "But she wasn't here long... less than a year."

"The girl, do you remember a name?"

Mrs. Rothamul tapped her forehead. "It was so confusing then. There were arguments in your backyard... barking and howling noises from the house even though your family didn't have a dog... your father got worse and worse. Then one day the young girl was gone." She stopped for a moment and shook her head. "But for the life of me, I can't remember her name. I just can't..."

Paula's voice boomed from the house. "Grandmother!"

The royalty drained from Mrs. Rothamul's face. She sighed, shrugged her shoulders. "Roles have switched around here."

Ted sighed. It felt as if he had been dismissed from the throne room. He stood and moved to leave, but before he reached the gate he heard, behind him, what sounded like a carnival barker forced to whisper.

"Esther."

He paused and turned around. "Pardon?"

"The girl's name." The Queen had regained her regal stance. "I just remembered. It was Esther."

Ted opened his mouth to speak but closed it again as she disappeared behind a hedge. He heard her call out to Paula, "Coming!"

Ted walked out of the yard, crunched down the gravel-covered alley and onto the unpaved street, already dried out and dusty. In the last hour, he had read about a king who had died on his throne and witnessed the dethroning of a queen, but in the process, he had picked up a piece of his puzzle. He felt lighter. Things had moved another notch. In fact, he had almost forgotten how hot he was.

Ted entered the Calvinato's house and was immediately drawn to an intense but friendly conversation between Elisa and Maria in the dining room. Elisa was trying to coax meaning from what Maria was trying to relate. The two words Maria was trying to pronounce, sounding different on each attempt, landed, like a flies on a glassy river, with Elisa snapping, trout like, to catch them.

"Lonely been? Lonny bean?"

Elisa was exasperated but in a good mood. She explained to Ted that Maria had heard from Mr. Calvinato—in one of his infrequent lucid moments—that Jacob had once worked in a place in which the name of the first word started with an "L", and the second word started with a "B" but that she couldn't figure it out.

Ted's memory of the sheriff incident and the talk with Mrs. Rothamul gave him an advantage. His guess, "Loony bin?" sent Maria into an escalating fit of joy.

She pointed at Ted and, as if he was the groom at a wedding, showered him with short, rice-like syllables: "Si, Si!" and "Bravo, bravo!"

Ted related to Elisa what he'd gained from the Queen. Though there were many hospitals in nearby Tampa, she told Ted she knew of only one state mental institution located almost three hundred miles north in Tallahassee.

Ted thought for a moment. "Almost three hundred miles?" He looked at his watch. "Then I better get going." He walked to his room with Elisa trailing behind.

Elisa stopped in the doorway. "You're driving up there?"

Ted dropped his suitcase on the bed and opened it. "Of course. You know the run around I'd get if I called."

Elisa crossed her arms. "But didn't Mrs. Rothamul say your father worked closer?"

Ted continued to fill his suitcase. "She was confused." He stopped packing and faced Elisa. "Look, my father worked at the hospital where he was finally taken. Where else would that have been but a mental hospital?" Ted shook his head. "Even your father remembers he worked in a loony bin."

Elisa dropped her hands to her hips. "But what about all the regular hospitals in Tampa? Surely some of them must have mental wards. "

Ted threw a shirt into the suitcase. "Call them if you like, but I'm leaving for Tallahassee as soon as I get packed."

Elisa gave up and agreed to phone as many hospitals as she could in the Saint Pete – Tampa area. Maybe Jacob had worked in one of them.

***

Thirty minutes later Ted studied the features of a gas station attendant not far from his old neighborhood. Florida's history was etched in the old man's face.

"Best to avoid the interstates." The mechanic waved Ted's dipstick like a dowsing rod. "Both 75 and 10 are still in pieces between here and the capital." The old man spat into a can he carried like an appendage to his body. "The coast road's just as fast."

Taking the attendant's advice Ted decided to take old highway 19, which hugged the gulf coast for the first third of his two hundred and eighty mile journey, and then shifted inland and oozed through the heart of swamps and bogs, eventually turning west into the panhandle of Florida and on to Tallahassee. Glimpses of the sun reflecting off the gulf lifted his spirits for the first part of the trip. But as soon as the two-lane road turned away from the water, Ted began to have second thoughts. Was he being impetuous? Was this trip just another waste of time?

Ted braked just past a sign that simply read: VIEW. His car ground to a dusty halt on a gravel patch off the road, just feet from a marsh. He watched a Great Blue Heron inch one stick leg upward and slowly step ahead, barely disturbing the mirror-like waters of the lagoon that stretched for miles away from the highway. The heron, in its time-lapse speed search for a meal, seemed oblivious to any danger that might lurk below. Ted wondered if his personal alligators would soon rise out of his bayou and drag him into the muck below.

Ted arrived in Tallahassee by the middle of the afternoon and tried to shake off his nagging pessimism. Most of his life, Ted had managed disappointment by keeping his expectations low. The Florida State Hospital building did nothing to move him in an optimistic direction. Security gates and heavy mesh screens on the windows greeted Ted with suspicion. An iron fence and gate denied easy access even to the parking lot. A uniformed guard, who glared at him through a closed sliding glass window, defended the entrance to the lot. Ted got the impression the guard was in a debate with himself about whether Ted was worth the effort. Finally, with a curt wave, the guard indicated that Ted should leave his car and come into the guardhouse.

Ted opened his car door and realized why the guard had been reluctant to open his window. Suffocating humidity stabbed his lungs. He coughed and moved quickly to escape the sweltering heat.

"Shut that damn door." The guard shook his head and glowered. "You stand in the door and all my cool air leaks out."

Ted did as he was told, then walked to the counter where he leaned and let the conditioned air revive him.

The guard, dressed in khakis at least two sizes too large for him, crossed his arms. "Well, what do you want?"

The man's head disappeared comically up to his eyebrows into his huge cap. But the fact that this clown was another potential roadblock kept Ted from smiling.

A few minutes later the gate yawned open and Ted eased his car into the parking lot. He breathed a sigh and touched the pass that was clipped to a lanyard hanging around his neck. He lifted the plastic pass and read: *Administration Building Only.* Thankfully his bowing and scraping had gotten him at least this far.

The sound of the door closing firmly behind him in the lobby of the ancient administration building echoed in the chasm of high ceilings and marbled floors. Light flooded into the room from tall wood-framed windows cheerfully free of the metal mesh Ted had seen on the windows of other buildings. Floral wallpaper extended upward from six-inch-wide chair molding, and period high-back chairs lined the sidewalls. In the center of the room sat a lonely and rugged oak desk, identified by a plaque as the reception desk, which shared its polished top with a black phone, an electric typewriter—humming expectantly—and an open appointment calendar, but it lacked an actual receptionist.

A door behind the reception desk opened suddenly, and the sharp report it made demanded Ted's attention. The door, one of three spaced along the wall, could have been straight from a 1940s detective movie. It had a milky white glass panel upon which had been stenciled: Personnel. Peeking out from behind the partially opened door was the head and left shoulder of a Marilyn Monroe look-alike.

Ted swallowed. "Hello."

"You don't have to whisper." She punctuated her statement with a beguiling giggle. "It's not a mausoleum, you know?"

When the woman moved into the room, all resemblance to Marilyn Monroe disappeared. Her hips were enormous. She introduced herself as Debbie, director of personnel. Ted briefly explained his mission. Debbie smiled and waved him toward her door. Buoyed by her good nature and openness, he followed her into her office.

"So." Debbie exhaled the word as she dropped into a large, padded high-back office chair, which complained with a groan in spite of its sturdiness. "Are you looking for a former patient or employee?"

Ted sat in chair in front of Debbie's desk. "Actually... both."

He gave her some more background on his situation. Then he asked whether his father had ever worked or been a patient in the hospital. Ted watched as Debbie leaned to her right, ducked below desk level and opened the drawer of a file cabinet snuggled next to her desk.

"By the way." Ted smiled when Debbie's head reappeared. "While you are in that drawer. Could you also check on an..." Ted felt awkward as the name crossed his lips. "Esther Miller?"

Debbie gave her chair a torturous workout as she leaned again to work her way through the file drawer. Ted could tell by her expression when she sat up that the search had been in vain. She suggested that Ted check with several smaller private mental institutions around the state and gave him a list of 12 hospitals in the state that offered mental health services.

Well, that was that. Ted sat for a moment in his car as he waited for the air conditioner to kick in and looked at the suitcase on the seat beside him. There was no reason to stay the night in Tallahassee. Ted drove through the gates of the hospital, expectations now underwater, lower than the oppressive swamp with its cat-o-nine-tail reeds dancing in the dim light of the setting sun pressing in on both sides of the levee highway leading back to Saint Petersburg.

Accusations bubbled up in his mind as if out of the marsh. Give up; you never finish anything, anyway. Plastic model cars and planes, unfinished or unpainted, had filled boxes and drawers throughout Ted's childhood. A tree house in a stately oak on the back of his Florida property had been misnamed; a house, after all, has walls and a roof. Not even trial runs of positive self-talk could lift Ted out of the mire. Each attempt at raising his spirits lay flattened like the hapless turtles that tried to cross the asphalt intrusion upon which he drove.

It was late by the time Ted reached the edge of his old neighborhood. Ahead, Elisa's car, parked in the Calvinato's driveway, loomed in his headlights.

"I'll see you tomorrow," was the last thing she had said before he left for Tallahassee. Had she come up with good news from her search? Something important that couldn't wait for morning? But wait; hadn't she assumed he planned to stay the night up north?

Ted parked his car and in his haste to see Elisa paid no attention to the heat that, in spite of the darkness, had refused to release its sultry grip. He surprised her as she leaned over the dining table, writing on a notepad.

"Ted I'm glad you came back tonight." She held up a note pad. "I was leaving you a note."

Ted dropped into a chair and scooted up to the large polished dining table.

Elisa stared at him for a moment and shook her head. "No luck, huh?" Then she sat in a chair across the table from Ted. "Your wife called."

Ted slumped even further in his chair. He rubbed his eyes and yawned. "Of course she did."

"Your boys will be on a morning flight. Here..." She shoved the notepad across the table. "That's the flight number."

Ted sat up and grabbed the notepad. He scowled first at the note and then at Elisa.

"Hey, don't be pissed at me." Elisa pushed her chair back and stood. "I'm just the messenger."

Ted closed his eyes and sighed.

"Call your wife tonight. She said she'd wait up for you." Elisa pointed at the notepad. "It's all in the note."

Ted looked at the note. *Confirm with your wife that you will pick up the boys. Someone named Stella also called. You can call her late as well. She has news about your father.*

When Ted looked up, Elisa had disappeared. He jumped up and was barely able to catch his chair before it could topple over behind him. He hurried down the hallway and caught up with Elisa already half way out the front door. He waved a folded paper he had pulled from his pocket. "Elisa, wait. I have a list of mental hospitals in the area."

"Sorry, got to go. I just wanted to be sure these messages were here as soon as you got back." She nodded at the paper in Ted's hand. "That'll keep till tomorrow. I got nowhere with my calls." Elisa ducked out and closed the door behind her.

Ted stood motionless, the paper in his hand moved slightly in a brief breeze of hot air pushed in by the closing door. Seconds later the door opened again. Elisa looked around the edge of the door. "Sorry again. I didn't have time to write this down. Stella also said she knows where Mrs. Reyes is. See you tomorrow."

9

The following day Jan was with Ted in spirit as he drove to the airport in nearby Tampa. He thought about his conversation with her the night before and how different Jan sounded. Was it something in her tone of voice or was it a shift in priorities? Perhaps she was more confident, or was it that she was being more distant than usual? As if at a carnival dart game, Ted missed the balloon-like choices over and over again. Sometimes he would brush a feeling, but it would jump aside, denying him a bull's-eye. But his confusion about Jan aside, Ted was sure about one thing. He had folded. The boys were coming. Nothing would change that.

Then thoughts of his phone conversation with Stella moved in. Her visit with Jacob at Arizona's state hospital revealed that his admission was precipitated by his inability to maintain his medication. Considering their common duplicity in regards to Sister, the fact his parents had kept the information that Jacob took psychotropic medication from him all these years wasn't a surprise. Stella then told him that, in spite of what Elisa had said, she had yet to locate Mrs. Reyes, though she was closing in on her.

When Ted arrived at the airport his invisible entourage—
Jan and Stella—followed him from the parking lot, through the
front doors and straight to the American Airlines counter. He asked
an agent to check on the boys' itinerary. He canceled the return
flight for the boys, scheduled for three days later, and rescheduled
the three of them for the next available flight back to Phoenix late
the next day.

In the back of his mind Stella protested. *You're giving up?*

Jan, who had moved further back in his subconscious, didn't
protest. Her indifference came through loud and clear. Ted had
popped the elusive balloon. Jan was no longer a puzzle. She just
didn't give a damn anymore.

Ted paced in front of the arrival ramp. The boys' flight was
an hour late. Reasonable explanations were obscured in Ted's mind
by visions of explosions and flames. He wondered if the PLO was
still active since the Air France incident just over a year ago. And
worse, wasn't it just six months ago when one fully loaded Boeing
747 crashed into another 747 on the runway in the Canary Islands?
Ted was visualizing the headlines from the latter disaster—*Worst
airline crash in history*—when a disinterested voice on the public
address system announced the boys' safe landing. Ted's heart rate,
however, refused to slow as thoughts of disappointing the boys
replaced his thoughts of imminent disaster.

Soon the door to the ramp opened and a few frowning
passengers slogged into the waiting area, then no one. Ted peered
down the tunnel to see what had stemmed the flow of deplaning
people and saw several passengers bunched in the middle of the
ramp. Ted heard Eric before he saw him.

"Daddy!"

Seconds later Eric popped out of the confusion and ran to Ted.

Ted swept Eric off his feet and staggered backward. It was
a game they played. Eric resembled Jan's brother, thick, athletic.

This time however, Ted was truly stunned by the possibility a son of his could be a Pee Wee Football linebacker. "Hey, Tiger. What's your mother been feeding you?"

Eric smiled and made a muscle. Ted squeezed Eric and let him slip to the floor. Was it possible that Eric was that much heavier in just three days? Or was he losing touch? The thoughts made his head buzz.

"Sir?" A woman's voice made him focus. "Mr. Miller?"

The first thing Ted noticed about the woman standing in front of him was her deep red lipstick, applied precisely, but ugly without the contrast of the white teeth of a smile. A glance higher revealed blond hair tucked severely under her stewardess' cap. Ted looked down at Eric for a moment, then returned his gaze to the woman's eyes, which in spite of their sparkle, were focused above Ted, emphasizing the message of her crossed arms.

Ted released one of his short, explosive, self-deprecating laughs. "Yes, I'm Mister... Ted that is... Ted Miller."

The red lips barely moved. "May I see some identification?"

Ted patted his pockets. "I just had my wallet..."

A voice behind the stewardess interrupted Ted. "Dad." Josh grunted, dropped a large canvas bag on the floor and threw a backpack in Eric's direction. "Idiot."

Eric took refuge behind Ted.

"Boys." Ted glanced back at the woman. "As you can see, they are mine."

She sighed and shoved a paper and pen at Ted. "Just sign for them."

Ted scribbled his name on the paper and watched the stewardess march back toward the ramp. He looked down at Josh, who had plopped down next to his bag. "What happened?"

Josh glared at Eric. "The little twerp dropped his backpack when he saw you and tripped a guy." He shot a few more daggers Eric's way. "Then he just ran away."

On their walk out of the airport, Ted basked in the memory of Eric's grip on his neck as he held him in his arms, the damp odor of an active seven-year-old boy—and maybe future star football player—when Eric's chest pressed against Ted's nose.

Eric stopped a few feet outside the airport's large sliding glass doors. "Dad, wait."

Ted looked over his shoulder. "Come on Tiger, the car's not far. And don't just drag your backpack like that."

Eric wiped his forehead. "It's sticky."

"It's called humidity." Ted turned toward the parking lot.

Ted waited until they were in the car before he broached the subject of their change in plans. He waited for a reaction as he watched Josh fuss with his seatbelt in the front passenger seat. Josh had won the shotgun argument with Eric based on the grief he'd experienced in the airport. He let the belt go and it snapped back into its holder and crossed his arms. "What? Only one day in Florida?"

Eric's head popped over the top of the front seat. "At least Dad's coming home."

Josh smacked the seat near Eric's resting head, forcing Eric to fall back to his seat. "Didn't you listen? Now we can't go to Disney World."

Eric sat forward, keeping his distance from the edge of the front seat. "But at least we can go to the Witchy Springs."

They were securely belted into their seats and headed north out of Tampa before Ted corrected Eric's interpretation of the name Weeki Wachee Springs. The promised visit to the tourist attraction that Ted remembered from his childhood was his feeble attempt to make up for the Disney World disappointment.

Eric stretched so that Ted could see his eyes in the rear-view mirror. "Is the mermaid real?"

"Don't be a dope." Josh still had his arms crossed. "And

stop kicking the back of my seat."

Ted looked at Eric in the mirror. "The mermaid's a woman, Tiger, but the costume she wears from her waist down looks just like the fish she's feeding." Ted pointed to a sign ahead. "Read that sign, Josh."

Josh uncrossed his arms and squinted. "Watch For Turtles On Road."

Ted glanced to his right and saw that both boys had their noses pressed as close to their side windows as their seatbelts would allow. "Your grandfather called this Turtle Road."

Several miles went by without a sound from the boys. Ted glanced at them a few times, remembering how intently he had watched for turtles on this same road when he was Josh's age. He wondered if the boys were noticing differences in the landscape on their first trip to Florida. No cactus here, where ground-hugging palmettos spread their sharp fronds, competing for space in the white sandy soil. But he kept his thoughts to himself. He was, after all, having enough trouble fighting with his image of Stella shaking her head in disappointment. But, in spite of her assurances when he spoke to her the night before, Ted was resolved to go home.

Finally, Ted slowed the car and Josh read a sign. "Welcome to Spring Hill."

Fifty feet beyond that sign was a billboard featuring a beautiful mermaid waving and inviting everyone to visit Weeki Wachee Springs. "Only one mile ahead!" warned a bubble, similar to the bubbles for dialogue in a comic book that extended from the top of the billboard. With the boys' attention now turned from turtles to mermaids, Ted had little time to puzzle about where he had read the name Spring Hill before.

From the road, the springs looked smaller and gaudier than he remembered. It was as if a circus had come to town 30 years before, put up temporary canvas signs, then just left. The rental car's tires made a grinding sound and kicked up the dusty spirits of departed shellfish as they pushed grooves into the crushed shells that made up the parking lot.

Eric was out of the car before Ted could set the parking brake. As soon as they could, Ted and Josh joined him at the edge of a huge circular swimming pool-like structure with walls two feet high.

The springs stretched 100 feet across and funneled into a small river which flowed toward the Gulf of Mexico, not more than three miles to the west. The crystalline water erased Ted's initial disappointment. Exposed rocks and shoals surrounding a chasm so deep that a nearby sign claimed no one had ever found the bottom of it fascinated him.

Eric stood on the wide wall and pointed. "Let's get in the boat."

The name painted on the side of a boat cruising across the spring – a boat crammed full of people, their attention turned inward – gave away its purpose: *Nellie The Glass Bottom Boat.*

Ted pointed to the entrance. "We have to pay first. Then we see the mermaids."

Stairs led them below ground at the edge of the spring. A door at the bottom of the staircase opened into a large room with stadium seating for 200 people. The front wall was constructed of thick aquarium windows twelve feet high that looked directly into an underwater playground. Mermaids, scales and tail from the waist down, but very much women in bikini tops from the waist up, cavorted with fish, reptiles and mammals. The mermaids had no breathing apparatus attached to their bodies. Occasionally one of the exotic creatures would wriggle away and take a breath of air from a hose dangling from a nearby outcropping of rock. Then she would spiral back, flipping and turning in a sensual underwater ballet that, Ted noticed, held Josh in a familiar trance.

Ted remembered when he had substantiated his own hetero-sexual inclinations in the same place. The viewing room had been smaller in the middle 1950s, windows half the size, but his reaction was the same as Josh's was now. Of course he had already gained solid clues about the mysteries of the feminine form from his salacious activities with Elisa and Paula, but his experience here was a turning point.

Eric moved from window to window. "Daddy, look, a walrus with no tusks."

"I think that's a manatee," answered Ted. He looked at the others seated behind them in the gallery. "Maybe you should sit down for a while."

Eric sat in a seat next to him. "The fish look like a rainbow."

Ted looked more closely. Schools of multi-colored tropical fish glided through the diamond studded water and did look like rainbows shredded and sprinkled through the springs. Ted was glad that Eric was paying more attention to the animals than he was to the mermaids. Soon enough he would be weighed down by the relentless burden of procreation.

Eric turned to an older woman sitting a row above them. She had agreed with him about the rainbow of fish. Now they were involved in a discussion about the turtles and river otters cavorting with the mermaids. Ted looked at Josh and saw again that his focus was still completely on the mermaids.

Alone with his thoughts, Ted gave in to an urge to close his eyes. It felt good to stop fighting his body. Several times on the way from the airport he had caught himself dozing off. Never before had he experienced such an exhausting, endless dance with his lifelong partner, anxiety. The boys, he could clearly see, were enjoying themselves, but he still felt that he had failed. He visualized boxing up his recent excursion to Florida and placing it with all the other unfinished projects in his life that had loomed from his memory on the way back from Tallahassee. He thought about his apartment in Phoenix, how he would unplug the phone and the one-eyed-monster as soon as he got home. Then he would sleep.

Ted's head nodded forward. He caught himself, and his eyes jerked open. He had to stay awake. He decided to focus on the fish in the underwater theatre in front of him. Then a vision caught his eye. A mermaid, floating inches from the gallery window, stared at him. Her piercing gaze made him shiver. Long blond hair caught in the upsurge of water from the bowels of the spring floated like seaweed in a tide. Bubbles of air floated heavenward as she smiled a smile he sensed was meant only for him. Then, with a quick pout and a wave, she was gone.

10

"Quiet, both of you! I'm reading." Ted stared at the instructions printed in bold letters on the pleated bag that he held in a death grip. The pink of his fingernails drained to match the white of the puffy belt of clouds Josh had described earlier from his window seat to Ted's right.

Eric strained against his seat belt. His arms were crossed and his bottom lip stuck out far enough to cover his top lip. "It's only a barf bag."

Josh looked away from the window long enough to mock Eric and smile. "It's only a barf bag." That provoked an encore from Eric's lip.

Ted jammed the bag into the pouch on the back of the seat in front of him. "That's enough!" He leaned to his left and lowered his voice. "You find something to do until it's your turn to sit by the window."

"But he's been sitting there for…"

"He's only been sitting there for 15 minutes. We agreed that you two would trade seats every half hour." The promised flight time back to Phoenix was three hours and 36 minutes, but on his flight to Florida, which seemed more like weeks than just days ago, the plane had encountered rough weather and had taken over four hours. Now he wished that he had lengthened the time between seat changes.

Eric pointed at Josh. "Tell him to stop smiling."

Ted turned to Josh. "Stop teasing Eric."

Josh kept his eyes turned toward the window. "Can't I smile?"

Ted closed his eyes, leaned forward, and pressed his fingertips against the areas on his temples where it felt as though someone had inserted ice picks. When he opened his eyes, dropped his hands and sat back, both boys were looking at him, each with knitted eyebrows. They quickly returned to their default postures—protruding lip for Eric and staring out his window for Josh—but this time they said nothing. For Ted, the less said, the better. He could feel the anchors holding down the edges of his emotional fabric beginning to strain, ready to pull free. If Ted's life had become a circus, then it was time to take down the tents and clean the cages. To the inventory of his troubles he added the craziness of flying around the country chasing ghosts. He pulled his checkbook from the inside pocket of his sports coat. Thankfully his school district had put him on paid leave. But those payments would stop as soon as he was officially removed from his position. He wondered if Paul had already hired a new teacher to take his place.

Ted took advantage of the lull in the battle for the window seat. He fluffed the small pillow he had accepted from the stewardess, nestled his head against it, and closed his eyes. Then from the edges of consciousness, the mermaid appeared and pushed aside his obsessively critical inner voice. For a moment he floated next to her, underwater yet breathing normally. He felt more relaxed than he had in years. The tightness in his chest had subsided. He drifted, free of gravity. On the opposite side of the thick glass windows, he saw his boys and next to them sat Jan. Her arms were crossed, joining her eyes and mouth frozen in accusation. His mother was there as well, frail but sitting up and smiling. Jacob was nowhere to be seen, and Ted searched for him in the unfamiliar faces of others in the gallery. Suddenly he felt a hand on his arm, tugging him toward the surface of the water. He gasped for air and tried to focus. He felt bulky, pinned again to his airplane seat by Newton's Law and the weight of his personal conundrums. Eric was pulling on Ted's left arm with one hand and holding up his other wrist, showing Ted his Mickey Mouse watch. "It's my turn."

***

Back in Phoenix, Ted stepped out of the taxi and stared for a moment at the home where he was no longer welcomed. He surveyed his lawn, blades of grass half eaten and dry, fairy circles throughout. A stranger, a gardener recommended by a friend of Jan's, now mowed the lawn that he had planted, nurtured, and protected from villainous insects and insidious centipede grass diseases. Paid hourly, the landscaper had little time to worry, as Ted had, about lawn invasions. Then he noticed that the fascia boards, the only wood on his block and stucco home, were losing their fight against the harsh Phoenix sun. They needed a good scraping and a coat of paint, but Ted could only stare. Then a terrible thought crossed Ted's mind. *I've become my Dad.*

The boys tumbled from the taxi. Eric refused to let go of the fact that since they had all fallen asleep on the plane after the first time Josh reclaimed his position, he had lost his other chances at the window seat. Josh reminded Ted that the trip to Florida had been too short. Ted asked the taxi driver to wait. Without further comment, he herded the boys toward the front door of the house. Their house faced east. When Jan opened the front door, Ted could see, over her shoulder and through the dining room to the rear windows and beyond, to where the fascia board's enemy was setting over the backyard fence.

"What happened?" Jan's tone favored indictment. Ted shrugged his shoulders. The boys quickly, and in unison, filled Ted's awkward silence with a litany of ways in which their father had failed them miserably.

Jan shooed the boys into the house. "Don't drag your bags on the carpet." When she returned her attention to Ted, she took refuge behind the front door. "Ted, I wish you could see yourself, you're scaring me."

Ted took a deep breath. "I'm running on empty. I just don't know what to...." Ted's voice trailed off in a deep sigh.

Jan closed the door further until only her face was showing. "Call Stella. She's been trying to reach you. Maybe she can help. I know I can't."

She closed the door, and Ted heard the thump of the deadbolt. It wasn't the first time she had locked him out, but it was the first time she had literally locked the door.

***

Ted startled awake. He took a stab at recalling the nightmare that had wakened him so abruptly. It was tantalizingly close but just out of reach and fading quickly. He held up his right hand to block a ray of sunlight that had sneaked through a break in a wooden window shutter, and he rolled off his sofa/bed. He stumbled to the bathroom heavy-eyed, one hand on his chest in the area where his heart tattooed his rib cage and with the knowledge that he had not met his goal of a good night's sleep.

Ted studied his face in the mirror, and the realization hit him that he had seen this expression before. A few months earlier, he had watched a boxing match on television. Jimmy Young and

George Foreman, scheduled to go twelve rounds, had completed eleven rounds, Young punishing Forman in every round after the middle of the fight. The television camera closed in on Foreman just before the bell announced the twelfth round. No one was home. The aggressive anticipation that had appeared on Forman's face before each of the first few rounds had now changed to passive acceptance. He would answer the bell, but his fight was already over. Within days Foreman claimed he had met Jesus during the fight and retired from boxing to become a minister.

A knock at his door interrupted Ted's thoughts. He glanced at the clock. Who would be knocking at 7 A.M.?

"Good morning. Are you Ted Miller?" The man standing at Ted's apartment door shifted from one foot to the other. His leisure suit was one size too small. His smile continued past friendly and stopped at serial killer.

"Yes, but isn't it a little early..."

The man held up a thick envelope he'd been hiding behind his back, then handed it to Ted. Ted automatically reached out and grabbed the envelope.

"Mr. Miller, you have been served."

By the time Ted recovered from the sneak attack, the man had moved out of earshot.

***

Later that same morning, Ted sat alone in Stella's office. Although her first two patients had canceled and she could work Ted in for a talk, she had not yet arrived, which gave Ted some alone time with the painting.

The darkness at the center of the painting was no longer his personal territory. He had managed to drag everyone in his life along with him, deep into its shadows. Rather than moving toward the blue sky above he had retreated deeper into the abyss.

He stared at the painting while flicking the edges of the unopened summons he held in one hand with the fingers of his free hand. It was too soon to read the actual words that he knew would lead to the dissolution of his marriage. Even worse was the thought that the early morning visit by that creep must have been instigated by Jan not long after he dropped off the boys the night before. She couldn't wait to close the front door, obviously to make her Judas phone call. He had been right all along about the change in her voice. She'd already left him, the summons merely the first evidence of her impending evacuation.

"So, back in the woods, I see." Stella walked straight to the coffee maker. "Coffee?"

"Black," he said. "To match my mood." Ted pointed at the center of the painting. "And to show where I live. Care to join me? Everyone else has."

Stella handed Ted a steaming Styrofoam cup. He thought of school and how he had demonstrated condensation to his students with a hot cup of coffee, its vaporized water swirling up and over the lip of the cup.

"Feeling sorry for ourselves, are we?" Stella folded herself into her chair and crossed her gangly legs.

Ted's lips tightened. "You too, huh?"

"So, everyone is ganging up on you?"

Ted handed the summons to Stella who hesitated. "Go on, open it."

Stella ran her finger under the seal of the envelope. She read the first few lines on the first page of the documents. "Ouch."

"Yeah, and risking the chances of me feeling any sorrier for myself..." Ted stopped for moment and stared at Stella, "I called Paul last night." Again he paused.

"And..."

"He said he was sorry."

"About?"

"He couldn't wait any longer. He hired someone for my position."

"Shit."

"Yeah, tough shit for me. But do you want to hear something funny?"

Stella raised her eyebrows and nodded.

"With all this crap falling around me, all I can think about is a mermaid I connected with for maybe 30 seconds in Weeki Wachee Springs, Florida."

"Weeki what?"

Ted described the visit he and the boys had made to the springs. Stella made her usual affirmative noises as he spoke. When Ted finished, Stella leaned as far forward as she could with a hot cup of coffee in her hand.

"So what now? You're going back, right?"

"Haven't you been listening? My life is falling apart."

"And staying here will fix that?"

"Josh and Eric need me, my dad needs me, I..." Ted covered his face with his hands. "I think I'm on the verge of some kind of breakdown."

Stella's expression didn't soften. "We've been through this territory before, Ted. You aren't going to be good for anyone, especially yourself, if you don't..." Stella sipped her coffee and put the cup on a table beside her. "... You know all this."

Ted sat up, took a deep breath, and exhaled. "I'm stuck."

Stella leaned closer to Ted. "I have some news for you that may help."

Ted sat up. "News?"

"I found Mrs. Reyes."

"You did? Did she say anything?"

"Your mother said something to her just before Mrs. Reyes was transferred." Stella stopped and waited.

"Well, come on what did she say?"

"Are you sure you want to hear this? I mean, you sound like you're ready to give up, right?"

"Don't be a shit. Tell me."

"Sister is in a hospital named Spring Hill."

11

"Magazine, sir?"

Ted looked into the large hopeful eyes of yet another airline stewardess. In one hand she held a few magazines splayed like a deck of cards. Her pasted-on smile proudly displayed the snowy white teeth—missing in the encounter with this woman's flying sister at the airport in Tampa—which were enhanced by her dark red lipstick.

Ted thought for a few seconds, and then he pulled out the airsickness bag from the pocket in the back of the seat in front of him. "No thanks." He smiled but didn't give her as much as a peek at his own teeth. "I have something to read."

"Oh." The stewardess's teeth disappeared. Wrinkles appeared on her forehead, and the magazines folded into a single pile.

Ted felt his stomach tighten as he watched the stewardess move to the seat ahead of him. Her teeth made an encore and the magazines opened again like a flower. He dropped the now-familiar airsickness bag in his lap. Ruining other people's days was becoming a regular occurrence for Ted. What was he doing on this airplane?

Oh my god, the boys. He hadn't even called them in his rush to get out of town. He promised himself he would call them as soon as he was on the ground. His quick visit to his mother's side the previous day, just after his visit with Stella, offered no solace or any information. Her doses of morphine had been increased. Stella, in the meantime, had assured Ted that she would keep an eye on Jacob. Apparently, she had an in at the state hospital where his father was keeping the staff busy with his barking and howling. Stella had also given Ted the name of a friend of hers who was a divorce lawyer, but who was at the moment out of town. The knot in this stomach pulled tighter. What if he needed to contact the lawyer over the next few days? He made a mental note to call Stella again as soon as the plane landed in Tampa. Ted had to smile, at least for a second, when he thought about Stella's response when he asked her why she was doing all this for him. *"Your life is like a novel. I have to know what happens next."*

Ted pulled out a checkbook and a folded paper that the airsickness bag had covered when he dropped it on his lap. He opened his checkbook even though he knew nothing in it had changed since he looked at it the day before. Elisa had assured him, when he and the boys left that he was welcome to stay at her father's house if he returned. Ted felt a brief reprieve when he calculated that he had enough personal savings to last at least a month, even if he didn't stay with Calvinato's, and there was always the rainy day fund. Thankfully Jan had extra income from a trust her parents had set up for her. Then he picked up the paper. Debbie had given him the list before he left the state hospital in Tallahassee. He verified one more time that, although there was no hospital named Spring Hill on the list, there was an institution on the list named Quiet Springs located in the town of Spring Hill. *Spring Hill, amazing... right where I saw the mermaid.* This fact reversed the direction of his mood. He closed his eyes, took a deep breath, and released it slowly.

***

Less than an hour had elapsed since the arrival of his flight. Ted stood on a curb outside a rental car garage, sweating in the afternoon Florida sauna, waiting for a second rental car. Ted raised his eyes and pleaded with the heavens. He considered making an ecclesiastical bargain that involved a moratorium on the removal of motel room Bibles for a quick resolution of his rental car dilemma. The first car, a new Mercury Comet the rental clerk had assigned to him, had suffered a fatal vapor lock, instigating his latest downward spiral.

Thoughts of his phone conversation with Elisa shortly after his plane landed distracted him further. Mr. Calvinato had suffered some physical setbacks and was in the hospital. Meanwhile Maria had been quite homesick lately, and Tony's hospitalization gave her a chance to return to Italy for the time being. Elisa had offered him refuge at her own home, but Ted thanked her again for all her generosity. He told her he would get a motel when he arrived in Spring Hill instead. Ted patted the checkbook in his shirt pocket. Hopefully it would be a cheap motel.

Moments later the second rental car stopped in front of him. Ted gave the cloudless sky a half smile and a shrug. No need for a deal after all. As he turned onto the highway, whines of varying pitches emanated from both the car's transmission and air conditioner. The noisy transmission he could handle; the air conditioner, on the other hand, was a problem. Apparently, it was screeching because it couldn't quite remove enough of the relentless humidity from the saturated air.

Ted tried to focus on the goal of the day. He rubbed his eyes, once again targets of salty rivulets of perspiration. Between squints and rapid blinking, he noticed that the territory through which he now traveled conjured new memories—the ones he had made with his boys. He smiled when the signs about watching for turtles and the occasional turtle itself along the side of the road reminded him of Josh and Eric, their petty bickering suddenly sidelined as they pressed their noses against the car windows.

Then the billboard dominated by the image of the Weeki Wachee Springs mermaid came into view. Ted felt a sinking feeling in his stomach—a feeling different from his normal anxiety—something he hadn't felt since the day he first called Jan for a date after he'd agonized for hours about whether or not to call. He had experienced this exact feeling while finally dialing her number.

Considering the circumstances, it was ironic that thoughts of Jan would accompany him now, since it wasn't Jan who inspired this anticipatory tingle that Ted was experiencing in his midsection. All he could see in his mind's eye was the mermaid at the glass window just before the boys and he had left the springs. He recalled the pout on the mermaid's face as she hung suspended, staring at him, just before she swam out of view.

Ted shook off the mermaid's memory. He glanced at a map of the area he had purchased from a service station attendant who had marked the route to the front door of Quiet Springs Hospital located a few minutes' drive beyond Weeki Wachee Springs.

From the parking lot where Ted stood, Quiet Springs looked more like an apartment complex than a mental hospital. Several one-story buildings circled around a central structure. Sidewalks connected each building to the central outpost like spokes on a wheel. Along each sidewalk and between the apartments, trellises gave ivy a place to search for a new home. Other than the trellises there were no fences or gates, and none of the windows had bars or heavy metal screens. The lawns were mowed golf-green short, but occasional tuffs of Saint Augustine grass popped up as if to challenge the groundskeeper to a duel.

Ted paced for a moment in front of an arched opening in the

trellis, and then he stopped in front of a sign pointing the way to the administration office in the central complex. He closed his eyes for a moment. He couldn't move. He had no plan.

What if Sister was here? What would I do? What would I say? Hello there, I think I may be your nephew? Or, by the way, if Margaret Miller is your sister, she lives in Phoenix, Arizona and she's dying of colon cancer and I've come to take you home?

Panicked, Ted turned in the direction of his car and bumped into a man whom he suddenly realized had been standing no more than two feet behind him while he was agonizing and then choosing to retreat. Ted stepped back

"What's the matter, Bub? You lost or something?" The man had the body of a balloon blown up to its limit and looked as though he would float away if he weren't tied down quickly. His voice sounded as though it had been squeezed through the high 'C' pipe of a circus calliope.

Ted crossed his arms and frowned. "You scared the crap out of me."

The man began walking in a tight circle around Ted, moving counter clockwise, wringing his hands. "Sorry, sorry, oh no, oh no, I'm in trouble again. I'm in trouble again."

Ted responded by walking around within the corpulent fellow's circle in a clockwise direction, stopping when he came face to face with him, and then moving to meet him again when the man continued walking. Ted finally held up his hand like a traffic cop. "Will you please stop? Come on, you're not in trouble. Really, I..."

The man, whose shirt buttons strained to keep his girth contained within the cotton uniform he wore, stopped and put one hand on his forehead. He closed his eyes. "You're mad, oh no, you're mad."

Ted looked again to heaven for assistance but found only a cloudless sky.

Then from behind Ted, a deep bass voice with a Jamaican lilt came to his rescue. "Eldon, it seems we are getting upset again, aren't we?"

Eldon opened his eyes and dropped his hand. "Bobby, I didn't mean to scare the nice man."

Ted turned. Behind him stood a man with skin so black the contrasting white of his smile gleamed in the sun. He wore hospital scrubs with a nametag on his shirt pocket that read *Robert Swaby*.

"I know you didn't, Eldon." Bobby gestured toward Ted with an opened palm. "I'm sure Mister...?"

"Miller, Ted Miller."

"I'm sure our new friend Mr. Miller understands." Bobby caught Ted's eye and nodded. "Don't you Mr. Miller, or may we call you Ted?"

Ted shifted his weight from one foot to the other. "Of course. That is... yes, I do understand and of course you can call me Ted."

Bobby released a laugh that surrounded Ted and Eldon, provoking laughter from the two of them as well. When he stopped laughing, he smiled. "Good. Don't you feel better, Eldon?"

"Yes, yes. Much better, thank you."

"Come then." Bobby offered Eldon his arm. "I think it's time for art therapy." Bobby smiled at Ted. "But before we go, how can I help you, Ted?"

"Is there a..." Ted hesitated a moment. "Do you by any chance have a patient here named Esther Miller?"

Bobby's gleaming teeth disappeared, leaving a dark frown. "No... sorry. I haven't heard that name before."

Ted hesitated again. "How about someone called Sister?"

Bobby looked at his companion. "Eldon, do you know someone named Sister?"

"Sister, Sister?" Eldon hesitated. "No, nobody named Sister."

Ted sighed and thanked them both. He thought about the orderly's initial reaction to the question about Esther but chalked it off to his own confusion.

"Follow this path to the building in the center." Bobby pointed in the direction of the administration building. "Maybe they can help you. Come, Eldon."

The two had walked, arm in arm, in the opposite direction for a few seconds when Eldon pulled away from Bobby and turned back toward Ted, who'd been watching them leave.

"Oh, Mr. Ted."

Ted took a step in their direction. "Yes?"

"I just remembered..."

Bobby looked at Ted and shrugged.

Ted took another step in their direction. "Yes, yes?"

"I have a sister. Her name is Elaine." Eldon shrugged his shoulders. "She doesn't visit me very often."

Ted and Bobby exchanged glances.

"I'm sorry to hear that, Eldon," Ted said.

***

Ted entered the administration building through one side of a set of double metal doors and stepped into a cavernous room that reeked of the same peculiar odor that Ted had noticed a few times already here in Florida. He ran the smell through his olfactory memory. He chose the word musty, yet another problem to blame on the humidity. He wondered if residents here ever got used to it.

The center of the room had the look of an elementary school multipurpose room, its alternating green and white linoleum tiled floor empty, waiting for the next activity. Cubicles lining the walls of the room seemed an afterthought, bureaucratic and largely unoccupied. Various staff members, some in nurses' uniforms but most dressed in shirts and ties or dresses, gathered around tables placed in front of every other cubicle. The general tone of their conversations was social in nature. No one seemed especially busy or inclined to become so.

A piercing female voice echoed in the ceiling. "Hello, may I help you?"

Ted glanced around but couldn't see who was calling.

"Over here. Yoo-hoo."

One of the women dressed in white—dress, stockings and shoes—adjusted her winged hat, looked up from her conversation and pointed to the far corner. "Over there honey."

Ted nodded. Increasing numbers of employees stopped their chitchats and looked at Ted as he moved toward a waving hand. Once Ted had moved closer to the owner of the hand, the various conversations resumed. He was engrossed by the woman's deep red hair, pulled so tightly in a bun that her eyes looked like those of stagecoach horses being reined to a stop. Freckles dominated her face. Her mouth was shaped in a pucker that gave the impression that she was always ready to whistle. She was standing behind the only desk in the room not surrounded by a cubicle.

One of the men sitting on a table near her desk cleared his throat. "Stand up, Prissy."

Several workers in the immediate vicinity laughed.

"I am standing, Mike, you big goof."

More laughs followed her retort.

Prissy turned to Ted. "Ignore them." She glanced at Mike and frowned. Then she turned back to Ted. "How can I help you?"

"My name is Ted Miller, Miss...?"

"Just call me Prissy, everyone else does." Prissy smiled and surveyed the room. "It's not my real name but my momma named me Prissy when I was little because I was always so neat and clean and organized and that's why Doctor Fisher..." without taking a breath, she pointed at the small sign on the door behind her desk indicating *Dr. Fisher* "...says he keeps me working here even though he says I drive him crazy sometimes though I don't know why." Prissy smiled and finally breathed.

Ted's mouth hung open. He pulled up a chair, then sat and stared at Prissy, who began a nesting ritual in her own chair. He waited for her to get settled and leaned forward. "I'm here to find someone. She might be a patient."

"I'd be glad to check. What's her name?"

"Esther, Esther Miller." Ted hesitated. "At least I think she would go by Miller."

"You're not sure, Mr. Miller? Is she related to you?"

"She might be my aunt."

"Well let's not put the cart before the horse I always say it's just that if you're not related we might have a problem here Mr. Miller we have to protect the privacy of our patients you know you see we can't just go around giving out information about our patients to just anyone." Prissy took a breath and studied Ted's face as if she were trying to find a clue about his real intentions. "I'm sure you understand?"

Ted sat up. He opened his arms in agreement as well to assure Prissy that he had nothing to hide. "Yes, of course. You can't be too careful, can you? But, yes I am... related, that is." Ted fumbled with his wallet for a moment. Then he produced a driver's license and held it toward Prissy.

Prissy stood. She squinted as she leaned toward his extended hand and looked him over once more. "Well okay... let me check."

She opened the top drawer of a four-drawer file cabinet, dragged a footstool next to the cabinet, and climbed up. She talked to herself as she looked. "Let's see. Milger, Millard, Millford. No Miller." Prissy rose up on her toes and looked to her left, over the open drawer. "Pam?"

A woman peeked out from opening of a nearby cubicle. She frowned and pushed several strands of graying brunette hair away from her eyes.

"Do we have a patient named Esther Miller? My files aren't always updated."

"No, I'm sure we don't," answered Pam.

Ted's attention was drawn to the man who had teased Prissy, the man she had called Mike. At the mention of Esther's name, Ted noticed the man perk up and saw that he was listening intently to the conversation between Pam and Prissy. His mouth couldn't completely close over his teeth, and every few seconds he would lick his lips. His collar was unbuttoned and his wide paisley tie was loosened. His suit jacket hung open, but even if he had wanted to, there was no way he could have buttoned the jacket. The beginnings of a waddle in the Adam's apple area of Mike's neck helped Ted peg the beefy man as middle age—middle fifties was his guess.

Ted felt dizzy. He stood and turned his attention to Prissy. "How about Sister. Do you have a patient called Sister?"

Prissy looked at Pam and shrugged.

"No," said Pam. "I've never heard that name before."

Ted dropped back into the chair. When he looked over his shoulder again, Mike was gone, and Ted heard the sound of a door closing behind Pam's cubicle.

Moments later the door behind Prissy's desk burst open. A man Ted judged to be in his late sixties filled the doorway with the broad shoulders and narrow waist of a football quarterback. His salt and pepper hair jutted stylishly over his ears and the back of his buttoned down white collar. "What's going on?"

The chatter in the room stopped.

Prissy jumped down from her stool. "Nothing, Doctor Fisher." She pointed at Ted. "This man is just trying to find out if his relative is a patient here. Isn't that right, Mr. Miller?"

Doctor Fisher sized up Ted. "Miller, huh?" He cleared his throat. "Who is it you're looking for?"

Ted hesitated. He locked eyes with the disheveled man who

had disappeared moments before and who was now poking his head out the door behind the doctor.

Doctor Fisher turned, and Mike shuffled away from the door and back into Fisher's office. Fisher looked back at Ted. "Well?"

"Esther Miller, or Sister." Prissy answered for Ted. "Right, Mr. Miller?"

Ted nodded.

Doctor Fisher stepped into the room and looked past Prissy. "We don't have anyone here by that name, do we, Pam?"

Pam shook her head and retreated behind the wall of her cubicle.

"Well, there you have it, Mr. Miller." Doctor Fisher moved toward his office door, then turned back to face Ted. "If you will excuse us, these people have work to do." He looked around the room. "Right, everyone?"

***

Ted stood next to his rental car in the hospital parking lot. He opened the door but stopped when he noticed someone spying on him from behind a trellis. He moved toward the arch, but the figure walked away. Without stopping, the person looked back at Ted. He licked his lips and broke into a run. Ted realized there was no reason to chase the man, so he returned to his car and, without getting in, slammed the door he had left open.

"Shit!" He raised his eyes to the blistering sky. "Satisfied?"

Ted turned around, leaned against the car, closed his eyes and waited. A minute passed before he could no longer stand the heat of the steel fender on his rear end. He stood away from the car and decided that he had calmed down enough to drive. He took a deep breath and opened his eyes. Six feet away stood a mirage. It was the mermaid, but she wasn't in her fish costume. She was dressed as a nurse.

"Ted?" she asked.

Ted stared at her, but he couldn't speak.

"Your name is Ted, right?"

Ted nodded.

"We don't have much time." She looked over her shoulder. "Fisher's flunky could be back any minute, and I've got to go back to work."

Ted nodded again and looked toward the ivy.

The nurse stepped closer to Ted. "I was in the office. I heard what you said."

Ted opened his mouth to speak.

She shushed him. "Just listen. There is a patient here who calls herself Sister."

Ted's spine turned to butter. He stepped back and supported himself on the rental car again. "Sister ... she's..."

"We don't have time. I'm the only one who knows about her. I have some letters she wrote." The mermaid walked nearer to Ted and shoved a scrap of paper in his hand. "My name is Ruthie." She pointed at the note. "Call me tonight." She looked at her watch. "After eight."

12

Ted drove down the main street of Spring Hill's business district and immediately fell under its spell. On his left a winged horse still flew over a Mobil service station, and pure white globes sat atop the yet to be upgraded fuel pumps. The 1950s, it seemed to Ted, had squatted down on the town and never left.

He braked and made a quick right turn into the driveway of a motel directly across from the Mobile station. Nostalgia worked for Ted like a picnic near a babbling stream, bringing calming memories of vacations he had shared with his parents more than 20 years before. Visions of tiny bars of soap wrapped and decorated with pictures of the various motels they visited that Ted had eagerly collected mixed with a memory that at the time caused panic, but now brought a chuckle. On that occasion Jacob's bubbling pride in obtaining a 'killer' deal at a motel in Georgia deflated quickly in the face of a 2 A.M. retreat from a hoard of bedbugs. Lost momentarily in his memories, Ted lost track of how slowly he was driving while still in third gear, and his car bucked and nearly stalled. He depressed the clutch pedal, applied the brakes, and his car crunched to a stop half way up the gravel driveway of an establishment frozen in time. Ted shifted his car into neutral and marveled at the sight of tiny individual white-framed cottages that, like pioneer wagons circled for the night, surrounded a courtyard in a familiar horseshoe shape. A space barely large enough to park a car separated each cottage from its neighbor. Ivy slithered through latticework that arched over the entrance and closed in the back of each carport. In the center of the courtyard stood a cabana, covered with palm leaves and nearby, a shuffleboard court. A cottage at the top of the horseshoe curve stood out from the rest. It was wider and was the only unit with a second story. In its large front window, a red neon vacancy sign glowed brightly, as if defying the omnipresent sun.

Ted pushed in the clutch of his rental car and eased the balky transmission back into first gear. He parked in front of the office and shifted back into neutral but left the engine and air-conditioner running as he sat, eyes closed, breathing deeply. The image returning to his mind's eye now had a name: Ruthie.In his fantasy, she was still a mermaid. The nurse's uniform was too new a concept. He was captivated again by the intensity of her stare. She had once again lured him past the thick glass gallery windows into the sparkling waters of the spring.

A pounding on the driver's side door jerked Ted from his reverie. He turned off the engine and looked to his left but saw nothing. Then a hand appeared and knocked on the window.Ted moved closer to the window and saw the top of someone's head. He slowly opened his door, expecting to find a child, but the face that popped into view, sporting a thick mustache, was that of an adult male. Ted stared, and his mouth dropped open.

"Hey gringo, you freaked out?" The owner of the voice looked stern and frowned as he tried to fold his chubby arms over his rounded belly. "What's the matter, ain't you ever seen a Mexican dwarf?"

Ted closed his mouth and scowled. When he pushed the door

further, the little man backed up. Ted got out of the car, which made the man strain his neck as he looked up to maintain eye contact with Ted.

Ted put his hands on his hips and stood a tall as possible. "I was just sitting there minding my own business when *you* interrupted *me*."

The man held up his hands. "Okay, okay. Don't get your shorts in a bunch." The little fellow pointed at the motel office. "I own this place, see? I got errands to run. So if you want to get a room…"

Ted shook his head and sighed. "Oh, I get it. Sorry, I've just… I've had a pretty crazy day." Ted glanced back at the motel's sign near the street. "You must be…?"

The little man folded his arms. "You're sharp, gringo, but I don't have no time to gab or listen to stupid jokes about the name of my place."

"Jokes?"

"Yeah, you know, Paco's Inn… but he just left, so now it's Paco's Out?" Paco didn't smile.

"No, no, I just meant that… Ruthie told me to try Paco's place across from the Mobil station."

"You know Ruthie? Ruthie the mermaid?"

Ted nodded. Paco dropped his arms. Ted saw large white teeth appear.

"No shit? You know Ruthie? Why didn't you say so in the first place, man?" Paco reached up and patted Ted on the middle of his back. "Come on, let's get you a room."

Ted couldn't contain a smile as he followed Paco, whose walk reminded him of a penguin his sons and he had seen on a recent episode of Mutual of Omaha's Wild Kingdom. The thought also brought with it a sting of gloom, since where they had watched the nature show was in his cramped studio apartment in Phoenix, and the television they watched it on was an old black and white model he had taken from his former room at his parents' house.

In the office, Paco climbed on a stool behind the front counter. Watching him helped Ted shake his melancholy. He smiled again when he noticed that Paco was wearing a diminutive pair of Levis and a t-shirt, and he realized that Paco and Eric could shop in the same department of a clothing store.

While Paco copied information from Ted's driver's license, Ted had a chance to look around the office. Art deco had taken charge. The counter front bore rounded, varnished wooden panels. A Zenith standup radio from the thirties with a circular dial, a secondary short wave dial, and a polished wood case dominated one corner of the room. Then he noticed the sign: *NO CHECKS!* Ted opened his wallet. "Say Paco...."

Paco looked up.

"I think I might be a little short. Could you take a check? I'm good for it."

Paco returned his attention to the registration card. "Write your check." He turned the card around so Ted could see the amount he owed. "Since you know Ruthie."

While Ted wrote a check, Paco caught himself when he nearly fell off his stool. He laughed. "You're not the only one a little short around here."

***

Ted looked at his Mickey Mouse watch, which had always been a hit with his students, and tapped the dial at mouse nose level to be sure the watch was still running: *6:45.* Ted felt he was on glacial time. Had only 10 minutes passed since Paco had given him his room key and left the motel grounds in a hurry?

To get his mind off the time, Ted explored his room. The cottage was plain compared to Paco's well-appointed office. A small separate kitchenette and a bathroom too small for a tub were the only areas of retreat from the main room, where a double bed and a mismatched desk and bedside table, Goodwill rejects all, were squeezed into the space. Round water stains in the grain of the top surface of the nightstand revealed that many residents had ignored the neatly stacked coasters. Ted opened the drawer of the small table and found the Bible planted by the Gideons.

The book, written by men lost in a desert five millennia ago, containing propaganda that has divided mankind for centuries and myths presented as universal truth, reminded Ted how helpless he felt in its presence. For a moment he felt guilty, but that feeling was soon replaced with anger, outrage toward his father and the God who stood between them.

He closed his eyes for a moment while his anger dissipated and, as in the past, turned to self-doubt. His eyes blinked open and he looked at his watch again: *6:52*. He sighed and closed the drawer, leaving the Bible unmolested. *Stalemate*, he thought.

The air conditioner strained and gurgled, but louder still was the noise Ted could hear outside his cottage of water splashing on the ground. A portion of the air conditioner protruded from the bottom half of one of the windows in his cottage. Out a different window nearby he watched water, sucked from the saturated air by the groaning machine, cascade to the ground and pool momentarily before disappearing into the parched earth. He checked his watch to be sure again that the second hand was in motion: *6:56*.

"Shit." Ted stared at his suitcase, which he had tossed on the bed when he arrived and had ignored since. The luggage had caused a noticeable sag in the mattress. The sight made Ted moan as he rubbed a spot on his lower back that he knew would be knotted up in the morning. Hidden in that suitcase was something that could help him forget the lumpy mattress, but wouldn't, he knew, let him get any sleep. Anyway, it was his last envelope, and it would be crazy to complicate his life trying to make a drug connection here. Ted opened his suitcase and pulled out a double-folded pair of sox, from which he extracted the small package of cocaine. He opened the side table draw and placed the envelope inside the Bible.

Another check of his watch told him that he needed something to distract him while he waited to call Ruthie. Ted left the suitcase where it was and walked out of the cottage. He double-checked the door handle to be sure the door had locked and walked toward the Mobil horse, still flying high but motionlessly across the street.

Once Ted had crossed the street, he paused to watch a service station attendant fueling a car. He remembered full service in the nineteen fifties and sixties, but in the last few years most gas stations had become self-service. He turned south and walked past a mix of stores and homes that were clearly not part of a planned community, and in Ted's opinion, many of the buildings had never been treated to regular maintenance.

At one point, he focused his attention on the bulbous turret of a building across the street. He had finally guessed it to be a Russian Orthodox Church when he literally ran into Paco. They stood for a few seconds staring, first at each other, and then at the packages Paco had been carrying that were now scattered beneath their feet. Paco dropped to his knees, and Ted stooped to help Paco retrieve his possessions.

As soon as Paco was back on his feet, Ted nodded toward the door of an establishment that claimed to be a cocktail lounge but that Ted felt sure was just a beer joint. "I think we could use a beer. I'm buying."

Paco smiled. "I thought you were a little short."

"Not that short."

Inside, Paco tossed his packages in a booth and walked across the sawdust-covered floor to exchange what he called low fives with the three men slouched over the bar. Ted slid into his side of the booth and blinked to acclimate to the sudden change from bright sunshine to the dim lighting of the lounge. The last few bars of *Margaritaville*, where Jimmy Buffett finally admits it was his own damn fault, faded into what Ted felt was the much too lengthy introduction to the Eagles latest song, *Hotel California*. The old jukebox took Ted back to his days as a paperboy when he sneaked in the back door of a neighborhood bar. When he slipped the *Evening Independent* behind the bar, Jimbo, the crusty bartender, would take a drag of his cigarette and cough up mucus that would rattle around in his chest for half a minute before handing Ted a quarter marked with a swipe of red fingernail polish. The quarter got Ted five renditions of *Sixteen Tons* by Tennessee Ernie Ford, which he listened to in the back room of the bar while eating a cheeseburger Jimbo had cooked for him.

A loud laugh in the back of the Spring Hill bar pulled Ted from his trance. He breathed in the odor of overflowing ashtrays and spilled beer mixed with the smell of men who worked outdoors and had surely been in a bar fight or two. Above the bar the words: *From The Land Of Sky Blue Water—Hamms*, glowed in cursive neon light tubes. Near the front door two men in their early twenties swore as they struggled to best each other at the computerized game *Pong*.

On his way back to the booth, Paco called greetings to three men at the far end of the darkened establishment who were illuminated by a low hanging light fixture. One of the men was leaning over a pool table, sizing up a ball with his cue stick and dripping ashes from a stogie clamped in his teeth. The other two were upright and respectful. The player raised his pool stick and waved it in Paco's direction, then turned his head, plucked his cigar from his mouth, and spit on the floor. Paco laughed and crawled into his seat across from Ted. Moments later a barmaid appeared with two unrequested draft beers and two phone books, one pressed firmly under each of her arms. She had to curtsy so that she could set the beers on the table without dropping the phone books. Paco giggled and took the books from her. The waitress then tugged at the low-cut neckline of her costume, which threatened to set a nipple free at any second, while her smile revealed that visits to the dentist were not one of her priorities.

Paco struggled with the phone books and finally got them stacked under his butt so he could plant his elbows on the table. He laughed when he succeeded and slipped the barmaid two dollars, which she quickly stuffed into her blouse. Paco then pointed at Ted. "He'll pay for the beer later. That's for you, Rose."

Rose grinned again. "Thanks, sugar." The pool player called her name, and she rolled her eyes before she turned, hiked up her bodice, and walked to the back of the bar.

Ted took a sip of his beer. "I see you've lived around here for a while, huh?"

"All my life. My father owned the motel for years. I took it over when he died."

"I'm sorry."

"Don't be. That was 30 years ago."

"Thirty? But you don't look..."

"I'm almost 50, man." Paco shook his head. "Nobody believes my age."

Ted nodded and paid close attention to his beer.

"Hey, don't get morbid on me, man. I'm used to his shit. My dad had the hard life, not me. He was a teenager when he came here from Mexico to pick oranges. Saved his money, met my mom, bought him a motel." Paco thought for a moment. "Then they had a dwarf."

"So your parents were...?"

"Normal? Yeah, they were regular size. Guess their genes were fucked up, though."

Paco lowered his head as if praying to his beer, so Ted lowered his head as well.

A minute passed before Ted looked up at Paco. "Hey, what happened to your Mexican accent?"

"Oh, I save that shit for the tourists. But forget about all that. How do you know Ruthie, anyway?"

Ted opened up to Paco with the short version of his life and how it had changed so drastically. He told him about his brief contacts with Ruthie and how he could hardly wait until eight, when he could call her. Paco listened passively, but when Ted mentioned his encounter with Dr. Fisher and that creep Mike, Paco frowned and played with his mustache.

Paco's reaction shadowed Ted with a dark premonition. Ted leaned on the table. "Do you know Fisher?"

Paco closed his eyes and thought for a moment. Then he opened his eyes, leaned toward Ted and lowered his voice. "I like you, gringo, so I'm going to give you some advice. Not much around here is the way it seems at first. So go slow, man. Check shit out before you take it as gospel. But, like I said, I like you. I hope you find what you're looking for."

***

Ted considered Paco's friendly warning as he approached his cottage a few minutes later. It took a moment for him to register that his door was ajar. His heart did a quick drum roll as he slowly pushed the door open. Once inside, he discovered that someone had unpacked his suitcase for him, but not very neatly. The contents were strewn over every flat surface. Ted sucked in his breath when he saw the drawer to the side table open and the Gideon Bible on the floor. He picked up the Bible and flipped the pages. The envelope was gone.

Ted ran to the office and banged on the office door for a few seconds until the remembered that Paco had decided to stay at the bar. He turned and looked around. Attached to the cabana was a large clock. It read *8:15.*

Ted was in such a hurry to get to the phone booth that he stumbled on the edge of the shuffleboard court. He reached out to break his fall and released the note from Ruthie. He sat up and found he was sitting at the bottom of the scoring triangle of the court in the rectangular box labeled: 10 OFF. The paper with Ruthie's phone number continued to flutter further down the court and came to rest in the top most triangular box. He groaned and looked at the lighted panel a few feet away on the far side of the court: Telephone. He felt his wrist and wiggled his fingers. Nothing broken.

A voice let Ted know that he had an audience. "Hey, gringo, this your first time playing shuffleboard?"

Ted smiled because for the first time, he found himself looking up at Paco, who had stopped at the top of the triangle.

"Maybe I spoke too soon," said Paco. He reached down and picked up the note. He handed the note to Ted. "You scored ten points with this."

Ted grunted and rolled on to his knees. Paco grabbed his arm and lifted. Together they did an awkward dance in the middle of the scoring triangle. The smell of beer on Paco's breath made Ted glad that he had stopped after one. Otherwise, they might both have ended up sitting on the court.

"I was going to use the..." Ted pointed at the telephone booth and waited for a reaction from Paco.

Paco just shrugged and turned toward the office.

"Paco, wait. I need to show you something."

Moments later, Paco stood just inside Ted's room with his arms crossed. "Are you sure you locked the door before you left?"

"I'm sure."

"Anything missing?"

Ted looked around the room then focused on the open drawer. "I didn't have much, just clothes. I had my wallet with me."

Paco frowned. "You want me to call the cops?"

Ted looked at Paco and shrugged. "No, you know how that goes."

Paco turned and walked out the door. "Oh yeah." Paco didn't look back. "I do know how that goes."

Ted washed his hand and checked for blood. He only had a minor scrape on the palm of one hand, but the time it took to clean up was enough time for Paco to get back to the office. Ted's uneasy feeling about how Paco had reacted to the mention of Dr. Fisher's name flashed in his gut. Outside his cottage, Ted checked his lock twice and headed for the phone booth. As he neared his destination, Ted carefully stepped up and over the lip of the shuffleboard court. He stopped in mid-dial when he heard yelling. He couldn't make out what Paco was saying, but he could see him through the office window. Paco was on the stool behind the desk shouting into the phone. He occasionally punctuated what he was saying by banging his fist on the desk. Ted looked at the note in his hand and resumed his mission.

"Oh, hello." Ruthie's voice on the other end of the line sounded relieved. "I thought maybe you had decided not to…"

"No, no. Oh, god no." Ted glanced out the glass panel of the phone booth in the direction of his cabin. "I just ran into some… some interruptions."

Ted gasped for air in the stuffy booth, air that was tinged with the smell of urine. He thrust the folding door open, holding the mouthpiece of the phone against his chest to stifle the resulting metallic screech. From the earpiece he heard Ruthie's frantic voice. "Hello? Ted? Are you still there?"

Ted returned the receiver to his ear. "I'm here, I… Ruthie, hang on a minute."

Outside the booth, two boys had just arrived and were setting up to play shuffleboard. They argued loudly over which color disks each would use. Ted looked around and noticed the flying horse across the street. On the corner just under the horse's nose stood another phone booth. He asked Ruthie to hang up and promised to call her right back.

He was in the street before he saw flash of reflected sunlight in a car's windshield to his left. The last thing he heard was the sound of rubber gripping asphalt.

13

Ted woke in a fog, lying in a dimly lit tunnel. In the distance he could hear a repetitive squeak approaching, the chirping growing louder each second. It reminded him of the bicycle he had ridden daily from Christmas day when he was in the fifth grade until its rusty hubs froze when he was in the eighth grade. Near the end of its life, the bike had sent out similar warning signals every time Ted rode up the street.

Then the end of the tunnel began to brighten, as if a train with a brilliant headlight had entered. He blinked and the tunnel became a room. He was in a bed. At the foot of the bed, two angelic faces peeked out of a fog. Behind the faces, a long cart bumped into the room carrying what looked like a morgue-bound body, except the sheet covering the prone figure failed to cover the face. The squeaking stopped when the gurney, pushed by a red-faced man who murmured with every hitch and change in direction, completed its turn around the end of an empty bed to his left and came to a halt. A nurse then pulled a curtain between Ted and the next bed. A voice counted to three, followed by grunts, groans and movement, as if an actor in a play was trying to come through the curtain to take his final bow.

"Ted, can you hear me?" The angel who spoke sounded a lot like Elisa.

"Can you see us, Ted?" The other angel waved. "It's me, Stella."

Ted felt as though his mouth was full of cotton. The angels moved to his right side. The one who had waved grabbed his hand.

A tall man with dark-rimmed glasses appeared and crowded between the women. "Mr. Miller, glad you could join us. I'm Dr. Howard." Holding Ted's right eyelid open, he shined the light from a small flashlight into Ted's eye, moving closer as if he were trying, from Ted's perspective, to climb into bed with him. "Good," he said, as he moved to Ted's left eye.

"Water," Ted said.

Dr. Howard finished his examination and reached past Stella. He spilled water on a tray as he tried to fill a glass for Ted. "Sorry, they didn't cover this in medical school."

Stella took the partially filled glass from the doctor, put her arm behind Ted's neck and helped him raise his head. "Okay pal, drink this slowly."

Ted coughed. Then he took a few more sips. No more cotton.

"Stella?" Ted slowly rose up on his elbows. He felt a sting and a tug and realized he was attached to a bag, hanging from a tall steel pole, by a tube and a needle taped firmly to his forearm. Ted blinked and searched Stella's eyes, trying desperately to make sense of his situation. He closed his eyes, and a face flashed from his mental haze. "I've got to call Ruthie."

Ted's head fell back against the pillow. It was all coming back to him: The flying horse, the phone booth across the street, the headlights... Yes, he could remember now.

"So I got..."

"Hit, Ted." Elisa glanced at Stella. "You were hit by a car.

Someone tried to hit you."

Ted reached and felt the bandage swirled around his head like a turban. "What's this?"

The doctor who had retreated to the foot of Ted's bed looked up from a clipboard he had been scribbling on. "We were worried at first. But apparently it was just a glancing blow. There were no skull fractures and no internal bleeding or swelling in your brain. We induced a coma until we were sure. That's why you're so groggy." Dr. Howard moved between the women and fussed with the bandage around Ted's head. "I'll have them take this off today. You have some minor contusions, but a smaller bandage will work."

Ted moved his left leg and winced. "Broken?"

"No." The doctor moved back to the end of the bed. "But you do have several deep bruises. You're a very lucky man, Mr. Miller."

Ted rubbed the left side of his chest and gritted his teeth. "No internal injuries?"

"Your MRI was negative. Depending on how you're moving around, you could leave as early as tomorrow."

Ted focused on Dr. Howard. "MRI?"

"It's new, better than an X-ray."

"How long have I been here?"

The doctor smiled. "Two days. I was on duty when you were admitted."

Ted stared at the doctor. *Of course, how else could Elisa and Stella be here? Two days. My God!* Ted looked at Stella. "So how did you...?"

"You had our numbers in your wallet," said Stella. "Jan and the boys know. I told them I'd call as soon as..."

"As soon as you knew if I would rejoin you?"

"You did have us worried for a while," said Elisa.

"My dad. Does he know?"

Stella bit her lip. "He's not ready to deal with this."

Ted closed his eyes. He wasn't surprised that Jan hadn't come right away. Their marital problems notwithstanding, Jan always chose flight over fight. She had never handled confrontation well. A closed bedroom door, behind which she had retreated, usually separated them during arguments. Arguments Jan usually won by attrition.

Elisa changed the subject. "You said you wanted to call Ruthie? She was here earlier. Said a mutual friend told her about the accident."

Ted lifted himself up again. "Ruthie was here?"

Stella gently pushed him back against his pillow. "She had to go to work. Didn't say much." Stella lowered her voice. "She's very pretty, Ted. What's your connection with her?"

"It's complicated." Ted motioned toward the doctor, who was busy reading Ted's chart.

Stella cleared her throat. "Dr. Howard? Would you excuse us for a few minutes?"

Ted took a few minutes to bring his two friends up to speed. He shared in detail his experiences at Quiet Springs Hospital and described the people he met there, as well as everything else that had happened since his arrival at Paco's motel, including the burglary of his room—everything except his reaction to Stella's comments regarding Ruthie and of course what had been hidden in the Bible in the side table drawer. How could he explain the surprise of dizziness and the warm ache growing in his groin during his two brief encounters with Ruthie? Or how could he express the sinking feeling in his stomach when later he realized that in Ruthie's presence, his mind was void of images of Jan or the boys? As he spoke, Ted noticed that the two women had leaned closer to the bed with increasing looks of concern.

"My God, Ted!" Stella straightened and walked to the end of the bed. "You think things are merely complicated?" She gripped the frame of the bed. "I'm afraid for you. You're in real danger."

"Danger?" For the third time Ted raised himself on his elbows.

Stella paused. "I wasn't going to talk about your father before. But from what you said..."

"What about my father?"

"I looked in on him." Stella leaned farther toward Ted. "We've spent quite a bit of time together actually."

"I appreciate that, but..."

"Ted, Jacob talked about this Doctor Fisher you mentioned. There's a connection. Jacob has a lot of repressed anger, and most of it's directed at this man."

"Most?"

"The rest of his anger is turned inward. He told me God would never forgive him."

Ted grunted as he sat up again, even higher this time. "Forgive him? For what?"

Stella shook her head. "He wouldn't say."

"So why am I in danger?"

"Think about it." Stella paced around the room. "First this creep you mentioned..."

Ted nodded. "Mike?"

"Right. First this guy, Mike, who works for Fisher, shadows you, then soon after that your room is ransacked, and then someone runs you over?"

Ted looked at Elisa. "That's what you said before. You said someone hit me. Don't they know who?"

Elisa's eyes flashed, reflecting her fiery hair. "Ted, it was a hit and run."

"Hit and run? But I heard a screech when they hit the brakes."

Stella shook her head. "Nobody hit the brakes." She looked at Elisa. "Elisa's husband saw the police report. Whoever hit you was accelerating so quickly their tires squealed."

***

The next morning, Ted looked at himself in a floor-to-ceiling mirror that occupied one wall of the hospital lobby. A baseball cap hid the smaller bandage covering the back of his head. Otherwise, he looked the same. His left side as well as the back of his left leg was covered with deep painful bruises, but those were out of sight. He grimaced as a step toward the mirror reminded him they were there.

He looked through the file folder given to him by the discharge clerk. A brief accident description ended with a request that Ted contact the local police department as soon as possible. The description seemed clinical: *Victim struck on left side of body. Grazed by passenger side fender. Struck in back of head by side mirror. Witness vague on model of car and description of driver.* He also found note from Elisa reiterating her desire for Ted to stay at her home. Stella had to catch an early flight and needed a ride to the airport, so Elisa apologized about his having to take a taxi. They both wanted him to contact them as soon as he could. There was also a pamphlet from Dr. Howard, *"Danger Signs after a Concussion."* Ted was cautioned to seek medical attention at the first indication of blurry vision, nausea, or dizziness. The doctor had reconsidered his original estimate and recommended that Ted stay in the hospital a day or two longer, but Ted insisted that he be released.

"Oh, Mr. Miller? Ted turned toward the hospital receptionist, who was pointing in the direction of the front double glass doors. "Your taxi?"

Ted waved his file folder in her direction and mouthed the words, *thank you.* Then he turned his attention to a taxi parked just outside the tall glass doors of the hospital. From the corner of his eye he saw a small paper fluttering to the floor. Ted grimaced as he reached for the paper. "Jesus Chri…"

He was stopped in mid-profanity by the frown on the face of a woman sitting nearby with whom he had made eye contact as he stooped. Her disapproval made him think of the razor strap Jacob had used with relish when he'd overheard Ted using that same deity's name in vain when Ted was twelve. It was actually a double strap, attached at both ends, used originally by his grandfather to sharpen his straight razor. It made a popping sound as both belts snapped together and at the same moment took a bite out of Ted's skin. Jacob always forced him to take off his pants and his underwear. Then Ted had to bend over, hands on his knees. Anticipation of the coming strike always sent waves of nausea to his core. Jacob would prolong the agony with the same speech: "We stand naked and worthless before God, Ted. If I spare the rod, you will lose your soul." Even now Ted's ears and face burned at the memory.

Ted maintained eye contact with the woman as he retrieved the note. He touched the back of his left leg. "Don't worry. I've already been punished for that one."

The woman shook her head and looked away. He glanced at the note, turned, and limped out the door.

Ted caught his breath, still surprised by the stifling heat. But in spite of his desire to cool off as soon as possible, he paused to read the note he had noticed was from Ruthie. She apparently knew he was being discharged and wanted to meet with him at a local restaurant later that night. Ted slipped her note into his shirt pocket and slid gingerly into the back seat of the cab, thankful that the driver, who was apparently willing to sacrifice gas mileage, was running the air conditioner full blast.

The driver draped his arm on the seat back and smiled at Ted. "No luggage?"

Ted could see from the bright colors on the man's sleeve that he was wearing a Hawaiian shirt. From the way he had asked his question, Ted assumed he was, like his family, a transplant from somewhere in the Northeast.

Ted wanted to ask him the whereabouts of the restaurant Ruthie had suggested, but as soon the cabbie heard Ted's destination he turned, shifted into gear, and guided his cab into the morning traffic. He ignored Ted's attempts to interrupt his one-way conversation as they picked up speed. Ted grunted affirmatively every time the taxi driver said: "You know?"

Ted listened carefully. When he heard a short pause in the driver's rant, he shouted. "Is there a town called Bayonet Point near here?"

"Bayonet Point?" The driver stopped talking. He seemed stuck for a moment, trying to connect his previous point about the stupidity of former President Ford's *Whip Inflation Now* buttons— not that Jimmy Carter was doing any better—and Ted's question. "Oh yeah, Bayonet Point. It's down toward Saint Pete, on Highway 19, maybe, oh, ten, twelve miles south of Spring Hill."

Encouraged, Ted forced another question into the conversation before the driver could recover. "How about the Red Lantern restaurant?"

"Hopping place." The driver looked over his shoulder and smiled. "Peanut shells all over the floor in the bar. It's right on the highway. Can't miss it."

***

Ted spent the remainder of the day in his room alternately resting and exercising his left leg, which had stiffened, until it was limber enough to drive his car. He checked the motel office several times between bouts of do-it-yourself physical therapy to see if Paco had arrived. The balding middle-aged man who worked for Paco would just grunt and shrug his shoulders each time Ted asked about his employer's whereabouts.

Later that evening as Ted drove south he tried to time the traffic lights in an effort to limit the number of times he had to engage the clutch of his car. After a short drive the restaurant sign appeared, as promised, prominently displayed along Highway 19.

Ted parked his car. As he walked in the front door of the restaurant, he was glad that his limp had disappeared.

"Welcome to the Red Lantern, sir. Just one for dinner?"

Ted looked into the vacant eyes of an eighteen-year-old girl trying to look thirty-five. Her blond hair was parted in the center and flowed to her shoulders where it flipped. A mini skirt and go-go boots accentuated her long legs. Her smile and tone of voice said, *this is how I act when I'm expecting a big tip.*

"Thank you, no. I'm meeting someone. She might have made reservations." Ted looked at his watch. "I'm a little early."

The girl checked a list on her podium. "Ruthie for two at nine?"

Ted nodded.

"Follow me. She's waiting for you."

Thanks to the cabbie's warning earlier, Ted wasn't surprised to hear crunching under his feet as he followed the hostess past people sitting or standing up to and leaning on the black vinyl rim of the bar. From the merry sounds of the patrons Ted surmised that most of them had already made good headway in creating their next morning hangovers. Two couples and a single woman were swaying to the music of a three-piece combo on a small dance floor that separated the bar and dining area. The piano player blew a kiss to the solo dancer, a woman wearing a green sequined dress that was so tight it gave away every detail of her body's descent into middle age. The lady pushed aside a few strands of her platinum blond hair that had escaped her pinned up hairdo, sidled up to the piano and placed a tip in a jar. The drummer struck a quick drum roll and smacked a cymbal. Then, while still using one hand to finger his saxophone, the third member of the band moved the jar closer to the bar.

Single lanterns on each table were the only source of light in the dining area. The hostess led Ted on a circuitous route around several tables, ending at a booth at the far end of the dining room. She put a menu on the table and quickly faded into shadows and flickering light.

Ted stood still, enthralled. He watched as candlelight danced in Ruthie's eyes. Then, for a moment, all he could see was the top of her head.

Ruthie looked up and smiled. "Ted, please sit down. You're embarrassing me."

Ted winced when his butt hit the padded but firm seat.

"You must be really sore, huh? And your head?"

Ted removed his baseball cap and turned his head to show her the bandage.

"Ouch," she said.

They were in the middle of their dinner when Ruthie put down her fork. "I need to ask you something."

Ted stopped eating. Until that moment, the conversation had jumped and stalled like a car running out of gas. They knew so little about each other. Ruthie had apologized for not staying long at the hospital. She admitted she felt uncomfortable with Elisa and Stella. Ted assured her that the women had his best interests at heart. She told him that Paco had called her with the news of Ted's accident. The topic of Sister, which had brought them together, remained elusive, just out of reach, like chasing an important paper caught in the wind. "Ask," said Ted.

"Do you have a nickname?"

"A nickname? What could that possibly have to do...?"

"Look, one of the patients I work with hides the fact that her name is Sister. As far as I know, no one knows she goes by that name. Then you walk in and, bold as you please, ask if she's a patient at Quiet Springs." Ruthie stopped, took a deep breath and let it out slowly. Ted's mouth was open. Ruthie leaned back and sighed. "You seem like a nice guy. And I'm sorry about what happened to you. But I need to know if I can trust you." Ruthie took a breath. "Sister has a journal. She addresses each entry to someone and the name sounds like a nickname. So I need to know if you have a nickname."

Ted leaned toward Ruthie. "When I was little... just recently I... my parents called me Skipper."

Ruthie's eyes widened. "Skipper is the person Sister writes to in her journal."

At that very moment the band broke into their rendition of a Nat King Cole standard. The last notes of *"Unforgettable"* faded before either Ted or Ruthie said another word.

Ruthie pushed her plate aside. She took a manila envelope from her purse. From the envelope, she pulled a single sheet of paper and placed it on the table in front of her. Ted could see that the letter had been written in meticulous cursive script. "I want you to read this."

Ted reached toward the letter, but Ruthie pulled it back. "She says some things about me... some embarrassing things. So please... Oh my God. Don't turn around."

Ted had to steel himself against doing just that. "What is it?"

Ruthie shoved the letter back in the envelope and held it in front of her face. "Doctor Fisher just walked in and sat at the bar."

"Fisher, from Quiet Springs?"

"Yes, but it's dark at our table. I don't think he can see us."

"What should we do?"

"I think we should sneak out the back door... Oh sweet Jesus."

"What?"

"It's Paco, he just came in and he's talking to Fisher. I can't believe it. Not Paco."

14

The next morning, the first rays of sunlight sneaked through a gap in the stained curtains covering an east facing window of Ted's cottage and tapped on his eyelids. Soaked sheets stuck to his body. The air conditioner hummed valiantly, a noise he even heard in his dreams, but it had lost its battle with the sweltering humidity. Ted rolled out of bed to escape the clammy grip of the sheets. But he couldn't shake the childhood memory of waking to wet sheets, plus the acrid smell of urine and shame.

For their year and a half stay in North Carolina, Ted's father chose to worship with the Plymouth Brethren Church, one of the most conservative of all the Protestant brands. At age 13, hormones were sending new and confusing signals to Ted's groin when he was in the presence of girls his age, whose t-shirts revealed budding breasts or the outlines of training bras—a name that tickled Ted's funny bone when he tried to figure out what they were training the tiny breasts to do—and he was convinced that the main goal of this church was to keep these very hormones in check. Sue, a girl his age, challenged the church for Ted's soul. A simple smile followed by a giggle would set Ted's head spinning with thoughts guaranteed to fling him down the slippery slope that, according to the youth minister of the church, ended in eternal fire.

Ted also had a unique relationship with a boy at his church. Harold Yount wet the bed, too. Margaret Miller had uncovered the secret from Harold's mother and used the information to ease Ted's shame. The confidentiality allowed the boys to have sleepovers, something neither boy had been willing to try in the past.

For Ted, one particular Sunday morning began with the promise of good things to come. He had inched away from impending spiritual doom by winning a contest in Sunday school, demonstrating his piety by repeating from memory more Bible verses than any of his peers were able to recall. But more importantly, he had avoided any side-glances at Sue. Later, when the church services ended, parishioners gathered outside the church, congratulating each other on their decision to renounce sinful life, rejoicing in the fact that their decision had been a substantial down payment on the promise of eternal bliss. The Miller and the Yount families were in close proximity in the churchyard. Ted waited for the right moment to make a request that had, he thought, sounded simple. The next day was the first day of summer vacation. Already memories of seventh grade were receding to a distant corner of Ted's mind. In the final seconds before making his request, Ted had caught a glimpse of Sue's delicious smile. That she was within earshot of his conversation caused a brief malaise that Ted dismissed as more news from his new hormone companion.

"Mom... Dad, could Harold sleep over tonight?"

There it was, such a basic request. But the moment the phrase left his lips, Ted knew that the uneasy feeling he had experienced had nothing to do with hormones. He locked eyes with his father. He pleaded with the God he had recently begun to doubt. *Please dear God, he prayed, don't let my father speak.*

Ted clenched his teeth. His cheeks felt hot. His ears began to ring. Words tumbled from Jacob's mouth. A quick glance in Sue's direction—her mouth agape and her eyes wide open—verified that his father was saying exactly what Ted had hoped he wouldn't say.

Harold kicked a divot in the grass, his eyes welled with tears, and he turned and ran toward the parking lot. Harold's mother looked at Jacob, shook her head, and ran after her son. Ted sobbed and reached out to his mother. Margaret grabbed him and pulled him to her breast.

Jacob scratched his head. "What did I say?"

Ted pulled away from Margaret. He and his mother watched Sue disappear behind the church.

Margaret sighed and looked at Jacob. "You let the cat out of the bag."

Nearly dressed, Ted sat on the edge of the motel bed. The springs under the thin mattress complained as he forced on his socks. Ten minutes after a shower and in spite of the air conditioner's best efforts, his skin was already clammy.

Movement on the bedside table caught his attention. Ruthie's latest note, one edge held by the base of a lamp, fluttered in the air conditioner's steady, laborious breeze. Ted remembered Ruthie's hand shaking as she wrote her address down for him using the hood of her car as a desk in the Red Lantern's parking lot after their abrupt exit from the back door of the restaurant.

Come to my place tomorrow morning at ten. Ruthie had stuffed the note in his shirt pocket. *Thursdays are my only days off.*

Ted grabbed the note, reread it and shoved it into his wallet. He sighed. He was thankful that a misplaced note wouldn't join the mounting roadblocks he was experiencing. Then he checked his watch and placed it on his wrist. It was only seven. With time to kill, Ted opened the nightstand drawer and pulled out the Bible in which, he noticed, a former guest had placed a bookmark. He opened to the marked page, which was Genesis, chapter twenty-two. Immediately Ted recognized the story of the testing of Abraham's faith by God. God had ordered Abraham to take his only son Isaac, a son he loved deeply, to the mountains in another country, where he was told he would, first with a knife and then on a pyre, sacrifice Isaac as a burnt-offering to God.

As a young child, Ted had found the story abhorrent. In his teens, he had finally built up enough nerve to make his feelings known to a Sunday school teacher. The teacher had defended God's actions. For after all, hadn't God changed his mind in the seconds before the knife was plunged into Isaac's heart? God had even provided a lamb to be sacrificed in Isaac's place, hadn't he? Ted's response had been a question. First he verified that the teacher believed that God was our heavenly father. Then he asked what kind of father would put his son Abraham through such a harrowing experience, especially if it was merely to satisfy his own ego.

At home, Ted caught holy hell from Jacob for his insolence. By this time, Ted had grown taller than Jacob and the beatings had stopped. Still, Jacob was mortified by how the incident made him look in the eyes of the Sunday school teacher. Ted stopped Jacob's railings with a question.

"Dad, what if you were in Abraham's place? Would you have stabbed me with that knife?"

Jacob thought for a moment. "Things are different now. God doesn't speak directly to us anymore. He…"

"Answer the question! If God told you to, would you kill me?"

Jacob stared at Ted. "Don't ever question God's word or His will again."

Jacob turned and walked out of the room. Moments later, the hounds of hell echoed in the bathroom.

***

Ted gripped the steering wheel of his rental car as he pulled out onto highway 19. Barring further complications he would soon read the words of Sister, who had until this moment remained a figment of his imagination, planted there by his dying mother. And then there was Ruthie who, after the time they had spent together last night, caused him nothing but confusion. What was it he had seen in her eyes that day when she swam to the window at Weeki Wachee Springs? The only thing he was sure of was that by last night, whatever it was had disappeared. Ruthie was as much an apparition to him as Sister was, just out of reach.

A road sign announcing *Buccaneer Bay* distracted him. That morning at the motel he'd read a pamphlet on the history of the area. Pirates had at one time buried treasure at this very location. As Ted drove further south on the highway, he marveled at the housing developments that had been rescued from the swamps. Surely the residents must wonder if the packed sand supporting their homes was littered with buried swords and pieces of eight. A few miles further on and off to his right, Ted saw canals dredged to bring the Gulf of Mexico to the front doors of homes built on tiny islets. A sign planted in the white sand next to the road announced *Hudson, Florida*. He had arrived.

***

"Come in. Any trouble finding my place?"

Ted shook his head. The street signs had been easy to read. The numbering system was clear. But Ted was still having trouble matching the woman who stood before him and the mermaid who had looked into his heart. The dimples in her cheeks were the same, and her strawberry-blond hair that reached the center of her back still danced, though now it only moved when an oscillating fan, whirring just behind her, turned in her direction. But like the night before, he was soon seeing only the crown of her head. As a mermaid, Ruthie had no trouble returning his stare, but away from water she wilted like a flower too long out of the sunlight.

He entered her small mobile home and noticed that it was just as reluctant to reveal anything about her. The walls were bare. A sofa and love seat were hidden beneath drab slipcovers. Even the view of the canal that she could have enjoyed out her front window was hidden by heavy drapes. Ruthie pointed Ted to the covered sofa. Then she walked to her small kitchen and clicked on another table fan. Ted decided the fan's purpose was to redistribute the moisture her small air conditioner had been unable to wring out of the air. In spite of the heat, she wore a pair of Levis and a gingham blouse buttoned to her neck. Without asking if he was thirsty, she poured two glasses of iced tea. When she held one of the glasses out to Ted, rivulets of condensation from the glass dripped to her hand. After Ted took the tea, she wiped her forehead with the water from his glass and set her own glass on the small coffee table between them. Then she sat on the love seat and pulled her knees to her chin.

Ted drank half his tea and set the glass on the coffee table. He looked up and caught her staring at him.

Ruthie looked down at his glass. "Sorry I didn't ask. Would you like sugar?"

"Sugar?" Ted followed her gaze to his glass of tea already standing in a small pool of water that it had created. Ted shifted in the chair. "You really freaked out last night."

"I don't trust Fisher," she answered. "Not just about Sister... other things, too."

"I get that, but what about Paco? How do you know him, anyway?"

"He works part time at Weeki Wachee... on the glass bottom

boat. He's a good guy." Ruthie looked away. "He helped me through a rough spot... you know?" She sighed. "So why was he meeting with Fisher? I just don't get it."

Ted avoided her sudden stare by looking around the trailer and nervously flipping the edge of a manila envelope lying on the coffee table. "Nice place."

"I'm not here much. I spend four ten-hour days a week at Quiet Springs and two days a week under water."

Ted whistled. "Six days a week, no wonder..."

"Go ahead Ted, read it." Ruthie reached out and pushed the envelope closer to Ted.

Ted picked up the envelope. "You mean this is..."

"Get real, Ted." Ruthie laughed. "You've had your eye on it since you sat down."

Ted pulled the letter free of the envelope. The scent of perfume wafting out reminded him of his mother and the hardness of church pews they had shared in his youth. The missive was handwritten in perfect script on heavy stationery. Each line was parallel to the top of the page. Embossed in the upper right hand corner were the initials *EM*.

Ted ran his index finger over the initials.

"Esther Miller," whispered Ted.

"I'd forgotten." Ruthie dropped her feet to the floor and leaned toward Ted. "That was the name you gave Prissy... in the office that day."

Ted swallowed hard. His temples were pounding. "It's her, it's really her."

"I think so, too. Otherwise I wouldn't... I think I can trust you."

"I'm glad for that." Ted looked into Ruthie's eyes. "How did you get the letters anyway?"

Ruthie pulled her legs up to her chin again. "She carries

them around with her in a stationary box. I have an inbox at the nurse's station. Now and then she leaves one there."

"Does she ever talk about them?"

"Never... she just smiles and pats my arm when I ask about them."

"Have you ever shown..."

"No... you're the first. And no one knows she calls herself Sister."

"This narrows it down, you know?"

Ruthie nodded her head.

"If her last name is Miller... she's either my father's sister or my..."

Ruthie's feet hit the floor. "Your sister. Maybe she's your sister."

"Yeah... my sister, but, neither Prissy or the other lady..." Ted thought for a moment. "Pam, that's it, Pam. Anyway, neither of them recognized the name Esther Miller. Wait a minute... what's Sister's registered name?"

Ruthie sighed and shook her head. "Oh, Ted... her name is Edith Montgomery."

Ted sighed. "Nice theory while it lasted."

Ruthie raised her hands, palms up. "It doesn't matter... the initials are the same and, anyway, how many women call themselves Sister?" She pressed her hands on her thighs and leaned toward him. "Come on... read the letter. You showed up for a reason, Ted, I just know it."

Skipper,

They are watching me again. The doctors think I cannot hear their mutterings. My, how clever their opinions are of my condition. How shall I provoke them today? Perhaps I will give them hours of rhythmic rocking, or a fit? Yes, today they will witness writhing that will send them fleeing to their medical books. Then tomorrow I will be back to normal. They will be so proud that they helped me. They should listen to Ruthie, she knows, but they are so smug. Soon I will share my dreams with her.

Sister

Ted looked up. "What do you know that the doctors don't?"

"That Sister is as sane as you or me."

"How long has she been a patient?"

Ruthie thought for a few seconds. "Since 1945. But, I've..."

"1945? I was born in '44. That makes sense. I was a baby when Sister left. I..."

"Ted." Ruthie took a deep breath. "I've checked the admission records but they're not... complete. Doctor Fisher's signature was the only one on the forms."

"So Fisher has been at...?"

"That's right. No one working here now, except that creep Mike McCoy, was working at Quiet Springs when she was admitted."

"What's McCoy's story, anyway?"

"Later, Ted, okay? One thing at a time."

Ted held his hands up in surrender. "Okay, okay..." Ted thought for a moment. "So, have you ever told anyone that you think there's nothing wrong with Sister?"

"Fisher is difficult to work for. The doctors who stay for any length of time learn not to question him. When I was new I told some of them my suspicions about Sister. I even told Fisher once. But..."

"He wouldn't listen?"

Ruthie shook her head. "He told me that if I ever mentioned her to him again he would fire me."

"Jesus." Ted looked back at the letter. "What about her dreams?"

Ruthie stood and walked to the kitchen counter. She picked up a letter from the counter, turned back toward Ted and held it behind her back. "She hasn't shared her dreams with me yet."

"Is that another letter from Sister?"

"Yes it is... but I took it out of the envelope before you got here."

"Because...?"

Ruthie walked back to the love seat. "Because it has some personal stuff about me and I..." Ruthie laid the letter on the coffee table but pressed it down firmly with her fingertips. "And I'm still not sure if I'm ready for you to read it."

Ted touched the letter. "Ruthie, you can trust me... I promise."

Ruthie lifted her fingers and nodded.

Skipper,

I startled Ruthie today. Oh good heavens, I didn't mean to. She was sitting at her desk gazing at a spot far beyond the chart in front of her.

"Ruthie, they will never believe you," was what I intended to say. But all I got out was, "Ruthie," when she quickly informed me, in that cute little crude manner of hers, that it was no longer necessary for her to go the bathroom, since I had scared it right out of her.

Ruthie is such a sweetheart, 28, just out of nursing school. That is why they will never believe her, you know. It is they who have the medical degrees, but Ruthie? Why, she is just a beginner. In a way, I feel badly that Ruthie is so frustrated by the situation. But I have to be in real contact with someone. Ruthie is perfect. To begin with, she is so smart, and pretty. My, my, she is a real beauty. I was pretty once, too, but living here takes any attractiveness you may possess, twists it and mashes it into plainness that causes others to look past or even right through you. But, as pretty and smart as she is, Ruthie has her demons, too.

She never sees any young men. Don't get me wrong. I see the young male orderlies making fools of themselves in her presence. She just does not trust any of them. Something about her daddy, I think. I asked her about her father once but she just looked sad and then changed the subject. Maybe it is a woman thing, but sometimes I feel that Ruthie and I have been through the same thing. Something we share. Anyway, from what I have seen and heard, she does not date at all. She spends most of her spare time being a mermaid over at Weeki Wachee Springs. The girls there just swim around looking beautiful. People watch them through thick glass windows in an underwater gallery. It is not as if they are nude or anything, why, families visit the springs and the mermaids. The girls wear a full bathing suit with a tail contraption. But once, when I visited Ruthie on a field trip to the springs, I saw a sexual sight, as though Ruthie was making love to everyone behind the windows.

It was after I startled her, and after she reported that I had, in fact, frightened her, that I finally told Ruthie that the doctors would never believe her. Of course, Ruthie again asked why, since I was not committed to the institution, I had stayed. To which I, of course, replied that even though I did not speak to Him on a regular basis, God had made it perfectly clear that I was in this predicament for some wrong-doing, and that it was here I was to remain.

Sister

Ted reread parts of the letter then nestled the letter back in the envelope. Ruthie was biting her lip and peering at the ceiling when he looked at her.

"She's just guessing you know," said Ruthie. "About me, I mean." A tear dripped from her chin.

15

"You one of them developers?"

Ted's eyebrows narrowed. The man didn't look like a police chief to Ted. The top two buttons of his sweat-soaked tan uniform shirt were unbuttoned, exposing the tattered collar of a t-shirt, worn more than any wife would allow. Greased white hair was slicked back over his ears, and he held a cigar, one end chewed to a slimy pulp, between his thumb and index finger. Still, the nameplate on the desk he sat behind announced *George Todd, Police Chief.* Sure enough, above the badge on the man's pocket, a shiny brass name tag read *Todd.*

Todd stuck his cigar back in mouth and leaned back further. His ancient office chair groaned to a halt exactly where gravity should have taken over and dropped the chief on his head, wiping from his mouth the smirk that had already caused Ted some concern.

Ted thought for a moment about what Ruthie had said about Todd. Less than an hour ago, he'd left her with tears still in her eyes.

She had promised to call soon. He'd asked for directions to the station. The last thing she said was that the chief was kind of different. When Ted had reached the end of her sandy driveway, he'd stopped and looked back to make sure he had left footprints. When he was a child, his mother told him that when you dream, you never cast a shadow or leave footprints in the sand. Ted was relieved to see the dents he had made in the sand and that Ruthie still stood there too, her hair dancing in the warm breeze blowing in from the gulf, as real as the sand that had worked its way into his shoes. He remembered opening his mouth to speak, but nothing came out. He had just waved and folded himself into his car.

Ted released the image of Ruthie, leaned on the counter that separated him from the chief's cramped office space, and his focus returned to the question Chief Todd had asked. "Developers?"

"Hernando County ain't peaceful no more. They're coming up from Saint Pete and Tampa. Yankees mainly. Filling in our swamps. Building houses for the old farts from New York who used to just snowbird over the winter." The Chief took a puff of his cigar, chewed on it, took it out of his mouth and pointed the mucky end at Ted. "What you doing in Spring Hill, then?"

Ted coughed. Mixed with the acrid smell of cigar smoke in the muggy room was the faint odor of urine. "Just visiting, sir." Ted held up the report he had received at the hospital. "I'm the one who was hit by a car a few days ago."

The chief sat upright, put his cigar in an ashtray, stood, and walked to a rusting file cabinet. "In front of the Mobil station?"

"That's me," Ted said. "I'm staying at Paco's Inn."

The chief wrestled with a stubborn file drawer, one up from the bottom of the cabinet. A kick from his boot sprung the drawer loose. He fumbled through several file folders. "God damn that Leroy." Chief Todd pulled out a report and flashed it in Ted's direction. "Grown man, but he still don't know his A-B-Cs." He walked back to the counter, took Ted's form, and matched the file number to the lengthier version Leroy had misfiled.

Todd scratched his head. "I knew Paco's daddy when he bought that place."

Ted looked up. "I don't follow. You knew Paco's daddy?"

"Said you was staying at Paco's Inn, right?"

"Oh… right. Yeah, I'm staying at Paco's."

"Place is named after the daddy, not the runt."

Ted smiled and nodded.

The chief looked at Ted over the top of reading glasses he had slipped on to read the report. "You don't look too much the worse for wear," he said.

Ted touched the bandage on the back of his head. "Head's okay." He touched his ribs and rubbed the back of his left leg. "Legs and chest are still sore. The bruises are deep."

"Anywho," Chief Todd said. "No updates. No new witnesses found. No new details on who was driving the car or the model either." The chief glanced at Ted. "Driver tried to stop, then took off. Anything you can add?"

"No, I heard the… the screeching was from a fast start, right? Not from braking, right?"

"That's what they thought at first. The witness got confused. Sent Leroy out to measure the skid marks again. The car was braking." Chief Todd picked up his cigar and took a drag. He turned back to face Ted and blew a puff of smoke that made Ted cough again. "Anything else?"

Although the official report was bent in the Chief's grasp, Ted was able to see that several of the sentences had been deleted with a black marker. In a box labeled *witness*, the last name had also been marked through. Ted gasped. He could still make out the witness's first name.

***

Something strange and physical was happening to Ted as soon as he returned to Paco's Inn. His vision dulled, and his hand froze on the doorknob of his motel room door. He couldn't remember ever feeling this way before. Anxiety he understood. But this was new, a scream forming in his gut, moving up through his chest.

Ted tried desperately to understand the first of several messages clipped on the doorframe. *Call Stella? Why, to verify how I've fucked up my marriage, my job, my kids?* The mental list of screw-ups went on and on. The rest of the messages became a blur. The scream moved higher, pressure built behind his eyes. Still holding the doorknob, he rested his head on the door, choking back the pain in his throat.

It was at that moment, a breath away from losing the battle to keep the scream from erupting, that he felt pressure on his back, just above his belt.

"Hey, hombre. You sick or something?"

Ted turned around. His hands were shaking. "You little shit!" The dam broke. "You were the witness to my accident!" Ted thrust a finger at Paco, who stumbled backward. "There's a cover up! You're working with Todd and Christ only knows who else!"

The sight of Paco, sprawled on his butt, surprised Ted, and he backed off when he saw heads sticking out of nearby cottage doors. His hands still shook as he opened the door and stumbled into his room. The springs of his mattress complained, stressed by his weight as he collapsed. His head hit the pillow. The sharp pain in his left leg and the water-stained ceiling in his line of sight above became his only points of reference.

Ted's mind whirled and he lost track of time. His face burned. The stains on the ceiling went in and out of focus, some looking like animals or people. Then—after what seemed like an eternity—the rhythm of his breathing slowed and his vision returned to near normal. An elephant with ears bigger than Dumbo the flying elephant, materialized from an especially large stain on the ceiling. Slowly, like a cloud drifting into view, Paco's face replaced the elephant. Ted worked his way up on his elbows. Paco, who had been hovering over him, moved back.

The bedsprings fussed again as Ted winced, dropped his legs over the side of the bed, and sat on the edge of the mattress. He stared at Paco, who had backed to the door. "You still here?"

Paco held up two stubby fingers. "Two things kept me from going to my office and coming back here with a baseball bat in my hand."

"Oh?"

Paco pointed his index finger at Ted. "First, I'm pretty sure that most of that shit coming out of you is from a place where you've been keeping it bottled up."

"And the second thing?"

"I told you before. I like you. And I always give people I like a second chance."

A flash of Ted's anger returned. "I saw your name on that mucked-up police report."

"So?" Paco crossed his arms. "I was a witness."

"Yeah, the witness who can't remember much of anything. You even changed your mind about the driver trying to hit me."

"Now, wait a damn minute." Paco put his hands on his hips. "You were already in the ambulance when that idiot Leroy showed up. I told him it was a red Mustang that hit you. And I know damn well that I told him the driver peeled out... meant to hit you."

"And you didn't change your mind later? You didn't say you were confused?"

"Hell no." Paco held up his hands and spread them as if he was describing a large fish he had caught. "I haven't talked to Leroy about it since that day. And I haven't seen that lazy turd George Todd in a month."

From his seated position, Ted could look Paco straight in the eye. "What about the driver?" he asked. "You didn't see the driver."

Paco returned Ted's stare. "I'm standing on a stool behind my desk in the office. I hear a screech. I look up and see a car gunning for you. I nearly piss my pants. Sorry if I missed some of the details."

Ten seconds is a long time to stare into someone's eyes. Ted finally broke the silence. "Oh."

Paco crossed his arms and stood as tall as he could. "Anything else?"

"Well..." Ted threaded his fingers together. Then he made a steeple with his index fingers and tapped them on his lips. "Ruthie and I were at the Red Lantern last night."

Paco frowned and turned to leave.

Ted dropped his hands and talked to the back of Paco's head. "Ruthie was upset when she saw Doctor Fisher come into the bar."

Paco hesitated but didn't turn around.

Ted stood. "Ruthie was devastated when you joined Fisher. What the hell were you doing there?"

Paco stepped out the door, stopped, and turned around. "You weren't listening, were you?"

"When?"

"In the bar that night, remember? I said things aren't usually the way they seem at first around here. So, go slow..."

"I remember. Check shit out before I take it as gospel. Right?"

"That's right, amigo. You've got to trust me on this one." Paco walked a few steps away from the door. Then he stopped and looked back inside the cabin. "I can tell you one thing about Fisher though."

"Yeah?"

"Deal with him the same way you'd deal with a rattlesnake."

***

Less than an hour later, Ted drove toward Quiet Springs Hospital thinking about steam engines. His air conditioner was making a noise that could only mean that it had surrendered to the merciless humidity. But the sauna-like condition of his rental car was not the source of the steam engine metaphor running through Ted's mind. He was thinking that, although he had blown a relief valve 30 minutes ago, already he was building up another head of steam.

Of all the messages clipped to his door, he had only responded to Ruthie's. She was headed to the hospital—something she needed to pick up. He could meet her there if he wanted to. A hospital board meeting was scheduled for the afternoon, and Doctor Fisher would be tied up.

As important as the messages from Stella and Elisa probably were, they would have to wait. Could he trust Paco? What was really going on between Paco and Fisher? A car horn blared. Ted looked up and saw a steady green light. Had he been waiting for a signal light to change, or had he stopped at a green light? He wasn't sure, but, after a second honk behind him, his foot pressed the accelerator.

As instructed, Ted drove to the back of the hospital property. He entered a private driveway that circled around the remainder of the individual units. Unit C was the fifth building in from the street. After he parked, Ted noticed that a high fence surrounded the next building, and the windows were covered with wire mesh. It was hidden from the street, like a locked room in someone's house.

Ted heard his name. Ruthie waved from the door of Unit C. She had changed into Bermuda shorts and cotton blouse. Her hair was pinned off her neck in a tight bun. No time for idle chatter.

Ted caught up with Ruthie and pointed at the fenced unit next door. "Is that the only building with a fence?"

Ruthie fussed with her keys. "That's unit D." She turned her key and opened the door. "It's the only locked ward." She laughed when she noticed Ted staring at her keys. "This door is only locked for patient security. They come and go as they please from the door that faces the inner patio."

"So who do you keep in unit D?"

"Any person who has the potential to cause harm to themselves or others, mainly. A few are committed by the state."

Ted nodded. He imagined padded cells, and inmates running amok.

Ruthie led Ted through a small foyer and into a large room. In one corner, several comfortable-looking but decidedly institutional chairs huddled below a television mounted firmly to a wall, from which the unhappy voice of Chuck Woolery boomed. The TV was tuned to the Wheel of Fortune, and apparently a contestant had just spun the giant wheel and landed on Bankrupt. Across the room a ping-pong table waited for some action. Several square card tables, with folding chairs neatly tucked in, occupied the center of the room. Chess and checker sets and boxes of dominos were evenly distributed on the tabletops. The only thing the room lacked were the patients themselves.

"Hi Kathy, looks like everyone is at the pool." Ruthie solved the mystery for Ted without his having to ask.

Kathy sat at a desk near the entrance to a wide corridor extending to the other end of the building. Ted could see individual rooms opening off the corridor and half way down, a large nurse's station. Kathy wore a starched white dress and a white hat that looked as though a pretzel maker had folded it.

She pointed down the corridor. "The usual suspects are in their rooms." Kathy looked at Ted. "And you are...?"

"I'm sorry," Ruthie said. "Kathy, meet Ted. Ted is... he's a new friend of mine."

"Oh my." Kathy sat up and looked at Ted more closely.

Ted tugged at his collar.

"We don't ever meet Ruthie's... friends."

Ruthie stared at Kathy. "Give us a few minutes alone, will you?"

Kathy smiled, stood and disappeared down the corridor.

Ruthie took Ted by the arm and led him to one of the tables on the far side of the room, where they settled into creaky chairs. "You know why I asked you here, right?"

"To see Sister, I hope."

Ruthie bit her lip. "But now I'm having second thoughts. Whoever Sister really is, she's not crazy. What if we make things worse for her?"

Ted folded his hands on the table. "Even if you hadn't called, I was going to try to see her. I can't turn back now."

"Ted, I'm scared."

"You're scared? My accident was no accident."

"What?" Ruthie reached across the table with both of her hands and grabbed Ted's hands.

"Somebody tried to run me over. And that slime ball police chief I went to see today? He's covering up for someone."

"Oh my God, Ted," she said. "What now?"

Ted slowly loosened her grip, and then he grasped her hands. "Now," he said. "We think of a reason for me to meet Sister. We don't solve the whole thing today. We just begin the journey." Ted felt like Stella was sitting on his shoulder whispering into his ear.

Ruthie drew a deep breath and released it slowly. "I really did have something to pick up at the nurses' station. Let me do that first, then I'll check on Sister. She never goes to the pool." Ruthie stood. "Wait in here. I'll come and get you... but remember, she goes by Edith."

Ruthie was a few feet away when she stopped and turned back toward Ted. "Oh, Ted..."

Ted waited for her to speak.

"Later, I want to hear all about why you can't turn back."

Ruthie was out of sight when Ted moved closer to the corridor, to a table that had playing cards arranged for a game of solitaire. He sat down, dealt three cards, and dropped a queen of hearts on a lonely king of clubs. His impromptu game was soon interrupted by the sound of someone singing.

He stood and moved closer to the corridor. It was his song, the song that had played in his head for years. ... *Down came the rain and washed the spider out.* He followed the singing to the second room on the right. The door was open and inside the room, a rocking chair was turned so the man singing could see out a window into the courtyard between the two wings of Unit C. Ted recognized the man immediately. He was wedged so tightly in the rocker it looked as though his balloon body had been blown up from within the chair.

"Eldon, is that you?"

Surprised, Eldon's arms and legs flailed in an attempt to stand.

"Oh no, oh no, I'm stuck again!" Eldon's voice increased in pitch and volume. "Bobby, Bobby, I'm stuck again! I'm stuck again!"

Ted felt a hand on his shoulder.

"Excuse me, sir." Bobby squeezed by. "Be calm, Eldon. Don't fight it, you know you'll only make it worse."

As if performing a magic trick, Bobby maneuvered Eldon out of his rocking chair. Once on firm ground, Eldon continued prancing his legs and pumping his arms. Bobby danced around with Eldon until he slowly wound to a stop.

Bobby released a familiar laugh. "There Eldon, you see? You are not stuck after all." Bobby gestured toward Ted. "And look, our friend Ted has come to visit us." He raised his eyebrows. "Though I cannot imagine why."

Eldon smiled. "Mister Ted, Mister Ted! I remember you. Did you find your sister?"

Ted thought about his answer. "No, Eldon, I didn't. But maybe you could help me with something else."

"Oh yes, please!" Eldon clapped his hands.

Ted glanced at Bobby and then returned his attention to Eldon. "When I came into your room, you were singing a song."

"The spider song," Eldon said. "It's my favorite."

"Yes, Eldon, the spider song." Ted thought for a moment. "Eldon, do you remember who taught you the spider song?"

Bobby stepped between Ted and Eldon. His condescending expression had disappeared. He grabbed Eldon by the arm like a police officer might grab a criminal. "Eldon, maybe you should get ready for dinner."

Eldon's expression deflated. "I hate to be late for dinner, Bobby."

Ted glanced at his watch and thought. *A little early for dinner, isn't it?*

Bobby moved Eldon past Ted and out the door.

Then Eldon pulled free of Bobby's grasp. He turned and faced Ted. "Mister Ted?"

"Yes, Eldon?"

"Sometimes I play checkers with Miss Edith. When Miss Edith thinks about how to move her checkers, she sings the spider song. I learned it from her."

Bobby frowned. "Dinner, Eldon."

Ted hurried back in the opposite direction to the day room. Ruthie was talking to Kathy. Her hands were on her hips and she wasn't smiling. Kathy motioned in Ted's direction.

"Ted, there you are." Ruthie walked toward the front door. "Come on, we have to go."

Ted followed her to the parking lot. When she reached her car, she turned to face him. Her hands were shaking.

Ted took her hands in his. "What's wrong?"

She breathed deeply. "Fisher had Sister moved to Unit D."

16

Early the next morning Ted pulled into a service station and stopped next to a pump with a sign that read *Unleaded Regular.* He thought about his Datsun sitting idle in his Phoenix apartment complex parking lot baking in the desert sun. In the past year the newly mandated leadless gasoline had turned his high performance car into a choking, stalling wreck. He closed his eyes. Gasoline had caused him even more trouble when he was sixteen.

It was past midnight in mid-December and Ted's body shook as he watched the burly Phoenix cop standing next to him rap on the front door of his parents' home. More than a month had passed since the hellish summer sun had finally released its brutal grip on the desert. It wasn't uncommon this time of year for the citrus farmers, eager to protect their precious fruit, to resort to blazing hot pots and enormous fans to fight off nighttime winter temperatures at or below freezing. But Ted, who wore a black motorcycle jacket zipped up over a thick wool sweater, wasn't reacting to the weather. He was shaking because he could already imagine Jacob's reaction to his predicament. The door opened and Ted moved further behind the patrolman.

Ted's father appeared and leaned to his left. "Teddy, is that you?"

The officer turned, grabbed Ted by one of the shoulder straps of his jacket, and pulled him forward. "So this little hoodlum is your kid, right?"

"God will punish you, Teddy." Jacob's face turned deeper red as he spoke. He took a step, reached out, and pulled on Ted's sleeve. "And where on earth did you get that jacket?"

Ted felt another tug on his shoulder and found himself behind the cop again.

"Mr. Miller." The policeman blocked Jacob. "You need to calm down."

Ted peeked. His father took a step back. The color drained from Jacob's face. "What did he do?"

"Found him and his buddies parked about a mile from here, right where kids were reported messing with outdoor Christmas decorations."

"Dad, I swear, we didn't..."

"No." The cop frowned at Ted and then looked back at Jacob. "We can't prove they were unscrewing Christmas bulbs, but they did have a full gas can and a hose in their trunk."

"A hose?" asked Jacob.

"For siphoning. They use the hose to steal gas from cars." He waited a moment then continued. "Can't prove that either, though. But..." He hooked his fingers under Ted's shoulder strap once again and thrust him at Jacob. "It is past curfew."

Ted took a step past his father but again felt pressure on his shoulder. This time it was his father's hand catching the leather loop and spinning him around. Jacob pulled Ted with him as he closed the door until it was barely ajar and only his face showed out the door. "Sorry, officer. It won't happen again." His father closed the door, pushed Ted into an overstuffed chair and stood over him. "He's back, Teddy. Charlie is back." Jacob believed in a literal interpretation of the Bible, which said that Jesus cast demons out of people; Jesus even named them. His father also believed the Bible's assertion that a good Christian can do the same. Jacob bared his teeth. "In the name of Jesus, I order, you, Charlie." Spittle showered from his mouth. "Get out of my son."

Tears flowed down Ted's cheeks. He sat up, pushed his father backward, stood and ran. Ted stopped at the arched entrance to the hallway and looked back at Jacob. "There's no demon, Dad. Can't I just make a mistake?"

Ted shook his head, dismissed his thought of evil spirits, and focused on the map he clutched in his hand. Elisa's home was just a few blocks away. He had called Elisa the night before after returning to the motel from the hospital. Though Ruthie wanted to meet with him later that night–she had hoped to gain more information about Sister's transfer today, maybe even see her if she could–it was the news from Elisa that now occupied his thoughts. Her husband had sniffed out records of an incident in Spring Hill involving a Jacob Miller. She didn't elaborate except to say that the incident occurred in the 1940s. And as if that information wasn't enough to keep his leg shaking, his normal reaction to anxiety, Ted had decided that tonight he had to tell Ruthie about the letter his mother said Sister possessed.

Ted gripped the rental car steering wheel. Heat radiated from the hood of his car in oscillating fingers of disturbed air. Tapping— which had started, as a dull thumping deep in his sub-conscious, the place where he was wont to retreat—grew more insistent. It wasn't the sound of his heart beating, though his heart was almost in rhythm with the sharp clacking–like a woodpecker's futile attempt to peck a hole in a metal pole. Neither was it his leg, which shook hard enough to affect the suspension system of the car. The sharp reports were coming from his left, outside the car. Then a voice joined the banging. "Mister, you all right? Hey you!"

Ted looked to his left. A man's nose was pressed against the driver's door window, and his eyes peered through a layer of condensation. His hand was in motion, striking a metal object on the glass. Surprised, Ted rolled down the window.

The fellow let out a piercing howl. "What the Hell?" The man, dressed in grease-stained overalls, lurched backward. Already in a semi-squat, he looked like a Russian dancer, except instead of crossing his arms, one hand held his nose and with the other hand he braced himself from behind on a gasoline pump.

Ted opened the car door. Immediately it met resistance, and the man let out another yelp. Ted slid out of the car and found the man sitting in front of the gas pump on a cement platform. He was still protecting his nose with one hand, and he was rubbing his knee with the other. The attendant waved away Ted's offer of support, and as he rose, he steadied himself on the gas pump.

"I'm sorry if I hurt you... I... fill it up with regular, will you?" Ted looked up into the eyes of a man-child. He was tall enough to play professional basketball, but the way his overalls hung limp on his frame said he could never compete.

The attendant took a step backward, pulled an oily rag from his pocket, and dabbed his nose. He inspected the rag and held it up for Ted to see. "No blood." Without another word, he tweaked his nose, limped to the pump, and commenced with his official duties.

Ted slipped back behind the wheel. With the air conditioner off, he was met by stifling heat, but he couldn't face the doleful expression on the lad having difficulty inserting the nozzle of the gas hose into his tank.

Five minutes had passed when again tapping interrupted Ted's thoughts. The attendant was tapping on the hood, this time keeping the engine compartment between them. "Check the oil?"

Ted rolled down the window and held out his Mobil card. "No thanks... and sorry again... about the..." Ted pointed to his own nose.

Ted had been sucked into his shadow once again, and as usual someone else had paid a penalty. He worried about Elisa and her husband and their willingness to involve themselves in his problems. Would they feel the sting of his bouts of inattention? *Stay focused.* He repeated the phrase several times until he reached Elisa's street

Elisa's house was unique in the suburban clutch of rambling structures in address and color alone. Identical white picket fences surrounding each front yard were the only line of demarcation in a block-long sea of light green gravel where grass had been preempted. Heat radiating from Elisa's yard hastened Ted's retreat to a large covered porch.

A man in uniform answered the doorbell, his arms held out from his crowded service belt as if ready to challenge Ted to a gunfight. He offered his hand. "I'm Tommy, Elisa's husband. You must be Ted."

Ted clasped the man's meaty hand. "Oh, that's right... Elisa mentioned you were a policeman." He extracted his hand from Tommy's grip and noticed his knuckles were white.

"Highway patrolman, actually." Tommy smiled, but his eyes continued scanning Ted as if looking for clues at an accident scene.

Elisa appeared and nudged her husband to the side, interrupting his investigation. "Don't keep Ted out in the heat." She glanced at Tommy. "I made some iced tea. Would you bring it in from the kitchen?" She waited for him to leave, lowering her voice when she spoke to Ted. "Don't worry, you're innocent until proven guilty."

Ted laughed. "He is intense. Goes with the territory, I'll bet."

Elisa escorted Ted into her living room, pointed him in the direction of a large overstuffed chair and plopped down on a sofa. Ted stayed on his feet for a moment, his attention drawn to an entertainment center dominated by an eight-track tape player. He thought for moment about how glad he was that he hadn't succumbed to the hype of this fading, tape-eating technology. Yep, long-playing records were the only way to go. What did this say about Elisa and her family? No appreciation for the past...?

"Ted?" Elisa sat up on the edge of her sofa. "Are you okay? You look catatonic. Did you leave the hospital too soon?"

"What? No... I'm." Ted eased himself into the large chair, which enveloped his aching body. He removed his ball cap and turned his head, exposing the shaved area in the back of his head. "Guess I still get a little dizzy, but I'm fine, really." Actually he did feel pretty good, considering the circumstances. But how could he explain that he'd been sucked away once again, this time in a debate with himself on the merits of competing stereo equipment?

Ted saw in Elisa's expression that she wasn't convinced, so he changed the subject and began to fill her in on his visits with Ruthie and everything else that had transpired since he had seen her last. Tommy returned as Ted related his experience with George Todd. He set a tray of sweating glasses of tea on the coffee table and joined his wife on the sofa, ignoring the tray and listening intently. They both leaned closer when Ted talked about his visit to Quiet Springs.

When Ted finished his report, he shifted forward and took glass of iced tea from the tray. One sip and he realized how thirsty he was. Over the rim of his tipped glass he watched Elisa's face. From her expression she seemed stumped, not sure which question to ask first.

Tommy, on the other hand, had already decided on the part of Ted's story to which he would respond. "I got to know George a few years back. I worked state route 19 back then. Goes right through Spring Hill." Tommy adjusted his belt. "He's definitely a good old boy, but I never heard of any corruption. But if he changed the report..." He looked at his watch. "We'd better cut to the chase. I've got to leave for work soon."

Ted moved to the edge of his chair and placed his empty glass on the tray. "Elisa said you found something about my father?"

"Old stuff," said Tommy. "We're lucky somebody updated it to microfilm." Tommy checked his watch again. "Back in the forties, little places like Spring Hill counted on the patrol for law enforcement."

Elisa sighed. "Tommy."

Tommy held up his hands. "Okay, just the facts. The patrol got a disturbance report at the home of a Jacob Miller who lived in Spring Hill."

Ted leaned in. "What year was it... does it give an address?"

Tommy pulled a paper from his pocket and unfolded it.

Elisa jumped to her feet. "You didn't tell me you made a copy."

Tommy stood as well. "You didn't ask."

Elisa grabbed the report from her husband and reached it across the coffee table. "Here Ted, just read it yourself."

Ted took the report and then glanced at Tommy.

"No problem." Tommy held up his watch. "I've got to go." He looked at Elisa and walked passed her. "Just thought I could help, you know, interpret." He paused at the door. "For instance, 22:38? That's 10:38 P.M." Tommy grinned at his wife. Then he turned to Ted. "Oh, one other thing. I copied that on the Q.T. You can make notes, but leave the report with Elisa."

- 28 Sept. 1943 - C Troop - Spring Hill: 22:38 - Trooper M. Ward responded to a 1020 at 911 E. Diana Ave. Neighbors reported screaming and a car leaving quickly from the scene. Trooper Ward found the homeowner Jacob Miller, age 32, with facial contusions consistent with a physical confrontation with another individual. The victim's wife Margaret, age 32, was upset but unharmed. A daughter, Esther, age 14, had locked herself in a bedroom. Her parents said that she was upset but not injured. Mr. Miller reported that the family had surprised a burglary in progress. Mr. Miller described the two suspects as teenage white males both dressed in Levis and white t-shirts. Mr. Miller said that his assailant was the taller of the two suspects, thin and estimated to be 6 feet 2 inches tall. The second suspect was stocky and estimated to be 5 feet 10 inches tall. Betty Taylor, of 950 E. Diana Ave., the neighbor who reported the incident, did not see the suspects. The Miller's next-door neighbor, Mr. Paco Lopez, of 921 E. Diana, was at the scene and verified Mr. Miller's description of the suspects. Mr. Lopez reported he had left his house to investigate noises just as the suspects were running to their car. No evidence of forced entry was found. Mr. Miller explained he often left the house unlocked. Mr. Miller reported that nothing was missing from the residence. An APB was broadcast, including the descriptions of the suspects, as well as the make and model of the suspect's car, which was described as a 1942 two-tone green Pontiac. Mr. Miller said that although it looked new, it couldn't be a 1943 model since the car companies had switched over to the war effort last year and stopped making cars for civilians. Mr. Miller declined medical attention.

***

Esther was his sister and his parents were still high school age when she was born. Ted turned north on Highway 19 with those facts buzzing in his head. The steady blast from a horn jolted him from his stupor. He turned his steering wheel and squeezed his car to his right as far as the paved shoulder of the road would allow. On his left the horn blared again and Ted saw the flash of a middle finger. His heart raced. Surely he had looked to his left before turning, hadn't he? He checked his rear-view mirror and eased back onto the highway. Then he reached up and tilted the mirror so he could see his reflection and touched the dark puffy skin below both his eyes.

The added stress of the last few days was certainly a reasonable explanation for the exhaustion that plagued Ted, and how could anyone sleep well in the sauna of his motel room? But Ted knew that his fatigue was endemic to his psyche. What, he wondered, would it feel like to be completely rested? How long would it take someone like Stella to dig down to the bowels of his subconscious and discover why he always felt that he was running on empty?

A sign announcing Spring Hill jolted Ted from his introspection. When he pulled into the circular drive of Paco's Inn, Ted felt the urge to speak to Paco. The Paco Lopez mentioned in the report was surely Paco's father, but maybe he would remember something. But first, he thought, as he braked just short of the trellis at the back of his carport, I need to rest and think.

Ted found an official looking letter and a note clipped next to his cabin door. He tucked the message in his shirt pocket along with the paper he had used to take notes from the police report and tore open the letter. Words can hurt feelings; they can even cause physical pain. This letter went straight to his gut. The words, *separation agreement* and *child custody* set him pacing. It was an error to think that his life in Phoenix was on hold. Forces with the innocuous name of Johnston, Billings and Lamb were plotting his marriage's demise. Life was draining from the woman who gave him birth. In spite of his daily phone calls with his boys, Ted recognized that his absence was undermining their stability. And on top of all that, he had willingly derailed his career to go on a quest, which, appeared to have less and less of a chance of ending well with each passing day.

Ted stuffed the devastating letter in his back pocket. He fumbled with his key and missed the keyhole several times before he realized the key was upside down. Once inside the sweltering cabin, he squeezed into the bathroom, leaned against the sink and turned the white porcelain handle marked with a C. He splashed water on his face and peeled off his shirt, which he hung on the wall behind him. For a few moments, he stood listening to the sound of his breathing. His face was reflected in the mirror above the sink. Was it his imagination or had a few more gray hairs sneaked in line above his ears? He patted his cheeks. His skin was hanging more loosely than before. Then, in the mirror, he noticed the message sticking out of the pocket of his shirt.

Ted opened the stapled message and seconds later grabbed his shirt from the wall. He was still buttoning it as he ran toward the phone booth next to the shuffleboard court.

"Unit C, Ruth speaking."

"It's Ted, I got your message."

"Thank God you called!" Ruthie lowered her voice, but that failed to dampen her enthusiasm. "I found Sister."

Ted felt hope returning, like the first drops of rain on the parched earth after a long summer drought. "That's great, can I see her?"

"That's why I called. Instead of going to my place tonight, come to Unit C after eight."

Ted felt his heart pulsing in his neck. "I won't be late." He steadied himself on the ledge under the payphone. "Ruthie, you won't believe what I've uncovered about my family."

"We'll talk later." Ruthie's tone of voice changed then. "Thank you for calling, Doctor. I'll make sure I change the medications. Goodbye."

Ted hung up. The clock in the cabana said it was only two. The sun directly overhead promised a long afternoon.

Ted looked toward the motel office. Through the window he saw Paco's head bobbing behind the counter. He could see white teeth, so he knew Paco was checking in new guests. He touched the note in his pocket. Maybe this would be a good time to push Paco for more information.

Ted greeted an elderly couple as they left the motel office. He entered the office and found that Paco had already disappeared from behind his perch.

"Paco? You still here?"

Paco's voice was muffled. "I'm busy. Can you wait?"

Ted stepped around the counter and peeked into the apartment behind. None of the fine wood panels or art deco furniture of the office were evident. The small living room had a sofa and old chairs. In one corner, a desktop was hidden under piles of forms and receipts. To his right a staircase led to the upper floor.

Paco was pulling up his zipper when he emerged from one of the two doors leading to other rooms.

"Oh, it's only you." Paco frowned. "The joys of this world are so few. And you make me rush taking a piss."

"What gives?" Ted waved his hand around the room. "I'm surprised your office décor doesn't extend to your apartment."

"I don't live here. Sometimes a night clerk sleeps upstairs. But..."

"Bet you live on Diana Avenue." Ted pulled out his notes from Tommy's report.

Paco moved to his desk and hopped up on a stool. From the

center of his desk, surrounded by a pile of papers, he pulled free a glass of watered-down tea. He took a sip and looked at Ted. "You've been spying on me?"

Ted walked across the room. "These are my notes from a police report I saw today." He handed them to Paco. "Take a look."

Paco read the notes. When he finished he shook his head. "You're determined to keep digging around in this town until you hit shit, aren't you?"

Ted sat down on the sofa. "I told you why I'm here. And you know some of the crap I've been through since I arrived." Ted looked at Paco. "You said I could trust you. Can't you tell me anything?"

Paco kicked the edge of the desk. "I was sixteen when this happened."

"I did the math." Ted said. "Do you remember anything?"

"I was a kid, man. I had angst that you wouldn't understand."

Ted sat up on the edge on the sofa. "But do you remember anything about that night?"

"Wait a minute." Paco jumped off the stool. He reread the note. "Jacob Miller? Is this your family?"

Ted nodded and sank back down into the sofa. "I wasn't born yet. But, yes, this is my family."

Paco moved toward Ted. "Man, you've got to watch your back. You…"

Ted pushed himself back to the edge of the sofa. "Paco, what happened that night?"

Paco began pacing. "Something bad happened to the young girl."

"Bad?"

Paco dragged a chair close to the sofa and boosted himself up on the seat. "I didn't see anything. But after the police left, I heard my father talking on the phone to Fisher."

"Fisher?"

"My dad said the girl was just a child. He threatened to turn Fisher in."

"Turn him in, for what?"

Paco shook his head. "He didn't say why. Then my father caught me listening. Said he'd kick my ass good if I ever mentioned what I had heard." Paco climbed off the chair. "He sent me to my room after that. We never talked about that night again."

A full minute passed before Ted spoke. "That young girl is the woman I'm looking for. Ruthie and I are trying to find out why she's in Quiet Springs and how we can get her out."

Paco thought for a few seconds. "You've been seeing a lot of Ruthie."

"She's great. I couldn't do this without her help."

"Some advice?" Paco stared at Ted.

"I'm listening."

Paco crossed his arms. "Don't even *think* of getting under *her,* poncho."

"Christ, now you're the one who's not paying attention. Don't you think I've seen the hurt in her eyes? She didn't tell me much, but she did say you helped her through a rough patch."

Paco held up his hands. "Okay, okay, I believe you. But, that's exactly the reason I can't tell you why I was meeting with Fisher that night."

"Because of Ruthie?"

"It's a goddamned slippery slope." Paco began pacing again. "Shit runs deep in this town. I tell you too much and Ruthie could..."

"What?" Ted jumped to his feet. "Ruthie could what?"

Paco stopped pacing. "Ruthie's been hurt enough."

Ted opened his mouth to speak, but he was cut off by the jangle of the office telephone.

Paco walked into the office. Moments later he stuck his head in the doorway. "It's for you."

"For me?" Ted moved to the office and tried to take the receiver from Paco.

Paco wouldn't let go. "It's Ruthie." Paco stared at Ted for a moment, and then released the receiver.

Ted sighed and shook his head. "Yes?"

"Don't come to the hospital." Ruthie was frantic. "I got in to see Sister. Someone has taken her box."

"Box?"

"The box she keeps her letters in. I can't talk. Come to my place tonight, after nine."

17

The headlights of Ted's rental car splayed light across the front of Ruthie's mobile home. As his car plowed through the crushed shells of her driveway his tires made the sound of the sea retreating over the sand after the crash of a wave. He hit his brakes, turned off the engine, and killed the headlights. Ears ringing, alone in the dark, Ted stopped fighting the urge to close his eyes. Thoughts swirled, but none were in focus. He slumped, and his body nestled into the contours of the seat, creating a momentary vision of his father sinking into his La-Z-Boy that morning in Phoenix when he had gleaned the first hint of his relationship to Sister.

A sudden stab of light and a loud chiming from the dashboard brought Ted to attention. Ruthie stood next to the opened driver's side door, her hand still on the handle. The dome light cast an ethereal glow on her white uniform, transforming her into a heavenly cherub.

She touched his shoulder. "Are you okay?"

Ted rubbed his eyes.

"I heard your car drive up." Ruthie stood back. "You look terrible."

A quick glance in the rear-view mirror verified Ruthie's assessment. His eyes were red and swollen. The dark circles under his eyes weren't shadows.

Ruthie leaned into the car. She grabbed his arm. "Come on, sport. I guarantee that I feel as bad as you look."

Once inside Ruthie's home, Ted claimed the same spot as before on the camoflagued sofa. Ruthie curled up on the loveseat across the coffee table and returned his blank stare.

Ted sniffed the air. "Do I smell pot?"

Ruthie smiled and pulled out a plastic bag hidden next to her cushion. "I only smoke these as an umbrella when the shit starts raining down. Want to roll one?"

Ted shook his head. "Quit when I got married." He thought about the envelope missing from his motel, but the time wasn't right for sharing his own escape mechanism.

Ruthie shifted in her chair. "I wondered. I saw your boys with you that day at the springs, but I didn't see a woman."

"We're separated. I just signed the papers." Ted leaned toward Ruthie. "You remember seeing me that day?"

According to Sister's letter, Ruthie regularly gave bold and salacious looks to men on the other side of the aquarium glass. If she could remember him, was the heart-piercing look she gave him special?

Ruthie's answer did little to solve that mystery. "Never forget a face." Ruthie put the plastic bag away. "But there's a lot we don't know about each other." Ruthie stood and walked to her small kitchen. "Like why we're tiptoeing around things we couldn't wait to talk about just a few hours ago."

"I know," Ted said. "What happened at work?"

Ruthie brought two glasses of iced tea and set them on the table. "Bobby is what happened."

"Bobby?"

Ruthie sat back down. "Fisher shifted Bobby to Unit D. Made him responsible for Edith... Sister..."

"It is Sister, no doubt anymore. The day I was there? Eldon told me she sang a song I've heard in my head all my life."

"Eldon's part of this, too," Ruthie said. "He can't be without Bobby nearby, so they're together now depending on whether Bobby is in Unit C or D.

"And Bobby?"

"Bobby is a shit. I'm sure he told Fisher I had access to Unit D."

"Why would he call Dr. Fisher?"

Ruthie shook her head. "I don't know. Bobby's always been headstrong. He was an RN in Jamaica, but here, because of certification, he's only an orderly. He's bitter and resentful.

"What about the missing box?"

"I'll get to the box. Just listen, okay?"

Ted folded his arms.

Ruthie took a sip of tea. "I was able to get into Unit D because Pam... you remember Pam from the office?"

Ted nodded.

"Pam gave me the keys. That's when you called me, just before I went in to see Sister."

"You were excited."

Ruthie nodded. "But when I finally got in to see Sister, she was upset because someone had taken her box of letters. Bobby interrupted us, he and I argued, and by the time I got back to Unit C, I had a phone call from Fisher."

"Shit."

"Shit is right. Fisher said he would fire me if I went back to Unit D. Then he told me to get the keys back to Pam right away." Ruthie sighed. "That's when I called you."

Ted closed his eyes and shook his head. "We're screwed."

"Or…" Ruthie held up a letter. "Maybe it's just a setback."

Ted recognized the stationery and the embossed *EM*. "Where did you get that?"

"In my inbox. It was there when I checked out tonight. The box was empty thirty minutes earlier." Ruthie handed the letter to Ted.

Ted stared at the delicate curves of the handwritten script. He looked up at Ruthie. "Who put the letter in your box?"

She just shrugged. "Read it, Ted."

Skipper,

I had the nightmare again last night, the dream that has haunted me for years. They come once again, like insidious fingers of smoke through the crack under my bedroom door, to spread their pain and fear. Each time they come, their faces become a little clearer. The big one, the one who holds Father so the other one can do his filthy deeds, has always looked familiar. But the memory of his face is like chasing a piece of paper on a windy day. There was something different this time. When the short, sweaty one knocks me to the floor, I still feel his crushing weight as he falls on top of me. But this time, when he covers my mouth to stifle my screams, as my lungs ache for the slightest wisp of air, I reach out. I reach out and touch a scar that is under his chin. I remember it this time, as if a movie has stopped on one frame. In the midst of my panic and fear, I feel pity for this beast. As he always has, the big one urges him on like he's a trained animal. There is a quiet moment when all I feel is him tugging at my underwear. Then comes the searing pain between my legs as the beast *grunts and slobbers like a pig at a trough. Moments later the beast is up and off me. He pushes Mother away. Only hours ago she told me she was going to have a baby.*

Ted looked up from the letter. "Jesus, that's me." He turned the letter toward Ruthie. "Here, my mother is pregnant with me."
Ruthie nodded and Ted continued reading the letter.

We were so happy. Now all I hear are her cries to Jesus to help us, but they fall on deaf ears. I look down and see the warm liquid I feel between my legs is my own blood.

Sister

Ted laid the letter on the coffee table. "This isn't a dream. Sister and my parents have held this secret all these years."
"I can't imagine how hard it's been for them."
The stinging behind Ted's eyes increased. His chest began to heave. Ruthie reached him just as years of pent-up pain found voice in Ted's gut-wrenching sobs and groans. She held him until his body stopped its rhythmic motion and his breathing calmed. He watched her stand and move to the rear of the mobile home. Moments later she returned with a box of tissue. She set it on the coffee table and took several for herself. He watched her settle back in her chair and waited while she alternately sobbed and wiped her eyes.

Ruthie's tears made Ted think of the overnight trips his parents would take, leaving him home with a sitter when he was young and they still lived in Florida. Once, when he was five or six, his mother had been especially upset when they returned from one of the outings. Margaret went immediately to their bedroom while Jacob drove the sitter home. When his father returned, he told Ted to go outside and play, and he joined Margaret in the bedroom.

Of course Ted disobeyed. He crept down the hall and pressed his ear against door to his parent's room.

He heard his mother sobbing, and then he heard Jacob speak. "Your tears won't help her. We have no choice. You know that."

Why were his parents helpless? They must have been visiting Sister at the hospital. Had Fisher threatened them? Ted wanted to share these questions with Ruthie, and tell her about the police report, but he could tell something else was on her mind.

Ruthie blew her nose softly. "Sister was right, you know."

Ted breathed deeply to steady himself. "How's that?"

"She and I do have something in common." Ruthie drew a sharp breath. "That rough time Paco helped me through?"

Ted nodded.

"It was last year." Ruthie closed her eyes. "This is going to sound too weird."

Ted shook his head. "It's okay."

She bit her lip. "I was getting help for depression. I have... intimacy issues." Ruthie pulled up her legs and hugged her knees. "I tried hypnotherapy. It was just deep relaxation, really. Anyway, during one session I remembered being molested when I was little."

"My god. Who...?"

"I couldn't remember his face. I asked my mother." Ruthie reached for another tissue and wiped her eyes. "She was devastated. I don't know who my father is. He was out of the picture before I was born. My mother is sure the abuser was a boyfriend she had when I was little."

Ted stood and walked to the front window. He pulled back

the heavy drape about a foot and peered at a boat passing along the canal that flowed in front of her home. "Now I get it." He let the curtain fall closed and walked back to the sofa. "Paco was afraid..."

"What?" Ruthie dropped her feet to the floor, sat up, and leaned toward Ted. "Paco was afraid of what?"

Ted pulled his notes of the police report from his pocket. "Read this first."

Ruthie's mouth hung open the entire time it took her to read the report. It was still open when she dropped her hand, holding the report in her lap, and looked into Ted's eyes. "My God, Ted, this is Sister's dream."

Ted nodded. "Fisher's involved."

Ruthie hugged herself and shivered. "Fisher? How?"

"I showed the report to Paco. He was just a kid, but he overheard his father talking to Fisher on the phone after the incident. What he heard implicates Fisher as far as I'm concerned. He told me today that I've got to watch my back."

"Ted, you're scaring me. What else did Paco say?"

"It's what he won't say that bothers me."

"What do you mean?"

Ted thought for a moment. "I asked him why he was at the bar with Fisher that night we were there. He said he couldn't tell me anything because it might end up hurting you."

"Jesus, is that what you were talking about before I read the police report?"

"I thought I had something figured out, but... tell me how Paco helped you when you were in counseling."

Ruthie took a deep breath. "This is confusing the Hell out of me. But if it helps, Paco and I talk a lot. He took me under his wing when I started working at Weeki Wachee." She thought for a moment. "I needed a father figure, I trusted him. Opening up to him helped."

"You know he loves you, right?"

Ruthie nodded. "We've never discussed it, but he knows I don't have any feelings for him. Not that way, anyway."

"So it's more complicated than I thought."

"What is?"

"I thought Paco was just being protective of you. But it's more than that. He's afraid you'll discover something. Something connected to this Pandora's box we've just peeked into. Something dangerous."

"I don't get it. Two weeks ago you could never have convinced me that Paco would hide anything from me." She looked at Ted. "But since that night at the Red Lantern... I just don't know what to think."

"We've got to be careful." Ted shifted his position on the sofa. "But we still have things to check on and..."

"And...?"

"My mother told her hospital roommate that Sister has a letter that will explain everything. I don't think this dream letter is the one she's talking about."

"But what if we can't find Sister's letter box?"

"Talking to Sister is our only hope." Ted picked up the dream letter. "That's not all. We have to find out if my father worked at Quiet Springs. There has to be a connection with Fisher. But..."

"But... how do we get in, right?"

"Why are you smiling? Getting in looks impossible. But worse, you could lose your job."

She bit her lip. From a pocket of her uniform she produced a set of keys. She threw them to Ted. "Let me worry about my job. Would the keys to D Unit help?"

Ted stared at the keys. "Where... how?"

"Tomorrow is Saturday. No one will be in the administration office, and I don't have to swim until the late afternoon shift."

"You have the keys to the administration office, too?"

Ruthie just smiled.

Ted shook his head. "But I thought Fisher made you turn these back in."

"Ted, there's something I haven't told you."

"What's that?"

"Pam is my mother."

***

"Ted, wake up."

"Momma?" Ted's eyes fluttered but he couldn't focus. The thick aroma of frying bacon dulled all senses save his sense of smell. Even the crick in his neck seemed distant compared to the odor of sizzling animal fat wending its way through his nasal cavity. A sudden stab of light redirected his attention. He blocked the light with his hand. Through slowly parting fingers and squinting eyelids, an angelic figure appeared through the glowing light. He sat up, let his eyes adjust to the light and realized that he was sitting on Ruthie's sofa. She had thrown open the heavy curtains and, for first time since he had visited her, light flooded the front room of her mobile home. Ruthie turned from the window, her robe transparent in the sunlight from the window. That she had nothing on beneath the robe defied him to look away. He forced himself to rub his eyes. "I fell asleep... I don't remember..."

Ruthie sat down across from Ted. "It was almost midnight. You fell asleep in the middle of a sentence. I just let you sleep in your clothes." She smiled. "You thought I was your mother a minute ago?"

He thought for a moment. "My mother?" Then he remembered. "Oh, when I woke up. No, I wasn't even thinking of my own mother. It was the smell of bacon..."

Ruthie squealed, jumped up, and ran to the kitchen. She held up a smoking frying pan. "Just in time."

Ted stood, moved to the counter separating the small kitchen from the living room, pulled out a barstool and sat down. "My father had trouble keeping jobs. We lived in North Carolina for a year or so when I was in sixth and seventh grades. Momma was an older black woman who sort of... adopted me."

Ruthie stopped fussing with the bacon. "Adopted?"

Ted scratched his head. "Not really... look, a guy who went to our church owned a farm. I spent time on the farm during the one summer we were there. Momma was the wife of a sharecropper who lived on a small section of the farm. I spent a lot of time with them."

Ruthie nodded and smiled. "And the smell of bacon?"

Ted's stare didn't focus anywhere inside the mobile home. "Momma was always cooking things that smelled like bacon. I called her husband Old Paul. He had pitch-black skin, and his face looked like a relief map in a *National Geographic* magazine. He'd laugh with a rumble when he said I was a pinkish Yankee... taught me how to drive a tractor."

Ruthie leaned on the counter. "Sounds nice."

Ted thought for a moment. "Once I asked Old Paul why he couldn't come to our church." Ted closed his eyes and shifted on the barstool. "Old Paul poked his finger into my chest. He said, 'Teddy, some things going to break your heart.'"

Ted felt Ruthie's hand on his shoulder. He turned and opened his eyes. Ruthie was standing behind him, and her robe was hanging open. He tried to speak, but his words stuck low in his chest where his heart pulsed, the source of the warm glow spreading through his body. The gap in her housecoat exposed the white flesh of one of her breasts that defied gravity and curved up, disappearing where its hardened nipple dimpled the edge of the material. He stood and reached toward her, then pulled his hand back.

With a shrug of her shoulders the robe slipped to the floor. She took Ted's hand in hers and guided it. He sucked in a breath of air as his hand gently supported her supple breast. Moments later he felt her hand on the nape of his neck and pressure pulling him toward her face. He groaned once when their lips met. And again when he felt the pressure of her breasts on his chest. Ted was lost in the taste of bubble gum lipstick, the smell of baby powder, and the electric tingle of her touch.

Ruthie momentarily broke the spell. She unbuttoned his shirt and led him past the kitchen to her bedroom. Ted felt her fingers move over the buckle of his belt and grab the top of his pants. She tugged and pulled him on top of her on the bed. Her lips were next to his ear. "I want you so much, but..." She took his face in her hands. "Be gentle...it's been a long time since I..."

The end of Ruthie's sentence was lost in Ted's kiss.

Then a vision of Jan's back turned toward him in bed flashed in his mind's eye. "Don't worry," he said. "It's been a long time for me, too."

***

Ted parked his rental car on the street a block from Quiet Springs Hospital. In his rear-view mirror, he watched the reflection of Ruthie's car pulling in and parking behind him. What a surprise. Ambushed by love, yet a willing participant. Each time he stopped at an intersection on the way over, Ted fought the fears of their intended mission with the overwhelming rapture of seeing her face in his mirror. Together—that was the word Ruthie had used as they left her home. We can do this together—a new feeling.

He sat motionless, watching Ruthie get out of her car. Here, finally, was the remedy to the pain of being alone in a marriage, alone in a church surrounded by people, being alone in a classroom full of squirming adolescents.

Ruthie waited for him on the sidewalk. Ted searched her eyes for a hint of the enthusiasm he felt about the change in their relationship. But the flower had closed up again. He climbed out of his rental car, and as soon as he reached her she pressed a set of keys into his hand. Ruthie's hands were shaking, but she took his arm and tugged in the direction of the hospital.

As they walked Ted succumbed to his inner voice. Should he have stopped before they had gone too far? Had this added more to her pain? Ruthie's voice, urging him to try the largest key in the door to the administration building, stopped his self-interrogation.

Once they were inside, Ruthie steered Ted toward Doctor Fisher's office. "Mom said Fisher has files no one else sees."

Ted stopped. "How does she know about the files?"

"She's worked here as long as I can remember. Come on." Ruthie opened the door behind Prissy's desk and entered Fisher's office.

Ted touched Ruthie's arm. "My God," he said. "It looks like no one works in here."

"Prissy's a neat freak." Ruthie tried the top drawer of the only file cabinet in the room. "Damn. Is there a small key on that ring?"

Ted held up the ring. "Just door keys."

"Just our luck." She moved behind the desk. Ted heard a rattle. "These are locked, too."

A closet door offered the only other place to investigate in the sparsely furnished office. The door squeaked when Ted pulled it open. "Boxes," he said. "Lots of file boxes."

Ruthie joined him. "Look." She pointed at the only box that was out of place. "It's too high for me. Can you..."

Ted inched the box off the shelf with his fingertips. "Watch out!" Ted used his body to shield Ruthie from the falling box.

File folders and a smaller box spilled out around their feet. Ruthie gasped. "It's Sister's box." She picked up the tattered stationery box.

Ted flipped through a file folder he had picked up. "And look at this." Ted turned the tab so Ruthie could see. "It's a personnel file. It's for Jacob Miller."

A distant click and then a loud bang echoed in the high ceiling of the administration center.

"Listen." Ruthie grabbed Ted's wrist.

"Sounds like the front door." Ted stuffed folders back in the file box.

Ruthie slipped Sister's box on top of the last folder. Ted stood on tiptoe and pushed the box back into its place.

Ruthie tugged on his arm. "Come on. There's a side door, we'll come out behind my mother's cubical."

"What about the lights?"

Ruthie pulled harder. "No time."

Once out the door, they found themselves behind some file cabinets in the large administrative office. They circled the cabinets and stopped in front of Pam's cubical.

"Hello... anyone here?" The voice came from the front door of the building.

Ruthie lowered her voice. "It's Prissy."

Prissy moved into view, but her attention was on the area behind her desk.

"It's just me... Ruthie." Ruthie waved. "Over here."

"Oh thank heavens I just didn't know what to think you know and I felt a presence if you know what I mean and of course I never leave anything open when I leave and I was the last one out of here last night even after Max cleaned up so I was surprised to see the door open and lights on in Doctor Fisher's office, you see." Prissy pointed in the direction of the open door.

Ted leaned close to Ruthie. "Does she ever take a breath?"

Prissy walked closer. "Who is that with you Ruthie I swear I think I need to get my eyes examined as soon as possible?"

Ruthie whispered to Ted. "She is wound pretty tight." Then she took Ted by the arm and walked to where Prissy was standing. "You remember Ted Miller. He was in the office a few days ago."

Prissy shook Ted's outstretched hand.

"We were picking up something for my mom." Ruthie motioned toward Pam's cubical. "She..." Ruthie looked at Ted. "She loaned us her keys."

Prissy scrutinized the door to Doctor Fisher's office. "I see it's just that I can not stop thinking how sure I am that I turned out the lights in his office last night before I left and it is surely a puzzle to me that I am standing here seeing the door to his office as open as a hungry clam and the lights ablaze."

"Us too..." Ruthie looked at Ted. "We were just saying... just before you came in, that... that it was strange lights had been left on... knowing how conscientious you are... weren't we, Ted?"

"Conscientious." Ted took a deep breath. "Conscientious is exactly what we said."

Prissy examined Ted's eyes as if she was intensely interested in detecting his eye color. "Oh," she said. Then she walked to the open office door in question and poked her head in for a moment.

Ruthie entered Pam's space and began to rummage through a desk drawer. Ted stood in the open entrance to Pam's cubicle and watched as the lights in Fisher's office blinked off, and the door clicked shut. He smiled as Prissy sat at her desk, her full attention on him.

Prissy cleared her throat. "It's not like Pam to forget something especially when she will be out of the office for the weekend in fact I can't ever remember her forgetting anything as long as I've known her which is of course many years and which is certainly long enough to get to know someone well enough to know their habits which in her case is not forgetting things, you see."

"Got it." Ruthie brushed past Ted and held up a card attached to a neck strap. "Mom forgot her gym ID card."

Ted smiled. *Cool under fire,* he thought.

Prissy rolled a sheet of paper into her typewriter. "Oh," she said. She rested her hands on the home row. "I am so behind on Gordon's... I mean Doctor Fisher's correspondence that..." She looked at Ruthie. "I'm sure I'll be here for a few hours not that I'm rushing you of course I just don't want to offend you by the fact that I'll be concentrating on my work here and not able to give you my full attention, you see." Prissy put on a pair of earphones. Short clattering bursts of sound emanated from the electric typewriter.

Ruthie circled behind Prissy's desk. She motioned Ted toward the front door of the administration building. She tapped Prissy on the shoulder. "We're going now."

Prissy nodded.

Outside the building Ruthie grabbed Ted's arm. "That was close... and weird." She squeezed tighter. "Did you notice she called Fisher, Gordon, then covered it up?"

"I guess... I just wish we could have sneaked Sister's box out."

"It was empty."

Ted gripped Ruthie's shoulders and turned her toward him. "Empty? How..."

"I looked into her box. It was empty."

"Fisher?"

Ruthie nodded.

"A least we know my father worked here, but..."

"I know." Ruthie bit her lip. "I don't think we'll get another chance at that file box."

"You said something about Prissy covering up?"

"There have been rumors about those two." Ruthie ran to the nearest window and peered into the cavernous room. "She's on the phone."

Ted joined her. "What now?"

Ruthie tugged Ted's arm. "It's now or never. We have to talk to Sister."

They were halfway down an ivy-covered path, which ended at Unit D, when Ruthie, out of breath and trying to keep up with Ted, spoke. "I got a look at the letter Prissy was typing."

Sweat dripping from his forehead, stinging his eyes, Ted looked back at Ruthie. He squinted and rubbed his eyes, but he didn't stop running. "And...?"

"It was regarding a reimbursement." Ruthie grabbed his arm and reined him to a stop. "It was addressed to Paco."

18

It wasn't the pressure on his arm that kept Ted frozen in place. Ruthie's fingertips bore into his arm, but a quick pull would have freed him. Nor was it the wild dance of her eyes. He was riveted by an internal showdown that had festered for days. An enigma named Paco. For as surely as Paco was Ruthie's champion, he was also embroiled in recent roadblocks that had impeded Ted's search for the truth about Sister and the untangling of Jacob's involvement in her confinement at Quiet Springs. Paco was an open book about everything except his tainted relationship with Doctor Fisher.

"What's wrong?" Ruthie squeezed tighter.

Ted patted her hand. "Paco... I was thinking about Paco."

Ruthie released her grip. "I know... sorry." She rubbed the red marks on his arm. "But I'm sure he has his reasons."

"We should confront him together.... after...." Ted nodded toward the door to Unit D.

Ruthie looked at her watch. "It's almost lunch time. Patients in Unit D eat in their rooms."

"How about the staff?"

"Fewer nurses on the weekend. The orderlies will be busy."

"Are you okay with this?" Ted reached out, cradled Ruthie's face in his hands, and gently directed her attention to his eyes. "You have a lot more to lose than me."

Ruthie covered his hands with hers. "I don't have any choice."

"How so?"

Ruthie pulled back from Ted's grasp, but continued to hold his hands. "Sister chose me."

The heavy metal door of Unit D clanged behind them, shutting out more than blazing sun and sultry air. Hope vanished in the cramped lobby where a young male orderly hunkered in a caged nurse's station. Heavy wire mesh on the few windows filtered the sparkle from any sunlight that penetrated the gauntlet of metal and cloudy glass. A single door with a large window—reinforced with chicken coop pattern wire embedded in the glass—led to a corridor. Off the corridor, Ted could see individual rooms with smaller reinforced windows on the doors. None of these doors could contain the odor of cleaning fluids and human excrement in the unit, nor were they sealed tightly enough to muffle the groans or sharp cries of tormented souls.

"Ruthie?" The orderly, dressed in white shirt and slacks, rocked his chair forward, stood, and stuffed his book under the desk.

Ruthie pointed to Ted. "Toby. This is Doctor Miller."

She walked up to the cage. "Buzz us in please, will you? And I'll need the key to Edith Montgomery's room." Ruthie peeked at Ted. "Doctor Miller came all the way from Tampa to examine her."

Toby didn't move. His mouth hung open.

Ruthie moved closer to the small opening in the enclosure. "Toby. Are you okay?"

Toby scratched his head but didn't take his eyes off Ruthie.

"Yeah right, keys... but Bobby said..."

Ruthie leaned toward Toby. "What... what exactly did Bobby say?"

Toby licked his lips. He rubbed the side of his face. "That... that Mrs. Montgomery shouldn't be disturbed by... by..."

Ruthie leaned closer. "By whom, Toby?"

Toby took a step back. "You?"

Ruthie stared into Toby's eyes. "Bobby is an orderly and I'm an RN. What does that mean to you?"

Toby looked down, his chin resting on his chest. His position was familiar to Ted, who had on many occasions reamed out an adolescent caught in a misdemeanor. Toby slowly reached under his desk. A loud buzz echoed in the lobby, and the door to the corridor and the rooms beyond clanged open. He fumbled with keys on a board behind him, chose one, then reached through the opening in the cage and handed it to Ruthie.

Once past the door and into the corridor, Ted smiled at Ruthie. "Smooth."

They followed the hallway until it reached the back wall of the building where the corridor turned either left or right. One would need a ladder to see outside the unit through widely spaced wire mesh windows along the top of the back corridor wall, which filtered out optimism and defied escape. The groans were louder. A short scream came from deep in the bowels of the unit.

Ruthie tugged Ted to the right. She stopped in front of a room and peeked through the small window in the door. "Are you ready...? Ted, you're shaking."

Ted took a breath and slowly let it out. He nodded at Ruthie. "Go ahead, I'll be right behind you."

They stopped just inside the door. Ted eased the door shut behind him, but the sound of it closing echoed off the high ceiling.

Sister was sitting in a chair next to her bed. The piece she was knitting had yet to take on a familiar shape. Her strokes were deliberate, and her tongue protruded slightly from the side of her mouth as she performed what looked like a difficult twist of her circular needle. "I've already eaten." She kept her eyes on her work.

Ruthie stepped closer. "We're not delivering food. We've come to visit you."

Without raising her head, Sister peered at them over her half glasses. Her shoulder length salt-and-pepper hair hung straight, outlining her face, making it look like the mouth of a cave. Worry lines creased her forehead and crow's feet formed at the corners of her eyes when she squinted. She was almost forty-five, but her incarceration had added 10 years. "Who's that hiding behind you?"

Ted froze. Who was this person really? Was she his sister? In her eyes he saw sadness, a look of heartbreak that his mother had carried each day of her life. But deeper yet was a look of institutional acquiescence. If there had ever been a fire in these eyes, it had been quenched long ago.

Ruthie touched Ted's arm. She nudged him forward. "Someone's come to see you."

Sister removed her glasses. Her eyes, vacant moments before, now sparkled like a pirate's treasure chest pulled from a cave, and opened in the sunlight. "Skipper."

Ted opened his mouth, but a fist-sized lump rising in his chest blocked the words he so desperately wanted to speak. His eyes stung. Sister was just a blur moving toward him, but then he felt her hot tears against his chest and her bony arms encircling his waist. He wrapped her in his trembling arms as if she was a newborn. Ted's tears flowed as if from a hollow space within, now filling with the essence of Sister.

Voices echoed in the hallway outside the room and the door burst open, breaking the spell that bound Ted and Sister in their mutual cocoon and held Ruthie transfixed by their side.

A man dressed in a tan uniform filled the doorway.

Ruthie turned. "Leroy?"

Without releasing Sister, Ted turned so that they both faced the policeman. Ted remembered the name Leroy. He was the alphabetically challenged officer that Chief Todd had slandered when Ted visited the police station, and the man who had investigated and changed his mind about Ted's accident.

Tears still streaming down her cheeks, Sister looked up at Ted. "You shouldn't have come. Now they will hurt father."

The officer moved into the room, and Ruthie moved to screen Ted and Sister from him. Leroy removed his hat and ran his fingers through the stubble of his butch haircut. "Sorry Ruthie, but I've got to arrest this man."

Sister pushed Ted away. "Run."

Ted bolted past Ruthie and the cop and then collided with a man waiting just outside the door. He grappled with the man, and they both fell. On his back, Ted gasped for air. He tried to stand but couldn't move his legs. He raised his head and found a wheezing, swearing fat man sitting on him.

"You son of a bitch." The man spat out the words, unable to close his mouth over his protruding teeth.

Ted glared at him. "McCoy?"

Then Ted saw it, the scar that ran from one side of McCoy's chin to the other. Ted pushed McCoy and jerked his legs free, but before he could stand, Leroy jumped past the two of them and put a headlock on Ted.

The smell of stale tobacco and the acrid odor venting from Leroy's armpit made Ted gag, expediting his quick submission. He felt the bite of handcuffs on his wrists, then the helpless feeling of being dragged to his feet. Ruthie rushed out of Sister's room, pushed past McCoy, who was struggling to his feet, and stopped at Ted's side. Ted gasped for breath. He could feel Ruthie's hand shaking as she grabbed his arm.

Ruthie searched Ted's eyes. "Where are you taking him?"

Leroy retrieved his hat. "To the station, for now." He put on his hat, adjusted his utility belt, and crowded between Ted and Ruthie. "You work here... so I can't do much about you."

"But Fisher can." McCoy coughed and glared at Ruthie. "Don't worry... you'll hear from us."

***

Ted felt the release of the handcuffs, then a push toward the back of a cell, the third and last one on the dark and narrow corridor. He turned and saw Leroy reaching for the door made completely of bars. "Don't I get a phone call?"

The cell door clanked shut. Leroy made a fist to cover a cough that rattled deep in his chest. With the same hand, he pulled a pack of Camels from his breast pocket. He methodically shook a cigarette loose and removed it, tapped it against the pack, and pinched it between his lips. Then he produced a large kitchen match and, with a flick of a thumbnail, set it ablaze. The cigarette emerged from the hollow of his hands with an angry red tip. Leroy took a long drag and blew smoke into Ted's cell. "Ask the chief." He spit out a piece of tobacco left by the unfiltered tip. "Don't know when he'll be back though."

Ted listened as both the echo of Leroy's retreating steps and that of the cellblock door slamming shut behind him put an exclamation mark on Ted's feeling of hopelessness. A mixture of smells—urine, vomit, and something that smelled like a shirt he had worn for three straight days on a backpacking adventure—mingled in the back of his throat and made him gag. He fled to one of the two porcelain fixtures on the back wall that most closely resembled a toilet. He hadn't eaten since his early breakfast with Ruthie. Consequently his retching produced an unimpressive amount of clear liquid. Head buzzing and ears ringing, he stumbled to the bottom bunk and collapsed. The doggy smell of the thin mattress restarted his gagging response. Closing his eyes didn't stop the room from spinning.

***

"Why can't I see him?" Ruthie's voice was distant, but it roused Ted from his bed. No more than an hour had passed since his unceremonious entrance.

He pressed his ear between the bars. The voice responding to Ruthie was too low for him to make out words, but he recognized the patronizing tone. The rest of the conversation took on the same pattern. A door slammed and the jail returned to a silence that rang in his ears.

Five minutes later, the sound of the cellblock door opening brought Ted back to his feet. With his face pressed against the bars of the cell door, Ted could smell the cigar before he saw George Todd. The police chief carried a chair. He placed it against the block wall across from Ted's cell door and sat down. Todd chewed on his cigar, and then took it out of his mouth. "Still sure you ain't one of them developers?"

Ted took a deep breath and let it out slowly. He silently counted three of his own heartbeats. "Don't I get a phone call?"

The chief smiled and stuck the cigar back in his mouth. "Them developers are always causing trouble, is why I ask."

Ted gripped the bars of his cell. "My phone call?"

Todd scooted his chair forward so he could tip it back against the wall. "You been causing quite a ruckus since you been in town. Stirred up a few hornets' nests."

Ted bit his lip and looked at his feet. "What are you charging me with?"

"You been making some pretty powerful folks nervous, son." The chief removed his cigar with one hand and spat into a can he held with the other. "But I think I have a solution for you."

Ted lifted his head. "A solution? Aren't I under arrest?"

Todd placed the cigar back in his mouth and lowered his chair to the floor. "You got your wallet?"

Ted felt his back pocket. "Yeah."

The chief nodded. "Anybody read you your Miranda rights?"

Ted shook his head. "No."

George Todd stood up. "Then you ain't been booked yet." He moved close to Ted. He slowly removed his cigar and smiled, revealing bits of tobacco stuck to his stained teeth. "Of course, breaking and entering and resisting arrest are felonies in the state of Florida." The smile disappeared. "Things found in Bibles stored in side table drawers in crummy motels won't help either." The smile reappeared. "Catch my drift?"

Ted stepped back and breathed a sigh. "What's the solution?"

***

An hour later, Ted sat down in a wooden phone booth in the corner of Chief Todd's office. He tried to close the door, but its accordion-like panels were jammed. George Todd removed his foot from the track of the folding door but kept his hand on its edge. "The phone will shut off after three minutes." He blew a cloud of smoke into the booth and closed the door.

Ted tried Ruthie first but, when she didn't answer, he dialed the only other number he had memorized. "Paco, it's Ted. I'm being held at the Spring Hill Police Station."

"I know. Leroy picked up all your things. What the Hell happened?"

"I got caught in a locked unit at Quiet Springs. Ruthie was with me, but she's okay..." Ted thought of McCoy's scar and his scowl when he threatened Ruthie. "At least for now. They're putting me on a plane today. Fisher told Todd that he wouldn't press charges if I left the state and didn't come back. Otherwise I'd probably get jail time. I said I…"

"Hombre, take a breath. Where's Ruthie now?"

"I don't know. She was here trying to see me a couple of hours ago. But they wouldn't let her. You've got to find her. Tell her I'll call her as soon as I can. Christ, Fisher's going to fire her. You have to help us. You're the only one who…"

"Ted, get a grip. I'll watch out for Ruthie. I know a guy at the hospital, I'll…"

"Who? What guy?"

"Calm down, amigo."

"Calm down? They're going to cut us off soon." Ted took a breath. "Okay, what guy?"

"His name is Bobby, he's an orderly."

The phone made a loud click. Ted heard a dial tone. "No, not Bobby!" Ted started to dial Paco's number again.

The door to the booth opened. George Todd snatched the receiver away from Ted and hung it up. "You got a plane to catch. Ticket's one way… if you know what's good for you, you'll leave it at that."

19

"Sir?"

Barely awake, Ted wiped dried spittle from the corner of his mouth.

A cookie cutter blonde stewardess hovered over Ted. Her facial expression moved from concern to irritation. "We've arrived in Phoenix." She nodded toward the window on Ted's right.

Ted saw heat waves rising from the tarmac. "Oh?" Ted looked back at her as if she had just arrived from Mars.

"You'll have to get off the plane... We've landed."

Ted sat up, rubbed his eyes, and looked around the cabin. Except for another stewardess folding a blanket a few seats ahead of him, they were alone.

Ripped from the retreat of slumber, Ted's head buzzed with the image of Sister urging him to run. He thought of Ruthie and was not surprised to feel a sting of guilt. He was in the middle of the divorce process, legally separated, and yet ecclesiastically he was on shaky ground. He realized that from the moment he had reached inside her robe, Ruthie had not been able to look him in the eye for more than a few seconds. Then Ted had a sudden vision of Paco and Bobby together, conspiring against him. His hands began to tremble.

The stewardess took a step back. "I'm sorry sir, but this is our final destination."

**

The taxi stopped in front of Ted's apartment the moment the sun retreated behind the roofline. Ted waved away the offer of change from the driver, then sat on his suitcase and watched the taillights of the taxi disappear into the glimmer of dusk. The battle in his head had ended. There was nothing left to do now but bury the dead and bind up the wounded.

In spite of their new amber color, the streetlights above him still conspired to hide the Big Dipper and other heavenly bodies from its citizens. The edge of Ted's suitcase pinched his gluteus muscles, causing him to shift his weight, but he remained, eyes raised to the muted heavens. Where was the face of the deity that was surely laughing at him? All his life he had lost skirmishes to this faceless divinity over the attention of his father, but there was a deeper confrontation, a struggle in the deepest reaches of Ted's soul involving the very existence of God. His mind wandered to a time years ago in Sunday school when the doubts had begun in earnest.

Ted looked around the Sunday school classroom for support, but the stony faces of his buddies did not reflect the normal, hormone-driven rebellion he had hoped to see. Ted's face felt hot in the glare of his Sunday school teacher. In her late twenties, Mrs. Hathaway was a source of consternation for Ted. She did everything in her power to hide her sexuality: ankle length baggy dresses buttoned to her neckline, minimal makeup and bushy eyebrows, but she had a glow to which Ted's highly charged hormones gravitated.

He had broken at least two of the Ten Commandments with her in his mind. The lust he felt for her held him in perpetual guilt and penitence.

Recently, Ted had been part of the church's effort to read the Bible in its entirety, from Genesis to Revelation. Every Saturday for several weeks in a row, volunteers stopped by the church to take a turn reading. Jacob insisted that Ted take part. On the Saturday he attended, Ted's assignment was to read a few chapters from the Book of Numbers. In chapter 31, God told Moses that he should punish the Midianites for some offense against the Israelites. The upshot was that they were to kill all the men, boys, and the women who had known a man. Spared were the women of any age who had not known a man. Although Ted and his friends had no personal experiences upon which to rely, they all had a good idea what it meant to "know a man." The worst part was that God had said they could keep the young girls, who hadn't known a man, for their own uses.

"Ted." Mrs. Hathaway folded her arms. "Where do you get such ideas?" She looked at the rest of the class and smiled. "God is real, and he does love everyone." When her gaze returned to Ted he saw that she wasn't smiling. "What makes you think he doesn't?"

Ted swallowed. "He doesn't love the Midianites."

Mrs. Hathaway sat back in her chair. "The Midianites?"

"In the book of Numbers." Ted held up his Bible. "Chapter 31."

Before Mrs. Hathaway could respond, the rustling pages of fifteen Bibles sent her on her own search. She, with the class, read silently until titters spread through the group. Mrs. Hathaway's Bible closed with a clap. Gasps, then tight-lipped silence gripped the class.

Mrs. Hathaway closed her eyes and covered her mouth with her hands. The wall clock ticked 30 times before she dropped her hands into her lap and opened her eyes. "This is one of those times when faith…" She thought for a moment. "Life in those times was..." Mrs. Hathaway's eyes searched the group. "Sometimes we just can't understand what God...." She locked eyes with Ted. "I think we need to have another one of our talks with your father."

Ted readjusted his position on the suitcase. The crescent moon high above his head spoke to him. It had been there in the heavens when the Midianites had been slaughtered, and when his father had bruised Ted's butt and legs for bringing up the subject of the massacre. Neither his father nor Mrs. Hathaway had been able to explain the tragedy to Ted, and the moon had refused to talk. What Ted did know was that there was still a hole in his soul, and it was as big as the night sky that was keeping his rear end glued to his uncomfortable luggage.

Moments later, Ted stood. He rubbed his behind and the back of his right leg. His right foot was numb. He swore quietly as he limped toward his apartment. At the door the key slid in easily, but he hesitated. Inside things would be the same as the day he left, so full of hope. He pushed the door open. The one-eyed-monster flashed in its ceaseless attempt to gain attention. Ted dropped his suitcase, leaned on the door, and listened to it click shut. Ignoring the answering machine, he headed straight to the laundry bed. The dirty pile of clothes hit the floor, and what was left of the clean pile became his pillow. The last thing he was conscious of was the stale smell of dust that hadn't been disturbed for several days.

***

Twelve hours on the laundry bed didn't make much of a dent in Ted's accumulated sleep debt. According to Stella, the fatigue that shadowed Ted was just a symptom. The disease was the shame Ted packed up his personal mountain of life like a Himalayan Sherpa.

Ted's chest tightened with each message he left, first for

Ruthie, then for Jan, Paco, Elisa, and Stella.

Jan was the first person to answer his call. "Come to the house, I'll be home from church by 12:30." Her voice had a lilt. "The boys are at camp. We can talk."

Ted cradled the phone, but kept his hand on the receiver, waiting for a return call from the other Jan, the one who, if she were a cannibal, would choose Ted from the menu. When the phone didn't ring, Ted checked his watch. It was only eight A.M. He remembered Eric telling him about going to camp when he had called his boys the day before he met Sister. Ted rubbed his temples where his head throbbed the most. Only now had he made the connection. The boys always went to camp the week before school started.

Ted felt as if the last mooring line had snapped. His former school would be starting without him in less than a week. He had sacrificed everything, but to what end? He had failed miserably.

***

Directly overhead, the sun made Ted squint and dab at his forehead with a handkerchief rescued from the clean pile back at his apartment. He leaned on the fender of his car and stared at his house. It was still his house, but the rules of the separation agreement had reduced his status to that of an intruder.

The short blast of a car horn interrupted his pity party. Jan's car passed him and turned into the driveway. Moments later she emerged from the garage where she had parked. Jan walked to the front door of the house, stopped and turned in his direction. For a few moments they stared at each other across the weeds that had gained complete control of their lawn. Jan's frilly dress, hemmed below her knees, and her white hat reminded Ted of the agreement they had made when they married. Jan had insisted that their future children be raised Catholic. He remembered Jan's scowl that day when he joked that their future kids would be as likely to get their necessary allotment of guilt from the Catholics as from his own Protestant faith.

Jan raised her hand—a hand covered with a white glove that, in spite of the heat, extended to her elbow—and waved him toward the front door.

As soon as Ted stepped into the house, his nose told him that a roast had been steeping in its own juices, swapping flavors with carrots, potatoes, and onions for hours in the family slow cooker. Ted looked around as Jan removed her hat and gloves. He smiled when he saw the new color of the walls in the living room. He had stalled that painting project for years.

"Let's eat." Jan led the way into the dining room.

While they ate, Jan shared what Stella had told her about Ted's activities in Florida. He filled in blank spots, including an abbreviated version of why he was suddenly home, being careful to avoid anything that would get him thrown out before he had finished eating.

"It's too bad." Jan shook her head. "You got so close."

Ted nodded.

Jan bit her lip. "Is Ruthie the mermaid?"

"Mermaid?" Ted cleared his throat. "Did Stella mention…?"

"Actually, it was Josh. He said you were… gawking, I think he said."

***

An hour later, Ted was back at his apartment. Stella's message was the only one waiting on the machine. When he called her back, Stella invited him to her home in an hour. He and Stella had talked about how their arrangement was skirting the edge of the accepted client psychologist relationship. Stella had covered her tracks with her supervisors and her husband, but she and Ted had decided that she would drop him as a patient. Still, Stella had gone out on a limb for him, continuing their relationship as friends. Stella had just said, "I'm a rebel Ted, just like you."

Besides thinking about Stella's statement, Ted passed the time worrying about his sons. They couldn't be put on a shelf. They had lives of their own, and their relationships, like with their mother, were separate and dynamic. He realized that over the last few weeks he hadn't truly considered their needs and opinions. Now, when he wanted to hold them in his arms and beg for their forgiveness, they were miles away.

***

While Ted waited for Stella to answer her doorbell, he wiped his forehead on his sleeve and pulled his shirt free from his sweaty skin. Ted rang the doorbell again. He had never visited Stella's house before, and besides wanting to get out of the heat, he was anxious to see what it would be like talking to her away from the neutral territory of her office.

Finally Stella opened her door and studied him for a few seconds.

"What were you doing?" Ted crossed his arms. "It's hot out here."

"I've never invited a convict into my home before." Stella stood her ground for a few more seconds then stood aside. "Especially not when my husband is playing golf."

Ted shook his head and brushed past her. "I'm not a convict." Ted stopped and looked around her living room. "Put in jail, but not actually arrested."

Stella folded her lanky frame into a tan leather chair.

Ted sat on a sofa that looked to Ted like a small boat floating in a multicolored wall-to-wall shag carpet sea. He scooted to his left so he could see around a large flower arrangement in the middle of a low-slung coffee table. "You look perturbed."

Stella leaned toward Ted over her crossed legs. "I was checking on our waterbed." She shook her head. "It sprang a small leak last night, so we're... I mean I'm draining it."

"Big mess, huh?"

Stella flashed a momentary smile and then uncrossed her legs. "When you called, you said you had been arrested, so what really happened?"

Ted took a breath and sighed. He gave Stella an abbreviated rendition of the events that had culminated in his ouster from the state of Florida.

Stella pursed her lips. "Is Ruthie okay?"

"No word from her yet. Nothing from Paco either." Ted stood. "Where's your phone? I'll try again."

Stella pointed toward the kitchen. "In there, on the wall, it's..."

"I know." Ted shook his head. "It's a wall-phone."

In less than a minute, Ted was back. "Still no answer." He looked at his watch. "Two hours' difference. She could be working... at least she still has the job underwater." Ted sat down. "No pun intended."

Stella shook her head. "Very funny, but it's just a leak." She pointed toward the hallway. "We're not underwater yet." Stella smiled. "Good to see you joking, even if it at my expense."

Ted shrugged his shoulders. "No tears left."

Stella studied Ted for a moment, and then nodded. "When you called earlier, you mentioned visiting Jan this morning. How did that go?"

"We had lunch at our... her place."

"And how did that make you feel?"

"I thought you weren't my therapist anymore?"

Stella smiled. "Right. But, how did it make..."

"How much have you told Jan about Ruthie?"

Stella held her hands up. "Just that she's a nurse, and that she was helping you find out about Sister." Stella leaned back toward Ted. "Wait a minute. So you and Ruthie are...?"

Ted's face felt hot. "Jan is being nice to me. She asked me if Ruthie is the mermaid."

Stella sat back in her chair. "So you two are..." She intertwined her index and second fingers. "And Jan has figured it out."

"How could you tell?"

"Women's intuition."

Ted shook his head. "But Jan's divorcing me. Why would she care...?"

"Doesn't matter. Happens all the time." Stella laughed. "You've piqued her interest."

Ted centered his attention on his hands, making and unmaking a steeple with his fingers. "Perfect."

A few seconds passed, then Stella interrupted Ted's meditation. "Tell me more about you and Ruthie."

Ted shifted his position on the sofa. "Not much to tell. Ambushed by lust? Hell, I don't know." Ted shook his head. "I'm feeling guilty about it. I could tell it made her uncomfortable, too."

"Do you love her?"

Ted folded his arms and focused on a spot on the ceiling. "I don't want to talk about it."

Stella waited a few seconds. "Have you seen your mother yet?"

"Haven't you heard? I'm a terrible son, too." He sighed. "What about you?"

"I saw her yesterday. They can't understand why she's still with us. I think she's waiting for you."

Ted nodded. "I'm going to see her tonight. Dad, too."

Stella leaned forward. "I was going to call you. I saw Jacob yesterday. It was strange..." She leaned back. "He wanted me to warn you."

"Warn me? Warn me about what?"

"Well, first he said something about wishing he had fought back." Stella hesitated. "Then he said…. Ted, how old is your friend Paco?"

"In his fifties. Why?

"He would have been too young."

"Paco's father was named Paco, too."

Stella nodded. "That makes sense, then. Jacob said to tell you to watch out for Paco."

20

"Ruthie." Ted switched the phone to his right ear and checked his watch. It was five P.M. He had just walked in the door after his visit with Stella. "Where are you? Are you okay?"

Ruthie's voice was guarded, hushed. "I'm at Weeki Wachee, in the break room. Lucky I stopped by my house. I got your message."

"I heard your voice from my jail cell. What happened?"

"Todd threatened me." Ruthie's voice was now a raspy whisper. "He said I'd lose my job at the hospital if I didn't back off."

"Jesus. So Todd and Fisher…"

"Mom says Fisher has Todd in his pocket."

"That doesn't surprise me." Ted hesitated. "But how does Pam know?"

"I think my mom has something on Fisher. Even Prissy won't mess with her."

"Really? What does she know?"

"She's always vague about Fisher. It's just something I suspect."

Ted thought for a moment. "So what now?"

"Mom wants me to take a couple sick days. She wants to poke around."

"Sick days?" Ted's voice raised a notch. "I'm worried, are you in any danger? Maybe I should come..."

"No Ted, you..." Someone interrupted Ruthie. Her voice was suddenly distant. "This call is important. Give me just a few more minutes." Then she was back. "Sorry, there's only one phone in the break room. Ted, you can't come back right now. What good would you be locked up?"

Ted caught a mental whiff of the wretched cell behind Chief Todd's office. "Yeah, maybe you're right." Ted bit his lip. "At least for now. But what about you?"

"Don't worry. I'll lay low for a few days. They need me here at the springs. Still lots of tourists." Ruthie was quiet for a moment. "I haven't heard from Paco. I..."

"Oh shit." Ted voice rose again. "I forgot. I called Paco before I left. He's going to talk to Bobby. I didn't have time to tell him what Bobby's been doing."

"You're kidding." Ruthie stopped and lowered her voice again. "Paco knows Bobby?"

"And there's more." Ted gripped the phone. "My father told Stella to warn me to watch out for Paco."

"What? It's been years since your father has been around here."

"I know. I think he's talking about Paco's old man. I'm seeing my father tonight. When can I call you again?"

Ruthie was quiet for a few seconds. "I'll call you as soon as I can." Ruthie hesitated again. "Ted... did you... have you spoken with your wife?"

An alarm went off in Ted's head. Something in Ruthie's voice warned him to think about his answer. It was a simple question, but something in her tone reminded him of Jan when she asked about Ruthie. There was vulnerability in Jan's question as well, a subtle shift in the conversation that for most of his life he might have overlooked. Cues missed. Opportunities lost. Yet even his silence now was revealing, so he spoke with confidence. "We discussed the boys. They're away at camp. Last hurrah before school."

There was a muffled noise on Ruthie's end of the phone. Then Ruthie spoke. "I've got to go, sorry."

"Ruthie." Ted felt a twist in his gut. "Be careful."

***

Ted stepped off an elevator on the 12th floor of the hospital where Jacob was being warehoused. The route to his father's room had been circuitous at best. It reminded him of his short active duty stint in the Naval Reserve just after high school.

Fresh out of boot camp, Ted had joined his ship docked at the U.S. Naval Station in Yokosuka, Japan. Rather than spend his free time in town, Ted chose to remain on the ship to unwind in the crew's lounge. The television there was, of course, only able to draw Japanese stations. Fascinated, Ted would watch a silly quiz show anyway.

One day, a gruff first class boatswain's mate named Peters shook his head and lashed out at Ted. "Damn it, boot, if you're going to watch that God-damned thing, go down to the engine room and get a translation tube." So began a 45-minute pilgrimage. From the engine room he was sent to the mess hall, where a mustachioed cook with nicotine-stained fingers and twinkling eyes sent him to the officer of the deck. The OD that day was a chief petty officer named Luck. The word *fuck* was scattered throughout each sentence he uttered, the word used variously as a noun, verb, or adjective. Ted visited three more sites on the ship after seeing Luck before he was sent to the mailroom.

The mail clerk didn't look much older than Ted. He stared at Ted for a few seconds. "Think about it, boot. A translation tube?"

Ted's face burned at the memory. Today he felt that same exasperation as incompetent hospital staff members sent him from one wing of the hospital to the next, through one locked door after another, searching for Jacob. At last he was in the long-term residential section. It looked more like a hotel than a hospital, but the odor of decay defied the possibility that the place was anything but a convalescent facility. Nurses in an office near the elevator assured Ted that he had finally found his father.

Jacob's room, the size of Ted's studio apartment, had a small kitchen and bath. The walls were bare and matched the expression on Jacob's face.

"Hi Dad." Ted eased himself into a chair he had retrieved from the claustrophobic kitchen.

Jacob was sitting in a padded chair crammed between the double bed and the wall separating the main room from the kitchen. Shocks of undisciplined, pure white hair and mismatched wrinkled clothing gave him a hobo look. "I want to go home." His lips were moving, but his voice sounded as though it were coming from a hidden cave.

Ted took a breath. "I know you do, Dad, but from what I hear, you can't be left alone."

Jacob stared straight ahead. "I hate it here. The pills make me tired."

Ted's chest tightened. What was happening between the two of them wasn't new. Jacob was caught in a medicinal embrace, but even at his most lucid, his father had always been a beat off in their communication. For five minutes they sat in the same room, miles apart. Jacob stared beyond the wall behind Ted's head. Ted struggled to pull himself together.

Finally Ted spoke. "Stella says she's been to see you."

Jacob shifted his position in the chair but didn't look at Ted. "She talks like a doctor."

"But she's here as a friend." Ted leaned toward Jacob. "She cares about you."

"Don't even have my own Bible."

Ted stood. In a nightstand drawer, he found a Gideon Bible. He held it up. "Here's one. Didn't you look?"

Jacob shook his head. "New edition. Mine's the King James version, written in Old English."

Ted reacted to the irony of Jacob's statement with the sting of a rebellious 13-year-old. "The way God spoke, right?"

Jacob stared into Ted's eyes for the first time since Ted's arrival. "Right."

Ted bit his lip. He realized that any talk of the original Bible being in Greek or Hebrew would fall on deaf ears. He slipped the blasphemous book, sans the thees and thous, back in the side table drawer. "I've been to Florida. I found Quiet Springs."

"Paco's in with Fisher."

"Which Paco?"

"The father. The dwarf was just a kid."

Ted thought for a moment. "How was Paco involved with Fisher?"

Jacob closed his eyes. "I checked the books."

Ted sat down. His head buzzed with the new information. But how could he frame the most important question? Jacob could shut down at any moment. "Dad?" Ted watched Jacob's eyes slowly open. "Who hurt Sister?"

Jacob yelped, stood and walked to the bathroom door where he stopped but didn't turn around. "I should have fought back. God forgive me, I should have fought back."

The door to the bathroom slammed. Gut wrenching howls filled the room.

***

Later, Ted emerged from an elevator. Different hospital, but it was still purgatory.

"Mr. Miller." Lois, Margaret's primary nurse, denied Ted even a glimpse of her normally sunny disposition. "You haven't visited for a while."

"I've been…" Ted looked at his feet. "Away."

Lois cleared her throat. "She's asked for Skipper a few times."

Ted nodded. "How is she today?"

"As usual, medicated. I don't think she'll respond."

Ted sighed. "How much time…?"

"She's a fighter. Your mother has the doctors puzzled. Medically speaking, she shouldn't…"

"I know." Ted looked toward his mother's room. "She's waiting for me to bring Sister home."

***

Ted drove back to his apartment. At three different intersections, automobile horns jolted him into action. His mother's condition haunted him to distraction. Fully under the influence of morphine, she had not responded to his touch during his visit. Her face was contorted but not as if in pain. She had a determined look. Her hands were clenched as if ready to resist an angel of death if it dared to appear.

The one-eyed monster greeted him when he finally made it home. The first message was from Tommy, Elisa's husband. He had taken it upon himself to do some research. Ted's felt his hand shaking as he turned up the volume of the answering machine. Tommy had run a check on the name Esther Miller. The story he shared from 1942, two years before Ted was born, was convoluted, but his conclusions were breathtaking. Esther was the daughter of a Paul and Elizabeth Harrington of Pinellas Park, Florida. Ted recognized Harrington as his mother's maiden name. His grandparents had been killed in an accident before he was born, an accident Margaret had always refused to discuss.

Tommy went on to say that police had investigated a suspicious fire at the Harrington's home in which both Paul and Elizabeth had died. In a follow-up story, Jacob and Margaret Miller had adopted Margaret's sister Esther, who had been rescued from the fire, and she was living with them in Spring Hill.

Ted stared at the answering machine. Sister was both his aunt and his sister?

Ted listened to the message again. He sat down on the laundry bed and raised his hands to the deity with whom he had alternately fought, ignored, or had doubted. "Who am I?"

***

Ted asked Stella the same question a day later at her office.

"That's a loaded question." Stella looked at her watch and laughed. "Especially this early in the morning."

Ted smiled. "Thanks for doing this, by the way... especially since we aren't..."

Stella yawned and stretched. "Are your kidding? With my schedule, Teddy boy, you are my main source of entertainment." She rose and began to fuss with the coffee maker. "As far as your question? I'm afraid we'll have to wait until they read your eulogy."

Ted watched Stella's face carefully as she brought coffee back to where they sat. "You're screwing with me, right?"

Stella sat and sipped her coffee. "Think about it. We're all in a state of flux. Only after we die can the people who know us answer that question."

Ted told Stella about the message he had received from Tommy. "Can't you see why I'm asking?"

"I get why you're upset. But I don't think you're asking the right question."

"What are you talking about?"

Stella leaned toward Ted. "Do you think you're the only person who has been lied to about their past?"

"No... but..."

Stella held up her hand. "The question you should be asking is: Who will I be, now that I'm faced with insurmountable problems that are keeping me from reaching my goal?"

***

Ted drove aimlessly around his old haunts. The question Stella had posed, and her parting remark, weighed on him.

Stella had hugged him before he left her office, and then held him at arms length. "Lots of people love and care about you," she told him. She patted his chest. "But your answers are all in here."

He looked up and saw the familiar flat roof of the junior high school where he was no longer employed. Instinctively he pulled into the parking lot. The whining of his air conditioner reminded him his car was idling, wasting gas. Since the oil crisis three years before, the price of gas had doubled to eighty cents a gallon. But, he hesitated. If he turned off the engine, the relentless September heat would bake him in a matter of minutes.

His indecision registered in his gut. There it was, that familiar sinking feeling in his solar plexus. Known by many names—anxiety, dread, shame, indecision—it was, in fact, fear. Ted saw clearly that his life had always been driven by fear. It was fear now that was keeping him from returning to Florida where the answers to many of his questions remained hidden. His leg began to shake, his heart pounded. Ted had absolutely no idea what to do about any of it. At that moment a car pulled into the parking space next to him.

He recognized the driver immediately: Paul's secretary, Joanie. Her car door slammed. Joanie hurried toward the front door of the school but paused in front of Ted's car. She recognized him, waved, and said something that Ted couldn't hear over the noise of his car's engine and air conditioner.

Ted turned his engine off and stepped out of his car. The heat ambushed him. He reeled, unsteady. "Hi...sorry, I didn't hear..."

"I said you look like shit." Joanie giggled. "What are you doing here?"

Ted took a deep breath, let it out slowly, and shrugged his shoulders.

Joanie unlocked the office door and motioned for him to follow her inside. Once inside, Ted hesitated while Joanie adjusted the thermostat. Moments later, a blast of cool air revived him. He stood silently, watching as Joanie settled behind her desk, moving stacks of paper as if they were sticks and feathers for her nest. "He's got you working on Labor Day, I see."

Joanie stopped fussing and looked at Ted. "Paul always has his best ideas at the last minute." She thought for a moment. "He hired a cute young thing for your position." Joanie raised her eyebrows. "Just out of the university."

Ted thought about the group of kids who would pay the price for the new teacher's inexperience. "I haven't even met those kids, but I guess I've failed them, too."

"So let me get this right." Joanie leaned back in her chair. "You're responsible for kids you haven't even met?"

Ted studied the floor tiles. "Yeah, something like that."

Joanie shook her head. "What's happened to you?"

Ted sat in a chair near Joanie's desk. He brought her up to date on the events of his life since he had last talked to her.

Joanie nodded. "Must be hard." She bit her lip. "Being the new Savior, that is."

Ted stared at Joanie. "You should talk. The school stops functioning when you're gone."

Joanie looked at the ceiling and shook her head. She stood and pointed to the back of the office. "Let me show you something."

Joanie escorted Ted to a large conference room, which, since the school was located on the side of a mountain called Camelback, overlooked a vast swath of the city.

Phoenix is called the Valley of the Sun. Although the city is high desert and has the surprising elevation of twelve hundred feet above sea level, the broad space between mountain ranges is as flat as a checkerboard. On his most recent flight into Phoenix, Ted imagined God using the city's street grid for a quick game with one of his favorite angels before bedtime. For a moment he and Joanie watched ant-like cars and trucks moving in streams along ribbons stretched in straight lines from one end of the valley to the other.

Joanie pressed close to one of the floor-to-ceiling windows. "I like to come here when I have my Savior days. Makes me feel small and insignificant."

Ted nodded. "You can't help them all."

"I think you're missing the point." Joanie turned toward Ted. "You're a part of something much bigger than yourself. It sets you free. Don't you think?"

***

The sun was directly overhead when Ted drove out of the school parking lot. That meant that every local living creature was either in a hole, under a rock, or sitting close to an air conditioner. Since he had promised Jan that he would pick up the boys—who were now home from camp—at noon, it also meant that Ted would have to break a local motor vehicle law or two if he was to make it on time.

Jan had been acting strangely since his return. But the old Jan was apparently hiding just around the corner. When she told him he could see the boys, Jan had slipped into a tone of voice he recognized. "Don't be late. You know how you are."

The first thing he noticed at the house was the pile of camping gear and hiking boots on the front steps. Jan had a specific regimen that dictated what condition things had to be in for them to pass into the house. In a few moments he would find out if he still had priority over soiled sleeping bags or if things had returned to normal.

Jan answered the door. "Hi, come in."

"Daddy." Eric leaped into Ted's arms.

"Wow." Ted staggered backward. "What did they feed you?"

Eric laughed. "Tiger meat."

Ted let Eric slide to the floor. He saw Josh hovering in the dining room. "Hey bud, too old to hug your old man?"

Eric walked halfway across the living room and stopped. He stared at Ted. "Are you home to stay?"

21

Ted dialed Elisa's number and held the phone close to his ear. He'd taken the boys home and was now back at his apartment. For a few precious hours at least, laughter and arguing had made him feel as cozy as if he were snuggling with a good book on a rainy day. But Jan wanted the boys to sleep at home before their first day at school.

Now he was pacing, stopping only when he reached the limits of the telephone cord. The apartment seemed smaller than he remembered. "Three." He said. Should he hang up after the fourth ring? The answering machine on most phones might trigger after that. He glanced at his watch. It was only nine P.M. in Florida. What was the social rule? No calls after 9:30, right? Or was it nine? Neither Paco nor Ruthie had answered their phones. Ted readied his thumb to cancel the call.

"Yeah."

Ted held the phone away from his ear. "Tommy?"

"Who's this?"

"It's Ted... I..."

"Ted. Elisa's having a fit. You got my message?"

"Yes, it's amazing. But how did you know that I was...?"

"You should have called us. Stella let us know."

"Sorry." Ted closed his eyes. "I need your help. My dad says Paco's father was involved with Fisher."

"I'm way ahead of you. I'm seeing your friend Paco tomorrow. I'll try to talk to Todd as well. He's a skunk, but he's connected to some county big wigs. So I'm not sure how much I can do."

Ted felt as though something was stuck in this throat. "Maybe you shouldn't. You could make things worse."

"Damn it, Ted. Who's the cop here?"

The dial tone droned in Ted's ear. "You are?"

***

Ted's eyes fluttered but he couldn't focus in the pitch darkness of his apartment. Clamorous ringing, at first invading his dream, now came from across the room where he had moved the phone to keep it away from the boys. Shaking and disoriented, he slipped off the sofa and moved toward the sound.

"Shit." Ted dropped back on his couch and grabbed his foot. Still in a fog, he wiped drool from his chin and snapped on the lamp. The cap pistol and holster that had ambushed him in the dark lay where he had kicked it.

"Goddamn it, Eric."

The phone persisted. He checked his toe for blood. No blood, but the big toe of his left foot throbbed in rhythm with his heart, which felt as though it was going to beat a hole in his chest.

The answering machine clicked on and the message began. He made it to the phone just before the beep. "Hello?"

"It's me."

Ted blinked and looked at a nearby clock. "Ruthie?"

"I'm at a phone booth," she said.

"At two in the morning?"

"My phone might be bugged."

"Bugged?"

"Someone left a message. They said they'd know if I tried to contact you."

Ted was sitting on the edge of his seat. He told Ruthie about his phone conversation with Tommy and gave her Tommy's number. "Call him as soon as you can."

Ruthie promised she would. Then she said, "I talked to Paco."

"Did you ask him about Bobby?"

"He said I should forget about you."

A woman's voice intruded. "Deposit 75 cents for three more minutes."

"I'm out of change. I'll call you..."

Ted squinted at the travel-alarm clock resting on the corner unit where his single sofa beds joined. He wondered if the illuminating material on the hands indicating 3 A.M. was still radium but decided that they must have changed to another material by now. This was the third time he had checked since the passionless voice demanding more money had interrupted his call from Ruthie a few minutes after 2 A.M. After each check he had slipped close to sleep, in the zone where dream-like images can appear only to be snatched away as one is pulled back to reality. And each time he checked only 15 minutes or so had passed. When Ruthie appeared in the first segment of false sleep, her eyes refused to meet his—so different from the first time at the springs when she gazed without shame into his inner core. In the second vision, Sister was reaching out to him. From 2:55 to 3 A.M. he stared at the soft halo created by a streetlight at the edges of his curtains.

***

Late the next morning, Ted paced from one end of his tiny apartment to the other and back again, trapped in a loop, no thought lasting longer than two steps. Every time he reached his kitchen area, a glance at his watch caused a sinking feeling because he was again reminded that he was even later to a lunch date with Jan. A step back in the other direction and he was already thinking about the boys and what a shitty father he had become, followed two steps later by an image of Sister urging him to run. He was on trial, and every step or two he received a verdict: Guilty as charged. Bad husband, bad son, bad friend, he had failed everyone in his life.

Something in Jan's tone of voice when she had called to arrange their meeting told Ted that she was setting him up for ruination. "Ted I've got a list… things we need to agree on if we… to mend things."

They had agreed to meet at Bill Johnson's Big Apple Restaurant. Jan had resisted Ted's suggestion at first, but reconsidered when Ted reminded her that they had gone there on their first date. The Big Apple was not Jan—It was sawdust on the floor casual, Frisbee sized hamburgers, and gum smacking waitresses with guns on their hips.

Once he had extracted himself from his apartment, Ted let visions of individual deep-dish apple pies mitigate his otherwise continuous self-flagellation. For once he was glad for the distractions of alternating his hold on the scorching steering wheel of his Z-Car and pampering the balky hand choke as he occasionally drove but mainly lurched toward the restaurant.

Waves of heat radiated off the asphalt of the Big Apple parking lot as he pulled into an open space right in front, facing one of the large plate glass windows of the restaurant. The air conditioner had finally kicked in, so he left the car running and adjusted the vent so that a full blast of air could evaporate the sweat on his face. Jan was sitting in a booth by the front window, but he could tell that she hadn't noticed him. She looked so out of place with her frilly white blouse buttoned at her collar and her hair knitted in a prim bun. Her arms were folded and Ted felt the urge to wait a little longer when he saw her squint to check her watch, frown, and shake her head. It looked as if the jury was back, and the news wasn't good. Soon, the realization that any further delay would not help matters pushed Ted to abandon his cool observation post and move through the oven of a day into the fire of his near future.

Jan pushed a paper across the table as Ted slid into his side of the booth.

He rubbed his eyes and tried to focus on the list, which he saw contained seven numbered items. "Sorry... I know I'm late, but..."

Jan exhaled, released her flatware, which was rolled in a paper napkin, and placed each utensil neatly in its proper place on either side of her placemat that told the history of the restaurant. She nested in her seat, smoothing the napkin in place on her lap. Her spoon became an object of scrutiny. Her frown didn't change when she glanced up at Ted. "You look terrible."

Ted dropped the list on his plate. He pictured Ruthie in the phone booth searching for loose change. "I didn't get much sleep last night."

A waitress passed by but failed to notice the offending spoon Jan waved in her direction. Number four on the list caught Ted's eye. He picked up list and waved it at Jan. "Don't fight confirmation? I never..."

Jan put on her best Catholic face. "Josh is almost eleven. His confirmation classes start soon." Jan folded her arms. "You've never been supportive."

Ted read number one on the list. "Forget Florida?"

"We can still save our marriage. Father Maloney says..."

"I've got to change, right?" Ted focused on the other demands on the list. "This is all about me changing."

Jan leaned toward Ted. "Please don't raise your voice."

Ted recognized the look on Jan's face. Once, returning from the refreshment stand at a basketball game, Ted spilled popcorn on the person sitting next to them. Jan had the same look on her face then. "You are such a fool," she said when he'd sat back down.

Ted closed his eyes. He let the painful memory fade away. When he opened his eyes, Jan's focus was back on the spoon. "So we're back to square one?" he asked.

She reached across the table and touched the list. "That's completely up to you."

***

An hour later, Ted pulled up in front of the oldest Catholic Church in Phoenix. Spires on both corners of the cathedral pointed to where Ted's nemesis sat in judgment. He left his car and moved quickly toward the ancient wooden doors, behind which he hoped to find the natural cooling offered by original adobe walls, the mud and straw now hidden by plaster and overgrown with ivy.

The heavy door thumped closed behind him. He blinked to adjust to the dim interior, illuminated grudgingly by sunlight seeping through stained glass windows. Eric had once informed him that the windows told the story of the life of Jesus. Candles flickered in the foyer. Although he gave little credence to their purpose, Ted held his breath as he passed the flickering votives. If his own parents' conditions were similar to Purgatory, he didn't want to prevent any of the souls, for whom these candles burned, from deliverance.

Ted moved into the sanctuary and sat in an unpadded pew designed to keep occupants alert and pious. It resembled those in the fundamentalist Protestant churches of his youth. He and his friends always chose the back row so they could whisper in bible language. *If thou bumpith me again I will smite thee and thy family.* Ted chuckled out loud when he remembered the joke that went: *He who farts in church will surely sit in his own pew.*

"Mind sharing? I could use good laugh."

"Father Maloney. I'm sorry...I..."

A tall, middle-aged man dressed in a black shirt with a white clerical collar scooted in next to Ted.

"So you remember me. We haven't seen each other since your wedding."

Ted fingered a hymnal secured behind the pew ahead of him. "I promised you the souls of my children, not mine."

The priest nodded. "But you're here now?"

Ted thought for a moment. "I've been competing with your boss for my own father's attention for years. Thought I'd drop by for a chat."

Father Maloney cleared his throat. "And what did He have to say?"

Ted looked into the expansive interior of the church and pointed to a mural painted on the edges of the central dome at least sixty feet above their heads. "That picture of Him is a close as I've come." He looked at the priest. "And I'm pretty sure that's all there is."

The priest ran his hand over his bald head. "I have my doubts, too."

Ted's mouth fell open. "What?"

"I majored in Biology and Physics," Father Maloney said. "Walking on water started my questioning." The priest put his hand on Ted's shoulder. "Don't mention that to your wife, though." He pulled his hand back. "Sorry to hear about the separation. I'd like to help."

Ted leaned back and clasped his hands as if in prayer. "She gave me a list of the changes I'd have to make."

Father Mahoney nodded and stopped his smile before it got carried away. "Sounds like you're carrying a heavy burden."

Ted looked up and nodded at a large crucifix hanging above the altar. "Not like him of course."

"Maybe not the weight of the sins of mankind, but something." The cleric hesitated. "What is it?"

Ted thought for a moment. "Guilt I suppose." Ted took a breath. "Seems like I can't get enough forgiveness."

Ted watched as the priest's face gained ten years.

Mahoney nodded. "I know what you mean. Lately I feel I'm just a conduit for guilt." His quick smile disappeared. "In spite of absolution, everyone I see returns. It seems they're continually running from shame or chasing redemption."

The priest's words bunched up in Ted chest. He needed air so he stood to leave.

"Ted? Before you go."

Ted squelched his desire to run from the man who had seen into his soul and whose words spurred his need to put the huge wooden doors of the cathedral behind him so he could once again breathe, even though the air outside had been routed through the flames of Hell. But he waited.

The priest pulled at his collar. "You know, you can't fight with someone and deny their existence at the same time."

***

Less than an hour had passed since Ted left what he'd often referred to as the Church of the Immaculate Deception. He stood in front of the reception desk in the mental health office of the health maintenance organization, which had dropped him like a hot stethoscope as soon as he had failed to renew his contract with his school district.

"I'm sorry sir, but I can't seem to find your name on our patient list." The receptionist's braces sparkled, and her blue eyes gazed beyond the room.

Ted rubbed the back of his neck. "As I said, I am no longer a patient here, but I did receive a message from Mrs. Bloomberg-

Stein asking me to meet her here."

With an officious insistence on proper protocol, the young lady lowered her voice. "Sir, your name does not seem to be on Ms. Bloomberg-Stein's appointment list for today."

"Nevertheless." Ted raised his voice proportionately to the amount the girl had lowered hers. "She said I should come here, and that she would fit me in."

The braces disappeared and the girl reached under her desk. Seconds later, Ted was joined by a man whose blue uniform strained to contain his body.

Ted tried to explain his situation to the security guard.

The young man's voice was calm, and he enunciated each word as if he were speaking to someone to whom English was a second language. "Sir, I'm afraid that you will have to come with me."

Ted hesitated and felt pressure on his right arm. The hand applying the pressure nearly encircled his bicep. More resistance merely increased the security guard's grip. "Okay, okay." Ted relaxed. "I'll go, but tell Stella that..."

"Clarence." Stella called from her office door. "That won't be necessary."

Tingling signaled the return of blood to Ted's fingers. He rubbed his arm and smiled as Clarence did a little "yes boss" tap dance and disappeared.

Ted looked at the receptionist. Her braces reappeared, but her eyes still focused somewhere in space. Stella huddled momentarily with the receptionist and then waved Ted into her office.

Once in Stella's office, Ted found it impossible to ignore the painting. It had come to define the nature of his existence. He was still stuck in the pitch-black darkness in the center of the painting with no obvious path to reach the blue sky of enlightenment. Like the heavenly home of his father's God, whom he had tried to dismiss, the bright blue sky taunted him, just out of reach above the outstretched limbs of aspen trees that were rooted in his personal inky Hell.

"Still in the dark, I see." Stella plopped down in the chair from which she daily directed the paradigm shifts in her patients' thinking.

Ted looked away from the painting. "Even deeper." Ted sat down across from Stella and was immediately troubled by a look in her eyes. She had always focused on the topic at hand, but at this moment her mind had wandered or she was anxious about something. Whatever it was, it made Ted uneasy so he hijacked the conversation. "Talked to Father Murphy this morning."

"Father Murphy?"

"Jan's Priest." Ted filled her in on the conversation.

Stella smiled. "Sounds like he pegged you pretty well."

"I know, right?" Ted looked away. "It hit me in the gut. I couldn't breathe for a minute." Ted rambled for a few minutes, remembering that even Viet Nam had made him feel guilty. He had served a two-year hitch on active duty in the Naval Reserve right after high school. When Ted was discharged in 1964 things had just begun to get hot in Indochina. He spent the next decade watching friends either dodging the draft or actually being drafted into the war. Ted had been safe from war but not from his conscience.

For several minutes, the two discussed other events in Ted's life since they had last spoken. The topics: Jan and her list, Josh's comment about Ted staying, and Ruthie's early phone call. The discussion flowed easily until Ted mentioned his brief phone conversation with Tommy.

Stella leaned closer to Ted. "Elisa called me last night." She sat back, crossed her legs, and set her loafers into action. "That's why I needed to... why I asked you to meet me."

Ted's gut went into panic mode. That's why Stella had looked preoccupied. Ted opened his mouth, but Stella held up her hand in her traffic cop manner and continued before Ted could speak. "Tommy did some more sleuthing."

"What did he find... is Ruthie okay?"

Stella uncrossed her legs, stood, and joined Ted on the sofa. "Ted, you've got to focus. Tommy found adoption records. Your mother was adopted by the Harringtons."

Ted shook his head. "My mom adopted?"

Stella grabbed Ted's hands and pressed them against his knee to stop his leg from shaking. "Tommy thinks the Harringtons must have been unable to have children when they adopted your mother, but when your mother turned fifteen, surprise, along came Esther."

"Jesus." Ted knocked Stella's hands aside. "If my mom isn't Esther's real sister and she adopted Esther after the Harringtons died... then Sister and I aren't related by blood." Ted stood and pointed at the painting. "I'll never get out of the dark!" He hurried to the door.

"Ted, wait!"

Ted opened the door, stepped outside the office, and glared back at Stella. "Wait for what?"

Stella closed her eyes for a moment, shook her head, and sighed. "There's more."

Ted stared at Stella. "To tell you the truth, I don't think I can stand to hear anymore." Ted pulled the door shut and sailed past the receptionist. He stopped and looked back at the girl when he reached the outside door. "You were right. I'm not a patient here."

***

When Ted finally gave into rational thinking he pulled into a rest stop off interstate 17, the only freeway through Phoenix, which lead north to Flagstaff and south to Tucson. He recognized the location and calculated he was 50 miles north of Phoenix. His anxiety level had only declined marginally, not nearly enough to make a clear-headed decision about his immediate future. He stared at the door to the men's room, his engine occasionally sputtered and his air conditioner groaned. Then from nowhere, a girl approached his car. Her dyed black shoulder length hair was disheveled and matted, her cheeks were streaked with eyeliner and mascara, and one of her ears was pierced with a large safety pin. Ted guessed she was sixteen, but thought he would have to wait until the rest of her makeup was cried away to make a definite decision on her age. She was obviously committed to punk rock, which had recently swept the states with bands like the Ramones, and was more serious about it than some of the junior high punk rock wannabes Ted had tussled with in the past year.

Even though the sun was low in the sky, the heat barrage continued unabated. She stood next to his driver's-side window, wilting and staring.

Ted rolled down his window. "Need any help?"

The girl ran her hand through her hair and wiped her nose on her sleeve. "You going to Flagstaff?"

Ted thought for a moment. "I have no idea where I'm going."

She sniffled and stammered. "Me neither." Tears dripped on her blouse.

Ted reached across the passenger seat of his car and opened the door. "At least get out of the heat."

Once settled in Ted's car the girl lamented her situation, which she felt was unique, but to Ted a common complaint from teenaged girls, of unrequited love and lack of parental understanding. She and her boyfriend were running from unreasonable parents, but had, here along a blistering Arizona highway, engineered a falling out of their own. Ted waited for a minute when she seemed spent and at the end of her soliloquy. Then he put his own troubles on hold and used his counseling skills to reason with this disaffected yet puerile young woman. His main theme centered on personal responsibility and facing ones issues head on. An idea, at first impossible for her to grasp, but in the end a concept she realized she had no choice but to embrace. Ted ended his sermon with a suggestion that included a highway patrol car parked near the exit of the rest stop.

Lilly Parker, the name the girl had finally admitted to, waved to Ted from the window of the highway patrol car as it eased down the ramp and onto the freeway. At Ted's insistence she had scrubbed her face in the restroom before they talked to the trooper. Without her cosmetic mask Ted saw that she wasn't a day over fourteen. Ted waved until the state cop's car was out of view. He thought about what he had said to Lilly, got back into his Datsun, did a u-turn, and headed back to Phoenix.

* * *

As soon as Ted entered his apartment the answering machine demanded his attention. The message was from Stella but her tone was testy, not classic Stella, and Ted fumbled as he dialed her number. She answered on the first ring and when she heard Ted's voice she attacked. "Where the hell have you been?"

"Driving?"

"Get a pen, I got you on the first Continental flight in the morning."

Ted's chest seized from an adrenaline rush, he closed his eyes and saw the robot from the 60's science fiction television show *Lost In Space*, waving its arms and shouting, "Warning, warning, danger Will Robinson." He stretched the phone cord and walked behind the kitchen counter, as if could protect himself from the bad news that would inevitably come next. Of all the questions he could have asked, all that he could manage was, "A pen?"

"Ted, calm down. Take a deep breath." Ted could almost feel Stella gearing down to therapy speed. "There was an accident at Weeki Wachee Springs."

Ted looked at himself in a large mirror on the wall to his right. Ashen was the word that flashed in his mind. "Ruthie? Something happened to Ruthie?"

Seconds turned glacial. Finally Stella responded. "She's in the hospital, Ted... Elisa couldn't confirm anything about her condition."

22

Ted saw Elisa in the Tampa airport waiting area before she saw him. She was biting her nails and her hair was unkempt, exactly the way Ted had left his life in Phoenix.

Ahead of him, a man scooped up a child who squealed, hugged him and said, "Daddy, don't go away again."

Ted stopped suddenly. A vision of Josh, asking if he was staying this time, flashed in his mind. The force of a suitcase hitting him from behind buckled his knee and knocked him to the floor and into the man with the little boy in his arms. Looking up, Ted saw that the man had maintained his balance, but the child was crying. A woman with the looks and temperament of an NFL linebacker glared at Ted from behind. Dragging her fallen property, she banged his leg a second time with her heavy suitcase. The rest of the arriving passengers moved around the turmoil Ted had caused. He looked above the fray, searching for a familiar face.

Then, from the sea of legs, a hand appeared. "Grab on, Ted." It was Elisa's husband, Tommy.

Ted reached above his head. "Careful of my left..." Ted was up. "... Leg." He closed his eyes and hobbled in a circle.

"Shake it off, man." Tommy smiled and shook his head. "Can't be broken. You wouldn't be able to stand."

**

"She was in a what?" Ted asked his question to the back of Elisa's head. He was wedged in the backseat of her car. His left leg, stretched across the bench seat, throbbed from both the beating it had taken in the airport and residual pain from the hit and run.

For the 20 minutes since they had left the airport, Tommy and Elisa had competed with, and corrected each other, in a frenzy of facts about what had happened to Ruthie. The part that Ted understood was that somehow the breathing hose Ruthie used as a mermaid had been contaminated with carbon monoxide from the gasoline engine that ran the oxygen pump. Her fellow mermaids saw that she was in distress and got her to the surface in time to resuscitate her.

Tommy answered Ted's question. "Hyperbaric chamber... It's a pressure chamber. Helps get the carbon monoxide out of your blood."

Ted shifted his position on the seat. "I've got to see her."

Elisa turned and looked back at Ted, her hand gripping the top of the seat. "Not now. Maybe tomorrow."

"Tomorrow?" Ted leaned forward and grabbed Elisa's hand. "That's bullshit. I want to see her now."

Tommy glared at Ted in the rearview mirror. "And what if you run into Chief Todd?"

Ted sat back to get out of Tommy's vision. "Todd?"

Tommy glanced over his shoulder. "Ted, what the hell do you think is going on here?"

Elisa pulled her hand free, placed it on on Tommy's shoulder, and looked back at Ted. "There's an investigation. Someone tampered with Ruthie's air hose."

Ted sat forward again. "Oh my God. And Todd is investigating?"

Tommy slapped the steering wheel. "Leroy, too. And you're Mr. Persona non grata."

Elisa stared at Tommy for a moment, shook her head, and then looked back at Ted. "I went to see Ruthie. As soon as she's released from the hospital, she'll be at her mother's place. You can see her then."

***

Ted began his pacing at Elisa's house. Within an hour of arriving from the airport, Tommy left for work and Elisa went to check on her father, leaving Ted alone with his anxiety. Like a meat grinder, Ted's mind churned his predicaments into an unrecognizable mash that caused hyperventilation and more pacing, which sent his thoughts back for another thorough grinding.

Why had Tommy been so vague when he talked about contacting Paco? Was he hiding something? Who would try to hurt Ruthie? What was Jan up to, really? How much damage was he causing his boys? How was he ever going to help Sister?

As he paced, Ted kept each step confined within the borders of the large tiles covering Elisa's kitchen floor. Sometimes he made a quick, soldier-like 90-degree turn as he made a circuitous tour of the kitchen, then, with an abrupt 45-degree turn, he would head kitty-corner from the refrigerator to the dishwasher and double back to the refrigerator. The process seemed interminable, until the sudden ring of the phone on the kitchen wall stopped Ted's pacing. He touched the receiver and pulled back his hand twice before putting an end to the clamor.

"Hello?"

"Tommy. It's Pam... Ruthie's home... Has Ted arrived? How much have you told him?"

Ted held the receiver to his chest. He closed his eyes for a moment and then put the phone back to his ear. "This is Ted speaking."

"Ted?"

"How is Ruthie?"

"Ruthie is fine." Silence rang in Ted's ear for a moment. "She's sleeping, but the doctor... she's going to be fine."

"When can I see her?"

More silence from Pam. "I feel so... awkward. Ruthie's told me so much about you. But I don't really know you."

"But when can I see her?"

"It's dangerous for both of you... she could be hurt... there's more than you know."

"More?" Ted moved the receiver to his other ear. "What did you mean, when you asked how much Tommy had told me?"

"I've said too much. Ruthie wants to see you. Come after dark. Elisa has my address."

The next thing Ted heard was a dial tone.

***

Two hours later, Ted was still pacing. He felt caged. He was without transportation until Elisa returned and, although the summer was waning, it would be hours before the stubborn Florida sun would give in and provide the darkness Ted needed to complete the criminal act of visiting Ruthie.

In his teens, Ted had visited a volcanic mountain in northern Arizona, which was steep and covered with pebble-sized pumice. For each three steps he climbed, he slid back two. Florida was flat, but if solving the puzzle of Sister was the peak of his mountain, then he was slipping back, the summit out of view.

"Ted, are you okay?"

Ted stopped his pacing and looked up at Elisa, who was standing near the refrigerator. "Have you been standing there long?"

Elisa crossed her arms. "Long enough to see that you're going to wear a path in my tile."

"What's Tommy up to? Pam called. Thought I was Tommy. Wanted to know how much he had told me."

Elisa ran her fingers through her hair. "My dad is giving me fits. I've parked my kids with Tommy's parents, and I'm doing my best to help you."

"So you aren't talking, either."

Elisa took a long breath. "Tommy's been on the phone with this Paco character a lot lately." She opened the refrigerator and ducked out of view. "Are you hungry?"

Ted walked around the refrigerator door. "Please. Elisa. What's going on?"

"I've already said too much." She held up a package of ground beef. "Hamburgers?"

"Pam said the same thing." Ted thought for a moment. "About saying too much. Not about hamburgers."

Elisa smiled and put the meat on the counter. "How's Ruthie?"

Ted rubbed his eyes. "She's home. Sleeping... Okay, I guess. Pam sounded conflicted, but she said I could come over after dark."

Elisa turned toward Ted. A meat patty took shape in her hands. "You know we're on your side. Tommy doesn't want you to move too fast. You have to trust us."

***

The dark closed in on Ted as he drove north on Highway 19 in Elisa's 1975 AMC Pacer. He was glad the sun had finally set—the pacer looked like a giant yellow jellybean. Elisa was sure there was enough gas in her car, but she was embarrassed when she admitted that even though Tommy had admonished her to fix it, the driver's side headlight was out. There was no moon, and the single cone of light stabbing the night, reflecting occasional ribbons of moisture from the gulf, was like a flashlight beaming out of a bulbous coffin. Ted worried that approaching drivers would think he was a motorcycle navigating his lane near the shoulder of the road.

New Port Richey, where Pam lived, was 30 miles south of Spring Hill and out of Chief Todd's jurisdiction, but the chance he would be pulled over for a headlight infraction tied Ted's stomach in a knot. Tommy had mentioned a while back that Todd had connections. Who knew how far he could reach beyond Spring Hill's city limit?

The New Port Richey sign popped out of the inky night, giving Ted hope as he searched for the A&W Root Beer stand he'd been told to use as a beacon. His relief was short lived. Red lights flashing in his rearview mirror set his heart into overdrive. He pulled to the side of the road and waited, and waited. The officer who had pulled him over was in no hurry. Ted's mind went straight to the scenario: his driver's license did not match the car license, registered to a state trooper...

Finally, Ted heard the noise of a door closing from the direction of the pulsating red lights. Soon the beam of a flashlight shone though the driver's side window. Ted slowly rolled down his window.

The flashlight had a voice. "Step out of the car. Easy like, and keep your hands where I can see them."

Ted's hand shook as he grabbed the door handle. He stepped out and braced for the expected push to the ground and the shoulder-wrenching pain of his arms being pulled back so that his hands could be shackled together.

Instead, the flashlight lowered, exposing the Smokey the

Bear hat associated with the state police. The man wearing the hat squinted. "You Ted?"

"Yes." Ted pulled out his wallet and showed the officer his driver's license.

The officer inspected the license. "Arizona. Is the heat as dry as they say?"

Ted felt an intense urge to pee. "Most of the time. Still, pretty hot though. One hundred and eighteen, wet or dry, it's like an oven, right?"

The officer took off his hat and wiped his forehead with his shirtsleeve. "Lived here all my life. Never got used to this damned humidity."

Ted's breathing had returned to near normal. "Am I in trouble, officer?"

The officer plopped his hat back on his head. "You're lucky. I know Tommy. He's on duty tonight. Called him on the radio when his name showed up on the plate check. He'll fix the headlight. You're free to go."

Ted felt his shoulders sag with relief. He reached into his shirt pocket, took out a piece of paper, and handed it to the officer. "Do you know this street?"

The officer looked at the large *A&W Root Beer* sign above their heads. "Turn right, here at this corner. This address will be a couple of blocks down on your right."

***

Pam looked much younger this time. All Ted remembered from their first meeting in the office at Quiet Springs Hospital was the streaks of gray in her hair. Now, in the soft light of her front porch, her high cheekbones and intense hazel eyes left no doubt that she was Ruthie's mother. She must have been no more than twenty when Ruthie was born. She offered her hand. It felt soft and warm like a baby chick just out of the incubator. The furrows in her brow were not from age.

"Come in and sit down." Pam glanced down the hallway leading to the rear of her home. "Ruthie's been resting. I'll check on her."

Ted walked toward a chair that Pam had showed him. He stopped. "Pam?"

Pam turned back to face him.

"What you said on the phone, about the doctor. Is Ruthie...?"

"She'll be fine." Pam hesitated. "Exposure to carbon monoxide can cause permanent damage." She closed her eyes and covered her mouth as if trying to stuff the words *permanent damage* back in her mouth. Then she looked at Ted and squeezed out a smile. "But they think she will be okay."

Ted crossed his arms. "On the phone earlier, when you thought I was Tommy, you asked how much he had told me. What else is going on?"

Pam clasped her hands. "Talk to Ruthie first. She..."

"I what?" Ruthie appeared in the hallway behind Pam. "Ted, you're here."

Ruthie moved slowly into the room and steadied herself on the back of a sofa that divided the space in sections. She smiled. "Is it me or is the room moving?"

Ted froze in his position, standing in front of the overstuffed chair Pam had offered. For a moment he basked in the warmth of her expression. But there was something in the way her eyes darted away, a shyness, that kept him from moving in her direction. That the sofa separated them seemed appropriate.

Ruthie laughed. "You better sit, Ted. You'll fall with the room spinning like this."

Pam took Ruthie by the hand, led her around the sofa, and helped her settle. Then Pam collapsed next to her. "So, you're dizzy again?"

"I'm fine." Ruthie patted Pam's hand and glanced at Ted. "Really, Ted. The chamber thing was weird, but..." She shook her head. "I'm woozy, but I'm fine."

Ted remained silent as he watched her quickly shift her focus away.

Pam touched Ruthie's forehead. "Headache worse?"

Ruthie shook her head. "Who were you talking to on the phone a few minutes ago?"

Pam sat back. She clasped her hands and touched them to her lips and, as if in prayer, closed her eyes. She took a deep breath, opened her eyes, and dropped her hands into her lap. "It was Paco. We talked about what Eldon said to me about... about Sister."

Ruthie's mouth opened but she didn't speak.

Ted spoke for her. "Eldon?"

Pam grasped Ruthie's hand. "While you were in the chamber... I went back to the hospital to catch up on some work. Eldon saw me in the cafeteria getting coffee. He's a funny guy. He likes to talk to me... I..."

"Mom." Ruthie found her voice. "What did he say? Was Bobby around?"

Pam released Ruthie's hand, grabbed a throw pillow, and toyed with the lace on its edges. "Bobby was getting coffee, too." Pam smiled. "You know how Eldon is. He got a little worked up. He said, 'Oh Miss Pam, I hope I did the right thing. I gave Bobby the envelope from Miss Edith.' Bobby moved closer when Eldon started walking in circles. Then Eldon said, 'Now they're going to move her.'"

Ted jumped up. "Move Sister? Where?"

"I don't know... To another hospital, I'm sure. Bobby grabbed Eldon before he could say any more. He wasn't gentle with Eldon as he usually is."

Ted started pacing. "Do you know when they're moving her?"

Pam tossed the pillow aside. "I went back to the office. Fisher was out. I found a transfer file for Edith Montgomery on his desk..."

Ted stopped pacing. "So you do know where she's..."

"No." Pam stood and faced Ted. "Prissy came in. I only caught the transfer date." She bit her lip. "It's tomorrow. They're moving her tomorrow."

23

Silence was thick in the car, as dense as the fingers of ground fog now moving in from the gulf, heavier now than when he'd left Elisa's.

Pam had insisted that Ted and Ruthie take her larger Buick Regal. But Ted regretted his acquiescence since two headlights reflected more light in the broiling mist, making it harder to see the centerline. Ted sat forward, searching for the next white dash painted on the road to pop into view to verify they were still safely in their lane. A peek in Ruthie's direction revealed that she was still waiting for a response to her question. Sister was the reason for their foray, but it was Ruthie's interest in Jan that had caused the silence. She had leaned in close when she asked the question, as if trying to catch Jan's scent.

"Jan is in love with an image of what she wants me to be." Ted continued to stare at the road. "I never fit the image."

Ted glanced at Ruthie. Her mouth opened. But she didn't say a word. The corners of her mouth, though, moved up ever so slightly.

Ted squirmed in his seat, his attention drawn back to the road. "What if Sister doesn't want to be rescued?"

"Sorry." Ruthie touched Ted's arm. "I'm being selfish. She is a mystery. It's as if... as if she feels she deserves to be in the hospital."

Ted nodded. "Any ideas about how to get past the front desk this time?" He leaned forward and wiped condensation from the inside of the windshield. "Assuming we don't run up somebody's tailpipe first."

Ruthie joined Ted near the windshield. "I've seen worse." Then she produced a ring of keys and set them dancing on the dashboard. "My mom came through again. These are to the service entrance of Unit D."

***

Twenty minutes later, Ted braked to a stop at the three-way intersection in front of Quiet Springs Hospital. Patches of fog swirled in the beams of their headlights, alternately revealing and hiding the entrance to the parking lot ahead of them. Ted gripped the steering wheel. His right foot, braced against the brake pedal, shook.

"Go left." Ruthie pointed.

"I know." Ted took a deep breath. He lowered his voice. "I know which way to go. It's just..."

Racing out of the fog, a car suddenly ran the stop sign to Ted's left and disappeared down the street.

"Jesus. Did you see that?"

Ruthie stared into the fog. "It was so fast. Was it a police car?"

"I think so... yes, it was, and...

"And...?"

"There was a child in the passenger seat." Ted thought for a moment. "I didn't have time to read the emblem on the door. There were eyes peering at me just over the window ledge." Ted turned to

Ruthie. "It was either a child or a very short..."

Ruthie's eyes widened. "Paco?"

The tires on Pam's car screeched as Ted jammed his foot on the accelerator and turned the steering wheel hard to the left. In seconds they reached the driveway behind the hospital. Unit D soon loomed out of the fog. Ted braked, and they jolted to a stop behind the unit. Ruthie's legs were braced on the floorboard. One of her hands gripped the door handle and the other held tightly to the back of her seat. Before either of them could say a word, someone walked in front of the car and then disappeared into the fog.

Ted turned to Ruthie. "Bobby."

"Oh my God. Do you think he...?"

"No time to think." Ted opened his door. "Let's go."

Ruthie joined Ted, who was peering through a chain link gate. Behind it was an area large enough to accommodate a delivery truck. Through the fog Ted saw cement steps leading to a loading dock and under a security light, slipping in and out of focus in the swirling mist, the service door to Unit D.

Ted shook the handle of the gate. "Try the keys."

Ruthie tried each of the keys on the ring. "Christ. Not again. None of them fit."

"What?"

Ruthie tried each key again. "Damn."

Ted looked up. Razor wire topped the fence and the gate.

Ruthie tugged on his shirt. "Not an option. Come on." She moved in the direction of her unit. "I have an idea."

By the time Ted caught up with Ruthie, she was standing at the door of her unit swearing softly.

"You're not going to believe this," she said. "I left my keys at my mom's house."

Ted looked away. He remembered that, although this wasn't a locked ward, this door, closest to the alley, was always locked for the patient's security.

"Ruthie, the back door... Ruthie?"

Ruthie disappeared around the end of the building. Wisps of fog she had stirred up made Ted feel he was losing sight of a ghost. He bolted after her, trusting that the path was clear. In spite of the dark shadows beyond the reach of security lights and the lingering patches of fog, his confidence grew with each step.

Then he was airborne.

Ted had just enough time to visualize Superman in flight, arms in the lead, when gravity ruined his memory. First his hands and arms and then his face stung as hundreds of tiny pebbles tore at his flesh. Milliseconds later, his chest and legs walloped the ground. Then nothing. His body went numb and for a moment he didn't even blink.

Gasping for air, Ted came back to life. He had forgotten how to breathe. The process was unnatural and the sounds he made were haunting. Finally the heaving in his chest subsided. Only then did he feel the fire burning the palms of his hands and the blaze spreading to his arms and moving quickly to his face. A deep ache in Ted's left leg brought with it visions of squealing tires and waking up in a hospital bed. Ted gritted his teeth and sat up slowly. He squeezed his hands open and shut. They felt sticky and gritty.

"Mister Ted?"

An apparition loomed out of the mist above Ted. "Eldon? How...?"

Then Ted saw Ruthie.

She dropped to her knees and looked straight into his eyes. "Are you okay? I thought you were right behind me."

Ted turned and stretched out his arms. "I was trying out my Superman act."

"Superman?" Ruthie touched his face and gently examined his hands and arms. "Eldon. Help Ted... from behind. Gently... lift under his arms."

Eldon might look like a puff pastry, Ted thought, *but he is strong.* With Ruthie at his side, and Eldon behind him, Ted was guided down the path and into the unit. Once inside, Ruthie steered Ted into an examination room behind the nurse's station. She cleaned and wrapped the scraped areas of his arms where blood oozed and taped gauze pads to his palms. She carefully wrapped a strip of guaze over abrasions on his forehead.

Eldon giggled. "You look like a mummy."

Ted frowned.

"You should thank Eldon." Ruthie smiled at Eldon. "He let me in."

Eldon clasped his hands together.

"And that's not all." Ruthie held up a key. "He showed me where Bobby hid the spare key to Unit D."

***

At first Ruthie had objected. But she couldn't think of a better plan to get past the attendant, now that they had to use the front entrance of Unit D. Eldon was immediately in favor of his being included. Eldon would go into Unit D alone. If things went according to the plan, the attendant would leave his locked enclosure to deal with Eldon.

Ted read the sign on the door: Duty attendants, Nurses and Doctors only. No visitors allowed.

Ted looked at Eldon. "Ready, big guy?"

Eldon hesitated. "I hope Bobby won't be mad."

Ted whispered to Ruthie. "Where is Bobby?"

Ruthie glanced at Eldon, and then moved closer to Ted. "His name is on the duty list. He should have been in Eldon's unit."

"I've got good hearing." Eldon moved closer. "Bobby told the attendants to stay in the nurse's station. But they never listen. They went to the janitor's room to play cards."

Ruthie stroked Eldon's arm. "Thank you, Eldon. I wondered where everyone was."

Eldon began pacing in a small circle. "Bobby is going to be mad at me."

Ruthie grabbed Eldon's arm. "Ted, this won't work."

Eldon stopped. "I'm not as crazy as you think I am."

Ruthie's mouth dropped open. "Eldon?"

Eldon crossed his arms. "And Miss Edith isn't crazy at all." He pushed past them and stood by the door. "She needs our help, right?"

Ruthie caught Ted's eye and shrugged her shoulders.

"The man is right." Ted took the key from Ruthie and opened the door. "We'll be right behind you, Eldon."

Eldon walked quickly across the lobby and banged on the cage surrounding the nurse's station. In the confusion, the attendant didn't see Ted and Ruthie skulking by the front door.

"Eldon. For Christ's sake." The young orderly stood. He flipped a switch and the side door of the cage popped open. He was within arm's length of Eldon when Eldon crouched and raised his arms in a martial arts pose.

"No so fast, Toby," said Eldon.

Toby stopped and eyed an emergency switch nearby.

"Now," whispered Ruthie.

Ted charged Toby and grabbed him around his waist before he could reach the lever. Ruthie ran into the cage and retrieved some restraints. She returned and pushed past Eldon, who was circling Ted and Toby, jabbing the air like a Kung Fu master and shuffling his feet like a prizefighter. Ruthie and Ted struggled with Toby and were finally successful with the restraints. They wedged him into a chair outside the cage.

Ruthie knelt down next to Toby. "Can you keep quiet, or do I need to get something from the refrigerator to help you sleep?"

Toby shook his head. "Do what you have to do." He looked at Eldon. "Just keep Bruce Lee away from me."

Both Ted and Ruthie looked at Eldon, who was maintaining his martial arts posture. Ted's heart pounded. He felt light headed, and he grimaced as he replaced one of the bandages on his left hand. Then he did the only thing that had worked in the past when he was stressed, especially in awkward social situations—he laughed. Ruthie bit her lip but soon lost control as well. Toby, locked in a device that kept him in a perpetual self-hug, shook with laughter. Eldon, on the other hand, looked puzzled.

Ruthie stood and ran to the cage. "This is crazy." She opened a panel and took out a key. "We're breaking into a mental ward to kidnap a patient. And we're laughing."

There was a loud buzz and the lock on the door to the warren of rooms of Unit D clicked. Ruthie reached the door first and pulled it open.

Ted grabbed Eldon's arm. "What about Eldon?"

"He has to come with us." She waved them toward the door. "Come on."

Ted and Eldon followed Ruthie through the dank hallways. Ted fell back with Eldon, whose lumbering gait belied the image of his being a ninja. Ruthie disappeared around the last corner before Sister's room. Ted stopped to encourage Eldon, but before he could say anything Ruthie screamed. He abandoned Eldon and ran toward the commotion.

Ted turned the corner. "Bobby?"

24

"Let me go!" Ruthie's voice echoed sharply between the corridor's high ceiling and polished cement floor.

Ted focused on the incongruous sight of Bobby's eyes, always proud before, wide open and searching for an escape route.

"But I'm not..." Bobby looked to Ted for support. "Ted?"

Ted moved behind Ruthie. "Ruthie, he's not..." He grabbed her shoulders. "You're holding him."

Ruthie relaxed her grip and fell back against Ted.

Bobby winced and rubbed his forearm. Then his mouth dropped open. "Eldon?"

Ted felt a bump from behind. "Don't be mad, Bobby." Eldon's voice buzzed in Ted's right ear. "We just want to help Sister."

"Sister?" Bobby moved toward Eldon. "What kind of wild stories have you been telling?"

"You know, Bobby." Eldon scooted closer to the wall. "You know who Sister is."

Ruthie pulled from Ted's grasp and pushed her hair away from her eyes. She took a step closer to Bobby and planted her hands on her hips. "Yes, Bobby," she said. "Why don't you enlighten us all?"

Bobby's gaze shifted from the agitated trio to the space between them and the hallway behind, the only way out. "Okay." Bobby raised his hand as if to show he was unarmed. "Why don't we all just calm down?"

Ted glanced at Ruthie and then looked back at Bobby. "Going somewhere?"

Catlike, Bobby sprang past them, ran down the corridor, and disappeared.

Ted made a move to follow him but stopped short when Ruthie grabbed his sleeve. "No time," she said. They both watched Eldon turning in circles, his hands covering his face.

"It was stupid to chase him anyway. Who was going to help me hold Bobby?" Ted pointed at Eldon. "Ninja boy?"

A loud click sounded in the corridor in the opposite direction of Bobby's retreat.

"What was that," asked Ted?

Ruthie held her finger to her lips. "That came from the room beyond Sister's room." Her voice—like a serpent's hiss—slithered up the wall of the drafty corridor toward the ceiling. "A door just closed."

With Eldon in tow, Ted followed Ruthie to Sister's room. Ruthie unlocked the door. Inside, the light was on, and Sister was pacing. She reacted to the three of them huddled in the doorway as if they were a wind blowing her backward. She sat hard on the edge of the bed. Ruthie joined Sister on the bed and offered her hand. Ted was startled by the cornered animal look in Sister's eyes.

Ted exchanged a glance with Ruthie. Ruthie moved her lips without a sound, but he got the message: "Relax."

Ted took a deep breath and sat in a nearby chair. "We thought you'd be asleep."

Sister looked over her shoulder. "The room next door is

empty. I... I heard noises." She glanced back at Ted. "Then I heard voices in the hall... outside my door."

Ruthie squeezed Sister's hand. "Esther..."

Sister pulled away.

"May I call you Esther?" Ruthie's voice smoothed away the creases on Sister's forehead.

Sister reached for Ruthie's hand. "It's been so long since I heard that name." She closed her eyes and let the feeling wash over her.

Ruthie leaned toward the older woman. "Esther, are you saying that Bobby wasn't in your room a few minutes ago?"

Sister's eyes blinked open, and she shook her head.

Ruthie glanced at Ted. "We don't have much time." Then she looked back at Sister. "I know how crazy this sounds, but we have to take you away from here right now."

"Away?" Sister pulled away again. "But this is my home. Skipper. God put me here. You are in danger again." She gestured toward Eldon. "And what will happen to Eldon?"

"It wasn't God who put you here. Something terrible happened to you." Ted rose, took Sister's hands and gently squeezed them. "You know what happened. Doctor Fisher knows, too."

Sister tugged her hands free and covered her face. "You don't understand. They will hurt Jacob. Please, Skipper, leave me here. I'm to blame."

Ruthie grabbed a coat from a nearby closet and threw it across the bed to Ted. "Here, help her into this. She doesn't have time to get dressed." She reached under the bed, grabbed a pair of Sister's shoes and threw them on the bed. "Help her with these, too."

Ted kneeled to help her out of her slippers and into her shoes. He was still on his knees when the door pushed open and he saw the scar. Behind McCoy, Leroy walked in, but he was shoved aside by Doctor Fisher.

Fisher locked eyes with Ted. "Edith, are these people disturbing you?"

"No!" Sister was calm, the confusion was gone, and a hint of a smile passed across her lips. "Esther," said Sister. "You know my name is Esther."

Doctor Fisher cleared his throat. "Leroy, Mr. Miller is trespassing. Arrest him."

Sister sprang from the bed and moved in front of Ted. "No!" Ted could see that she was shaking. "No one is going to be arrested."

Leroy raised his cap and rubbed his stubby hair. "Ma'am, please. It's my job." He reached in Sister's direction. "Now you just step..."

"Unhand her, sir." Eldon moved between Sister and Leroy. He crouched in his judo pose, the fingers of his extended arm pushing against the badge on Leroy's chest.

Surprised, Leroy grabbed Eldon's arm and, together, they did a circular dance punctuated by a flurry of *oh no's* from Eldon. Ruthie ran around the end of the bed and tried to restrain Eldon.

Fisher pointed at Eldon. "What in God's name is he doing here?" He turned to McCoy. "You get Miller."

McCoy licked his lips and charged at Ted, but Ted threw up his arms and blocked McCoy's attempt to grab him. Like two bucks, antlers locked, they jockeyed for position.

Sister let out a mournful wail. All the combatants stopped and looked at her. Tears ran in uninterrupted rivulets down her cheeks. Her body convulsed as if teetering on the precipice of Hell. She pointed at McCoy. "It was you!" Tears, gathering on her lips, sprayed as she spoke with increasing volume and soul–piercing lament.

Ted felt a twist in his gut as he shared the pain released in her anguished sobs.

"It was you who took away my innocence!" Sister shook her

fist at McCoy. "It was you who made me bleed!"

Ted released McCoy, who fell back against the wall with a force that could have only come from a push, yet no one had moved against him. McCoy pointed at Fisher. "He made me do it!"

Leroy looked at Fisher. "What the hell is he talking about?"

"Don't be a fool," Fisher said. He pointed at Sister. "She's crazy." Then he glared at McCoy. "And she's making him crazy."

Hate for McCoy, suppressed for weeks now and mingled with a lifetime of unnamed anger, spewed from Ted's gut in an agonizing howl. He charged McCoy and grabbed him by the neck. McCoy flopped about, but in Ted's stranglehold he was defenseless. Leroy pulled on Ted's arm, but he couldn't pry him loose.

"Skipper!" Sister hurried to Ted and pulled on his shirt. "Don't kill him. He's your father."

McCoy slipped to the floor, gasping for air.

Ted's arms and legs felt heavy, his face burned, and the room was spinning. He turned toward Sister. She dropped to her knees, her hands covering her face as she sobbed. Ted moved to her, dropped to her level and held her face to his chest. Her warm tears quickly soaked his shirt. "Mother?" Ted voice cracked like an adolescent boy at his first dance. "You're my mother? But..." Ted held his breath for a moment. "The letter. Margaret was pregnant with me."

Sister looked up into Ted's eyes. "Skipper. A week after that terrible night Margaret had a miscarriage."

McCoy's wheezing was replaced by shuffling feet. Fisher disappeared behind the closing door. But before Ted could react, the door opened again, and Doctor Fisher was forced back into the room.

Ted gasped. "Tommy?"

Fisher struggled for moment and then hung his head as Tommy blocked any possibility of retreat. Someone pushed past Tommy, and Ted looked straight into familiar eyes.

"Hey hombre, you okay?"

"Paco? What the Hell?" Ted groaned as he, supporting himself on Paco's shoulder, stood, and then helped his mother to her feet.

"I was hiding in the next room with Tommy and…" Paco waved a chubby hand toward the doorway filled by two uniformed men. "… Some of his buddies." Paco cleared his throat. "This room is bugged. We were listening."

"What?" Ted guided Sister to the edge of the bed and back into Ruthie's charge. "Why?"

"We knew you and Ruthie were coming." Paco looked at Doctor Fisher and then down at McCoy, who was still sitting on the floor, massaging his neck. "It was the only way to catch these two."

"Why the Hell didn't you tell us?"

Paco crossed his arms. "It was important that Sister incriminate McCoy and Fisher."

"We knew it would be rough on her." Tommy nodded at Sister and then stared at Ted. "Come on Ted, you're emotionally involved, we couldn't be sure you would go through with it."

"What about my mom?" Ruthie asked.

"She helped." Tommy looked away. "She didn't know everything, but she let us know when you and Ted left for the hospital. She was… reluctant."

"Didn't Pam tell you about the letter?" Ted turned to Eldon. "Did you read the letter before you showed it to Bobby?"

Eldon twisted from side to side. "No, oh no. It was sealed. Ask Bobby, ask Bobby."

Tommy turned to the door. "Bobby?"

Bobby pushed past the two patrol officers and smiled at Ruthie. "Sorry, I couldn't tell you. I was helping, too."

Fisher struggled and glared at Bobby. "You bastard."

Bobby smiled at Fisher and then looked back at Ted. "I had

just gotten Tommy and the others settled next door when I ran into Ruthie." He glanced at her. "You got here faster than I thought you would."

Ruthie's mouth hung open. "So..." Ruthie shook her head. "Why did you run away?"

Bobby took a deep breath and released it noisily. "It's complicated... think of me as a double agent." He pointed at Doctor Fisher. "I had Fisher and his group stashed in another part of the unit waiting for you to arrive. I was supposed to get them once you entered this room so they could catch you trying to rescue Sister."

Ted shook his head. "Amazing. But what about the letter?"

Bobby searched his pocket. He held up a folded sheet of paper. "Nothing. The letter's blank."

Ted sat down next to Sister.

Esther scowled at Fisher. "He said he would hurt Jacob if I said anything." She pointed at the doctor. "He told me I was a sinner. He said God was punishing me."

Ted jumped up and moved toward Fisher. "You son-of-a-bitch." Ted's punch caught Fisher in his jaw.

Tommy stepped between the two men. "Take it easy, Ted."

"I'm the SOB?" Fisher nursed his jaw. "Talk to your little friend, Miller. He's up to his eyeballs in this."

Ted sat back down on the bed. He looked into Paco's eyes. "You?"

Paco shook his head. "I wanted to tell you" He looked at Fisher. "But he held all the cards."

Ted shook his head. "I don't understand. My father...Jacob said your father and Fisher were working together...but."

Paco sighed. "Before all this happened to Sister..." Paco squeezed a smile at Sister. "My father and Fisher were running an insurance scam. My dad gave Fisher personal information he got from guests of our motel, and Fisher used the information to bill insurance companies for non-existent services though his hospital."

Paco stared at his shoe tops. "Your father discovered the scam and threatened to turn them in."

"So to keep him quiet, they beat Jacob up and..." Ted looked at Sister.

"That's right." Tommy hesitated. "Bobby, maybe you should take Esther to another room."

Sister crossed her arms. "No." She offered her hand to Ted. "I want to stay with my son."

Tommy nodded and turned to Ted. "We've done a lot of checking. Once you were born..." He glanced at Esther and then looked back at Ted. " Once you were born, your family began to fall apart..."

"Ted." Paco hoisted himself onto the bed next to Ted. "After you were born, your father moved the family down to Saint Petersburg. Not long after the move, Esther had a nervous breakdown. From what we've gathered, Fisher forced your father to let him keep her here at Quiet Springs, to keep her from incriminating them."

"You mean my father kept working here? Even after...?"

"Fisher had him by the balls, Ted," Paco said. "Your father knew what Fisher was capable of doing. He was afraid for his wife. Afraid McCoy would hurt her too." Paco looked down. "Finally, he quit. He went a little crazy... you know the rest."

Ted shook his head and looked at Paco. He saw tears.

"You have to believe me, man. My father had nothing to do with what happened to Sister. But he couldn't do anything." Paco hopped off the bed. He wiped his eyes on his sleeve and then leaned on the bed. Ted could see that he was staring at the patterns of the bedspread. "I'm ashamed now, but I caved into Fisher's pressure after my dad died. He said that if I didn't keep the scam going and couldn't keep my mouth shut, he'd close down the motel and destroy my father's memory."

For a moment, the room went silent. Then Ruthie walked around the end of the bed. She stopped in front of Paco, who stepped away from the bed and faced her. She looked down, into his eyes. "Why didn't you ever tell me any of this?"

Paco searched the area around his feet. "I couldn't."

"But we were so close."

"I just couldn't." Tears formed in his eyes. He pointed at Fisher. "That bastard would have told you that…" Paco looked away.

"Tell her, you little shit," said Fisher. "You've ruined everything anyway."

Paco moved toward Fisher, but Tommy caught him before he could advance.

"What?" Ruthie glared at Paco. "Tell me what?"

Paco folded his arms and squeezed his eyes shut.

Ted scowled. "Just answer the question, Paco." Paco didn't budge. Ted looked at Ruthie and shrugged his shoulders.

Ruthie turned to Fisher. "What did you want Paco to tell me?"

Fisher glared at Paco. Then he locked eyes with Ruthie. "That you, my dear, are my daughter."

25

Ted checked the rear view mirror of Pam's car and caught a glimpse of an officer assisting a man into the back seat of a patrol car. He took a deep breath and pressed the accelerator. Twice in the last few hours he had imagined being in that exact position. The next time he looked up into the mirror, the lights of the Quiet Springs parking lot were gone and, for a moment, darkness overwhelmed them.

Ted glanced at Ruthie, who was curled up in the passenger seat, staring out her window. "Are you okay?"

She turned toward him, and her tears shimmered in the sudden glow of a streetlight. The interior of the car darkened again, and her gaze returned to her window.

Ted sighed. "Glad the fog lifted." He shook his head. Stupid, he thought. He was never good in awkward situations. Thankfully he hadn't explained why the fog had dissipated.

Ted glanced at Ruthie again. In the dim glow of the dashboard lights, he saw the rhythmic dance of her shoulders. He heard sobs that tightened his gut. Although he wanted to comfort her, instinct told him to let her grieve. Thoughts of Sister helped him give Ruthie the space she needed. He was thankful for the sparkle he had seen in his mother's eyes when she shooed him away. She would recover, and he would be with her as much as he could.

He smiled when he recalled Eldon with his arms crossed over his paunch, promising to watch over Sister until Ted returned. Bobby was more practical. He promised to move Sister back to her old room. They had all agreed that she would need time to acclimate. After all, this had been her home for more than 30 years. Acclimate indeed. His life, too, had turned upside down in a matter of seconds. But Ted knew he was in this for the long haul, now that the spider song was no longer a flickering hint of his past.

Ted's thoughts turned to the look on Ruthie's face when they led Fisher away. She looked like a masked Japanese Noh dancer, her face frozen in an expression that hid any emotion. Ted thought of how he had turned away when McCoy was put in handcuffs. He would have to deal with the reality of their relationship, but for now, even the thought of the scarred chin and the insipid way McCoy licked his lips sent a wave of nausea through his midsection.

He shifted in his seat. A crease in the seat's upholstery reminded him of a familiar pat on his lower back. Paco had already faced his responsibility in the fraud perpetuated by Fisher. Tommy said a deal was in the works and was sure Paco wouldn't have to serve any jail time. Ted recalled the confusion in the hall outside Sister's room and later learned that arriving late, Chief Todd had struggled with state troopers who held a warrant for Todd's arrest. Leroy was in the clear. He had just been following orders.

The root beer stand sign in New Port Richey brought Ted out of his reflections. The car's tires complained as Ted braked and turned the steering wheel sharply.

Ruthie sat up. "Thank God, we're back." She braced herself on the dash as the car screeched to a stop. Ruthie ran her fingers through her hair. "I hope she's asleep."

The front door of Pam's house opened. Pam's presence framing the doorway put Ruthie's hope to rest.

Ruthie squeezed Ted's arm. "I'm not ready for this." She studied the Kleenex in her lap. "Sorry." Then she opened the car door.

Ruthie brushed past Pam and disappeared into the house. He and Pam stared at each other for a few moments, and then she motioned for him to come in.

Once they were inside, Pam turned to Ted. "Tommy called. He told me what happened with Ruthie and Fisher. I should have told her sooner." She looked over her shoulder toward the back of the house, then walked to the sofa, sat down, and covered her face with her hands. Eventually she lowered her hands to reveal tears washing over her cheeks. "God help me, Ted, I should have told her."

Ted sat down across from her, reached over, and took her hands in his. "Why didn't you tell her? Why were you afraid?"

Pam pulled her hands out of Ted's grasp and sat back. "We weren't married, but Fisher and I were living together when Ruthie was born. I found out about what he was doing... the insurance thing."

Ted sat forward. "So that's why you left him?"

Pam clasped her hands, hard, as if she was wringing out the memory. "No... I mean yes. He threatened to involve me if I left."

"But you did leave him."

Pam thought for a moment. "I moved out of his house... but I stayed at the hospital." She looked at Ted. "I wanted to run way." Pam looked at the ceiling. "But I was weak. He said he would find me if I left."

Ted reached out and took her hands again. "Pam." Ted's tone was soft, as if he was speaking to a child. "When I asked if the insurance fraud was the reason you left him, you said 'no' at first."

Ted squeezed her hands. "Did something else make you move out of Fisher's house?"

Pam pulled out of Ted's grip and glanced over her shoulder. She turned back to Ted, took a deep breath and squeezed her eyes shut. "He touched her." Pam's sobs came from a place deep in her chest. "I should have turned him in." Her sobs became wails. "The bastard touched my baby! I should have turned him in!"

A sound like a wounded animal came from the hallway behind them. "Oh my God, I remember now." Ruthie's face was contorted and glistened with tears. She choked on the words. "His breath smelled like cigarettes. I pushed his hand away, but he wouldn't stop."

Ted stood, hurried past Pam, and took Ruthie in his arms.

She continued to weep. "He wouldn't stop… he wouldn't stop."

Pam stood and reached over Ted's shoulder and touched Ruthie's forehead. "I'm sorry, sweetie. Oh baby, I'm so sorry."

Ruthie pulled back from Pam's touch. She backed away from Ted but held on to one of his sleeves. "I can't talk about it… not now."

Ted followed her tug. Ruthie stopped behind Pam's car and threw herself into Ted's arms. For several minutes, Ted held her as she released her pain, which enveloped him and became his own.

Ruthie's sobs ebbed and her body stopped wrenching. Ted held her far enough away so that he could look into her eyes, recognizing the same desperation he felt. He knew they were at a crossroads.

"What now?" he asked.

Ruthie laid her head on his chest. She sighed. "My head is spinning."

"Can we solve this together?" Ted asked.

She stood back. "There's so much to sift through. I just don't know."

Ted looked away. "I've got a lot to settle in Phoenix... and you..."

Ruthie put her finger on his lips. "Take care of yourself. Go back to Arizona with an open mind..." She patted his chest. "... And heart." She smiled at him and nodded toward the house. "You know what I'll be doing." Ruthie held Ted's face in her hands. "You know where I live."

***

Two days later, Ted hesitated in the arrival area of Phoenix's Sky Harbor Airport. He touched the cassette tape in his shirt pocket. He searched the crowd for a familiar face, but all the waves and smiles were for his fellow passengers. Outside the airport's automatic doors, he staggered under the weight of the blast furnace heat.

"Hey, Ted."

Ted followed the voice to a car double-parked in the passenger pick-up area. Stella's lanky arms, waving over the top of her car, were hard to miss. Ted hustled to the car. A whistle startled him. It sounded like a referee signaling a foul at a basketball game.

Stella frowned and jumped into the driver's seat. "Hurry, get in and close the door. That guy made me drive around three times." She waved at the airport policeman and drove away. "Do you have the tape?"

Ted touched his shirt pocket again. "Got it... but I was hoping to see the kids first."

Stella waved to a driver who had let her merge into the exit lane. "It's noon. The boys are still in school."

Ted glanced at his watch. "Seasons, time. I can't keep anything straight."

Stella braked the car to a halt at an intersection near the entrance to the airport. "What? You were mumbling."

"Never mind." Ted tapped his pocket again. "Let's just go to the hospital."

***

A few minutes later, Ted and Stella stood in front of the nurses' station on Margaret Miller's floor.

Lois looked up from a chart she had been reading. "Mr. Miller, nice to see you." She looked at the portable cassette player in Stella's hand. "Dr. Stein, everything's ready."

Stella nodded and walked toward Margaret Miller's room. "I asked Lois to reduce your mother's…" Stella stopped and looked back at Ted. "I mean Margaret's pain medication."

Ted hesitated. "Don't worry. She's still my mom." He motioned for them to proceed and followed Stella and Lois into the room.

Lois checked Margaret's intravenous drip. "Mrs. Miller. Look whose come to see you."

Ted liked the way Lois always spoke to Margaret as if she could hear. He smiled at Lois and took Margaret's hand. He didn't know if it was just a reflex, but he felt her squeeze back. There was so little flesh on her hands that Ted felt as if he was shaking hands with a robot. Margaret's mouth moved. He leaned closer but only heard a hiss. Ted reached in his pocket, took out the cassette tape, and handed it to Stella.

Stella fumbled with the tape for a moment as she inserted it into the tape player. When she pressed the play button, Sister's voice filled the room.

"Maggie?" Sister's voice hesitated. "It really is me, sweetie… Esther. Skipper says you're very ill. It broke my heart to hear that. I wanted to come… but the doctors think it is too soon for me to leave. Skipper knows everything. He's confused, but I think it is all for the best, don't you? And such a good job you did raising him. He's such a fine young man. But do not feel guilty, sweetie. What is done is done..." There was a short pause on the tape. "Maggie... now I want you to listen closely. You always had a stubborn streak... but it is all right to let go."

Ted reached over and stopped the tape player. He blinked and wiped his eyes. "Look."

Margaret's mouth was quivering, and she was smiling.

***

The next morning, Ted sat in Stella's office. After the visit with Margaret, she'd dropped him off at his apartment. Jan expected him to pick up the boys later that evening.

"Well, how did it go?" Stella's question hung in the air like the stagnant brown pollutants trapped by the surrounding mountains, smothering Phoenix, a gift from the booming population and the automobiles they brought with them.

Ted stared at the painting behind her. He knew he hadn't made it into the sunlight yet, but he felt that he was at least in the upper branches of the trees. He could see the glimmer of light through the leaves.

Ted lowered his gaze. "I gave Jan her list back."

Stella sat forward. "And...?"

"I told her I was okay with the confirmation for Josh." Ted shifted his position on the sofa. "But I told her rest of the things wouldn't work."

Stella nodded. "How did Jan react to that?"

"She said I seemed different."

"Are you?"

Ted looked away.

Stella crossed her arms. "Are you different?"

"Jesus, Stella." Ted stood and walked to a window that overlooked a busy street below. He watched the flow of life. "The people I thought were my parents..." he pointed at the street,"...

are no more related to me than any of those poor bastards scurrying around down there. All my life I've been told that I'm too sensitive, too emotional and that it's not natural to feel as deeply as I do. Well now I see that's just BS, and by rejecting that nonsense, the one thing I'll stop being is a doormat." Ted stared straight ahead and chuckled. "Am I different?" He turned and faced Stella. "Even Josh says I seem different. And you know what? Maybe I *am* different. Maybe who we are is just made-up stuff we learn from our parents." Ted pointed at the painting. "And maybe, if I'm ever going to break out into that sunlight, I've got to make up a whole new life."

Ted walked back to the sofa and sat down. "Maybe the life I'll make up won't have anything to do with the fact that my real mother is someone I just met." Ted took a long breath. He stared into Stella's eyes. "And maybe, just maybe, the fact that I'm here on this earth, because that sweet woman was raped by the scumbag who I now find out is my father won't have any influence on who I'm going to be." Ted stood and walked to the painting. He reached up and touched the brilliant sunlight at the top. "Am I different?" He looked back at Stella. "You're God-damned right, I'm different."

Ted let the glow of the moment flow over him. A minute passed, and his arm felt heavy. He returned to the sofa, sat, and the overstuffed pillows of the sofa nestled around him. Ted took a deep breath. "Remember when you said you thought I was hiding something from you?

Stella uncrossed her arms.

Ted cleared his throat. "There was something more tangible than not wanting to expose myself." Ted told Stella about his occasional cocaine use and how the last packet of the stuff had been confiscated in Florida. Then he took a deep breath. "I got a call from Paco last night."

Stella leaned closer to Ted. "And…"

"Leroy asked Paco to let me know that he had a small

package with my name on it in his property room, and that I could pick it up any time."

The statement hung in the air between them for a few seconds. Stella leaned closer. "And…"

Ted smiled. "I told Paco that I wouldn't be needing it anymore. I told him to tell Leroy to destroy it." Ted narrowed his gaze at Stella. "You look awfully smug."

Stella rubbed her chin. "Seems I've cured you. And in less than twenty sessions."

Ted laughed. "But at what cost? How many patients have you cancelled to take care of me this week?"

Stella put her hands behind her head and stretched her arms. "I haven't bought a novel in weeks. But speaking of not being paid." Stella dropped her arms and leaned forward. "Did you give any thought to what I said about Jacob?"

Ted shrugged his shoulders. "I think you're right, we should wait to tell him about Sister." Ted hesitated for a moment. "And I don't think I'm ready to deal with the father thing."

"I took Jacob to see Margaret."

Ted leaned forward. "Why didn't you tell me before now?"

Stella thought for moment. "He kissed her good-bye."

26

Two days later, Stella and Ted inched their way toward the Phoenix airport in the stubborn early morning traffic. The whine of the air conditioner and the rush of cool air on Ted's skin was a given. The overnight low had reached only 86 degrees.

Stella tapped on her horn. "How did the boys respond?"

"Respond to what?"

Stella rolled her eyes and sighed. "Oh, I don't know, the huge changes that have occurred in your life, maybe? Or, how you are going to balance a life in two cities, two thousand miles apart?"

Ted stared at the brake lights on the car ahead of them. "Josh is growing up. He hugged me. He said he understood." Ted smiled. "Eric said he would look forward to visits so he could play at the beach."

Stella glanced at Ted. "So you've decided to stay in Florida for a while?"

Ted looked out his side window. He noticed that pedestrians were keeping up with them. "Maybe I should get out and walk."

Stella shook her head. "Not with all the extra luggage you

brought this time. And you didn't answer my question."

Ted stared straight ahead. "At first I wasn't sure what to do. Ruthie has a ton of shit to deal with. I honestly don't know where we'll end up. Sister needs me." Ted looked at Stella for a moment. Then he focused on the people walking next to them. "Okay... I guess I need to be with my mother for a while. But then I realized I didn't want to be the self-absorbed parent Jacob was. The boys need me. And I need them."

Stella glanced away from the stalled traffic. "I'm glad you recognized that."

Ted nodded. "I talked to Paul. We decided that I could be a substitute teacher this year. I can spend quality time with the boys, keep my fingers in my career and spend time in Florida with my mother as often as I can."

"Sounds reasonable." Stella glanced over her shoulder. "But what about all the extra luggage?

Ted stifled a smile. "It's complicated."

Stella shook her head. "Okay, be like that, but I couldn't help noticing." Stella nodded toward Ted's plane tickets, which had spilled out of the envelope on the seat between them. "Why the stop in Nashville?"

"I've got some business to take care of."

Stella glanced at Ted. "Don't leave me hanging."

Ted chuckled. "What, and ruin the plot for you?"

***

Berry Field, in Nashville, Tennessee looked different from any airport Ted had ever visited. The decor of the airport made it clear that he was in the country music Mecca. Though his musical tastes aligned more closely to Dave Brubeck and Mozart, he did know a little about country music. Merle Haggard's song about being in prison was playing on the sound system in the baggage area. Even though Ted was sure Ernest Tubbs hadn't had a country hit for a few years, large posters with Ernest's face welcomed Ted to Nashville, inviting him to the new Grand Ole Opry's home a few miles east of downtown Nashville. Other less-colorful posters reminded visitors that Elvis Presley had recently been laid to rest just a few miles down the road in Memphis.

From the air, Nashville had looked like a green gem split in half by the looping Cumberland River. "Don't miss the full-scale replica of the Parthenon," a toothy stewardess had reminded Ted as he'd deplaned. But all thoughts of tourism were dispelled when he reached out and grabbed his larger suitcase, the one that had already made an extra circuit on the luggage carousel. Ted managed to balance it on the lip of the conveyor system, but an even larger bag bumped his suitcase and knocked it back onto the belt.

"I'll get it." A man with a guitar slung over his shoulder wrestled Ted's suitcase to the floor. "What the Christ do you have in there?"

Ted waved to a nearby skycap leaning on a luggage cart. "Bibles."

The man adjusted his guitar. "Bibles? Do you sell them?"

Ted pointed the skycap toward his luggage. He then glanced at the man who had rescued his suitcase. "Actually, I'm returning them." Ted smiled. "It's complicated."

***

The Gideon International building was a short drive from the airport. It shared space with a bank and other secular businesses and was located at the end of a wide cul-de-sac. The center of the cul-de-sac was a grassy park, and perched in the middle of the park was a lonely gazebo. Behind the office buildings stood the remainder of the woods from which the land for the buildings had been confiscated.

Ted parked his rental car and walked to the gazebo. Here, fifty yards from a company with the sole mission of spreading the same word of God that had been forced on him in his youth, Ted felt further away from God than ever before. But one fact was clear. The battle with this God was over.

If God is truly all-powerful, and, all knowing, Ted thought, then why had He dealt such a crappy hand to Sister and to their troubled human brothers? Was He toying with them, testing them like He did Job thousands of years ago? Ted had once imagined God as a boy who owned a basketball. Play the game my way or I'll take my ball and leave. Except, with this God, you played His game or you burned for eternity.

Back at his car, Ted struggled with the suitcase he'd packed full of the Gideon Bibles that he'd taken from motel rooms around the county. He heaved the suitcase to the front door of the building and staggered through the portal. Then he entered the building, dragging the weight of eternity. When he reached the receptionist's desk, he pushed the suitcase on its side, released the latches, and opened the lid.

The young woman sitting behind the desk stood, leaned over her desk, and peered at Bibles packed like bundles of ransom money. Her mouth dropped open, but she didn't speak.

Ted pointed to the case. "I'm returning these."

The receptionist brushed aside strands of blond hair that seemed to obscure her view of the Bibles. "You're returning these?"

"Tell Him…" Ted pointed toward the ceiling. "Tell Him we're even."

The young woman straightened her body and looked up.

Ted bent down and took one of the Bibles from the suitcase. "If it's okay, I'll keep just one copy."

She nodded.

Ted held up the Bible and smiled. "Maybe I missed something?"

When he reached the door, he turned and saw the girl's mouth open as if to speak, but no sound came out.

"Oh." Ted again pointed at the ceiling. "Tell Him the ball is in His court."

***

The next day at noon, Ted sat parked in a familiar horseshoe driveway in a car he had rented at the airport in Tampa. He listened to the idling engine and felt the familiar prickling feeling on his skin as waves of conditioned air evaporated the sweat from his arms and face. He glanced out the back window and saw that the flying horse was still trying to escape its invisible harness, bound to the Mobil Gas sign across the street. Then he saw it. Perched on the flying horse was a vulture. It was the same species as the vulture that had circled him at his parents' home. Ted smiled when the vulture rose suddenly from the sign and, instead of stalking him, flew quickly out of view.

When he turned back, Ted looked up through his windshield. He saw the top of a person's head moving in the office window at Paco's Inn. He knew that soon he would be spending some time at Quiet Springs Hospital. But now that he had found the person who had sung to him so long ago, he relaxed; he had a lifetime to rescue the past. And soon enough, Ruthie and he would work through their individual—yet shared—pain. Time would tell if healing would bring them together. But for now, Ted was weary. His bones were heavy; fatigue tugged at is eyelids and overwhelmed his senses. Ted needed a shower, but most of all, he needed a bed.

The thought of finally closing his eyes and giving in to his exhaustion forced him to open the car door and urged him into the stifling midday heat. Once inside the small motel lobby, Ted collapsed into a chair. He looked into two piercing eyes.

"I just got back." Ted wiped his face with a shirtsleeve.

"Flew in this morning."

The eyes disappeared, and Paco walked out from behind the counter. "And this is the first place you came to?"

Ted grunted. "It's good to see you, too." He rested his head on the wall behind his chair. "What's up with you anyway? I'm beat, I need a bed."

"You're tired?" Paco crossed his arms. "I got up really early this morning. Working two jobs is no picnic, you know." Paco returned to his perch on the stool behind the counter and began writing in his ledger. "I like it at Weeki Wachee, but shit, I was up at four a.m. working on the motor of that damned glass bottom boat."

Ted thought he should cut Paco some slack. After all, this whole experience had been hard on him, too. He stood and walked to the counter. "I'm back for a few days. Think I could get a room?"

Paco didn't look up. "She's back in the water today."

"Ruthie?"

Paco kept writing in his ledger. "She asked about you."

Ted hurried to the door.

"Hey, gringo!" Paco leaned on the counter. "Don't you want a room?"

Ted opened the door.

"Ted!"

Ted stopped on the first step and looked back through the open door at Paco.

Paco laughed. "Welcome back, hombre."

***

Ted made a sharp turn into the parking lot at Weeki Wachee. His back tires lost traction in the crushed shells, and his car fishtailed. Ted steered in the opposite direction, hit the brakes and came to a stop in a cloud of fine white dust.

At the ticket window, an elderly man pushed Ted's money back to him. "Paco called." The man smiled a toothless smile. "Said not to charge the young man who would be in a real hurry."

Ted skipped down the stairs to the viewing windows. He pressed close to the glass. He watched two mermaids in the center of the springs undulating their tail flippers so they could stay in one place, feeding foot-long fish, occasionally shooing the fish away so the girls could take a breath from their nearby breathing tubes. He pressed closer to the window, afraid that he had come too late to see Ruthie.

Then from above, just a foot from the window, a mermaid drifted into view. Her hair moved independently, covering, and then revealing her delicate form. Bubbles from a drooping breathing tube hid her face for a moment and then wafted away. It was Ruthie, just inches away. She smiled and mouthed words to Ted. Her hand touched the glass, and she held it firmly in place. He couldn't make out what she said, but when he touched the glass opposite her hand, he didn't feel tired any longer.

About the Author

Frederick John Loase divides his time between the megalopolis experience of San Diego California and the hush of a tiny town in the Puget Sound—a ferry ride from Seattle and a bridge away from the grandeur of the Olympic National Park. Fred is a forty–year retired high school teacher. He co-authored a non–fiction book, and, according to Fred, has written many short stories that have been rejected by some of the finest magazines in America. He is also a ceramic artist. He shares a pottery studio on an island in the Puget Sound.

Made in the USA
San Bernardino, CA
08 April 2016